the UGLY DWARF

the UGLY DWARF

a novel

by William C. Gordon

[signature] 2012

Bay Tree Publishing, LLC
Point Richmond, California

Calligraphy by Ward Schumaker
Cover design by Lori Barra and Sarah Kessler
Interior design by mltrees

Library of Congress Cataloging-in-Publication Data

Gordon, William C. (William Charles), 1937-
The ugly dwarf : a novel / by William C. Gordon.
    p. cm.
ISBN 978-0-9836179-4-5 (pbk. : alk. paper) -- ISBN 0-9836179-4-5 (pbk. : alk. paper)
    1. Reporters and reporting--California--San Francisco--Fiction.
2. Murder--Investigation--California--San Francisco--Fiction. I. Title.
    PS3607.O5947U38 2012
    813'.6--dc23

                                        2012017505

This book is dedicated to Horacio Martinez Baca

Table of Contents

1

A Chunk of Meat

IN EARLY 1963 THE FAUX-AIREDALE with the missing ear broke away from his owner and ran toward a metal trash can whose top lay on the ground beside it. The can was pushed up against an elongated and ugly wood building. Several stories high and painted a dull yellow, the building was adjacent to a polluted inlet in San Francisco's China Basin that flowed under the Third Street Drawbridge. The landmark bridge was known for the heavy cement balancing weights that kept the roadway erect when elevated, which allowed barge traffic to maneuver in and out of the inlet.

As it approached the can, the dog was startled when it suddenly tipped over, its contents spilling out on the already littered ground, and a large raccoon scampered away from the still-rocking can and entered a broken air vent underneath the building.

The dog bolted after the frightened animal but stopped abruptly when it got to the overturned can. It sniffed intently, inserting its snout into something wrapped in burlap that had tumbled out onto the ground.

The owner of the dog caught up to him and grabbed the leash just as the dog began tearing at the burlap fabric with his teeth. The woman saw flesh and icicles being ripped apart, and blood flew in all directions. She yanked on the leash as hard as she could, pulling the dog back to stop him from making a bigger mess of things and covering her with red splatters, too. She then retreated to one of the wooden staircases that gave access to the abominable-looking building, tied the dog firmly to a post and sat down on one of the steps to figure out what to do. Melba Sundling, who was in her fifties, walked through that grungy industrial park next to the San Francisco Bay from her home on Castro Street on a daily basis. It was a way of getting fresh air and much-needed exercise, since her evenings were tied up with Camelot, a smoke-filled bar on Nob Hill whose ownership she shared with others but which she was responsible for operating.

She had just gotten over a long winter bout of bronchitis thanks to the help of several ancient Chinese remedies. Now she felt it was important to get in shape, and the daily walks with her dog helped. She noticed that they also improved her disposition and sense of humor, and, surprisingly, made her feel more competitive with her athletic daughter Blanche, who'd come to help her when her bouncer and confidant, Rafael Garcia, was sent to prison and subsequently killed while protecting another inmate.

The thought of what might be inside the sack shook Melba from her reverie and she got up and walked back down the stairs. She picked up a piece of discarded lathing that lay nearby and began poking at the burlap bundle, Excalibur, the dog, straining to participate. She pulled back the fabric until she was able to identify what looked like a big chunk of meat and what she thought might be skin. Not sure of what to make of it, she closed the flaps of the sack that had been ripped open by the dog and pulled the animal away. Melba walked quickly to a phone booth she'd passed earlier, all the while holding tightly to Excalibur's leash to restrain him.

She dialed the operator and asked for the medical

examiner's office, then quickly called the number. It was mid-morning and luck was with her—he was in. The clerk who answered the phone recognized her voice from his many nights at Camelot, and put her through to his boss.

"Hello, Melba," said the medical examiner, Barnaby McLeod, who was also one of her frequent customers at Camelot. "To what do I owe this honor?"

"I'm not sure, Barney. I was out walking my dog and he came across a chunk of meat wrapped in a burlap sack. Ordinarily I wouldn't have thought anything about it, but it looked like it had been sawed and it had icicles on it, so I didn't know what to make of it. I decided it was better to get in touch with an expert, because it might be human."

"You called the right guy, sweetheart," said the examiner. "Where are you? I'll come down there myself."

She explained where she was.

"Wait for me. I won't be more than twenty minutes. Keep everyone away from your find."

"That won't be a problem," she said. "Nobody knows it's there except you, me, my dog, the raccoon that tipped over the can, and whoever left it there."

When she hung up the phone, Melba wiped the sweat off of her pale forehead and patted her blue-gray hair under her nondescript bandana. Then she put another dime in the coin box and dialed again. "Samuel Hamilton, please," she asked the switchboard operator. The call was put through.

"Samuel here," a voice answered. The reporter was seated in his new and improved office, its only drawback being that he had to share it with another reporter from the morning paper. From there he could look out the window down onto the foot of Market Street and see the Ferry Building with its giant clock ticking off the minutes and hours. His khaki sports coat was draped over his wooden swivel chair. His white shirt was not pressed, but it wasn't quite wrinkled either, and what was left of his red hair was combed straight back across his freckled pate.

"Samuel, this is Melba."

"What a surprise," he answered. Then, more worriedly: "Did something happen to Blanche?"

"Are you kidding?" she said. "That broad's indestructible. But listen for a minute. I have a situation here. It may be nothing, but you never know. I'm down at China Basin and I just found a chunk of meat. I'm not sure if it's human, so just in case I called old Turtle Face and he's on his way down here. You interested?"

"I'll jump on the Third Street bus right now," said Samuel.

"Do I need a photographer?"

"I'll leave that up to you, big shot. Just hurry!"

"That makes it easy, I'll hitch a ride," he said. He opened his office door and yelled down the hall. "Marc, we've got a live one, let's go!" Then he hung up the phone.

Barney McLeod, the medical examiner, was a tall man with a small head, thinning brown hair and drooping eyelids. He wore a white medical jacket open over his shirt and tie. He was poking at the burlap bundle with a pointer when Samuel arrived with Marcel Fabreceaux, his photographer, in the latter's green '47 Ford coupe.

Samuel waved hello to Melba and scratched an excited Excalibur on the head before turning to greet Turtle Face. "Hi, Examiner McLeod. Haven't seen you since we were together at Mr. Song's Chinese herb shop. That was over a year ago." Samuel did his best to look past the tall man to see if he could make any sense out of the bundle the man was scrutinizing.

"Yeah," grimaced Turtle Face. "That son of a bitch Perkins. I still haven't forgiven him for dragging me through that mess with the claim check for the Chinese jar. Remember that?"

"How could I forget it?" answered Samuel. "That case made me the full-time reporter that I am today instead of a starving ad salesman." He turned to the subject at hand. "What do we have here, Chief?"

"News travels fast in this town," said the examiner, giving as much of a smile as anyone would ever get from him. He glanced over at Melba, who up to then hadn't said anything. Now she walked toward the group of men, pulling Excalibur, who was doing his best to get at the meat. Turtle Face extended his hand to stop her. "Don't get too close until I've had a chance to make a thorough examination. I don't want this crime scene contaminated."

"You've already decided it's a crime scene," noted Samuel, motioning to Marcel to take a photo of Barney McLeod, pointer in hand, looking down at the mysterious sack on the ground.

The examiner and the two men with him had cordoned off an eight-foot-square area around the overturned trash can, and were painstakingly going over every inch of ground, photographing every stray bit of flotsam that had accumulated there since whenever, or that had spilled out of the can when it was knocked over. Each piece was picked up with rubber gloves, examined for fingerprints, given a number and put in the evidence box. When they'd finished that task, the examiner focused on the burlap sack.

"You see the icicles on the flesh?" he commented absent-mindedly. "This meat must have been in a freezer."

Watching from behind the tape, Samuel could see several long, thin icicles stuck to the meat. "It also looks like the meat's been sawed," he said. "See those markings on it?"

"That's what I thought too," said Melba.

"Pardon me," said Turtle Face, coming back into the present. "I agree, it looks like somebody sawed it up a bit."

"Can you tell how long it was in a freezer?"

"Not right now. I need to get this to the lab, fast."

"Isn't there some writing on the sack?" asked Samuel. "See, it looks like an M near the bottom."

"Yeah, but I'm not ready for that yet," said Turtle Face. "First I need to make some slides and see if I can confirm my suspicions."

"That it's part of a human being?" asked Melba.

"Of course. Otherwise there's no need for all this fuss."

"How soon can I get a confirmation?" asked Samuel. "I'd like to write a story on this before you make it public."

"Let's talk this afternoon. By then, I'll be able to tell you if we have a part of a corpse."

"Will you also tell me what the letters on the sack say?" asked Samuel.

"Not for publication,'" said the medical examiner. "If there's enough to figure out where the sack came from, it may be the most important clue. Are we on the same page, Samuel?"

"Sure, I can just say that the authorities have an important piece of information that only they and the killer know about."

"That is, if there is a killer. It may be that it's just horse meat," said the examiner, giving a hint of a smile again.

"What about the significance of the other things you picked up today?" asked Samuel.

"Only time will tell what's significant. But when you stop by, I'll give you a list. That way you'll have the same one the police get and you can do a little detective work on your own. From what I've read in the newspaper, you've done a pretty good job over the last two years."

"Thanks, Barney." Samuel beamed as he walked over to where Melba and Excalibur were standing on the landing above the wooden staircase. He motioned to Marcel that he had enough. And it was true. Turtle Face had said the magic words—he knew he was going to get inside dope.

Melba was smoking a cigarette and leaning on the banister as he approached. Excalibur wagged his tailless fanny and Samuel petted him again. "Thanks for the tip, Melba. I hope it pans out. I was worried I wouldn't have anything to write about this spring."

She laughed; her limpid blue eyes were as calm as the day. "You're kidding, of course. In this town, something is always going wrong, and so far, you've been able to figure a couple of them out. But don't hold your breath. They won't all be so easy, and this one's a good example. It's pretty clear that we have a chunk of meat here. And if we're correct that it's part of a person, then it's your job is to find out who that person was and how he or she got this way."

* * *

The examiner had good news for Samuel that afternoon. The chunk of meat found by Excalibur that morning was, in fact, a piece of a human thigh. But he laid out specific conditions for providing that information. Samuel was given two lists. One was the evidence he could write about. The other was a much longer list of items to which he was being made privy but couldn't yet mention in any article he wrote. The examiner then turned the matter over to the homicide bureau of the San Francisco Police Department.

Samuel's article came out the next morning, accompanied by Marcel's photograph of the medical examiner pointing to the burlap bundle. The lurid headline read:

THERE'S A HATCHET MANIAC AMONG US

There wasn't much to go on, so Samuel's work would be cut out for him if he wanted a repeat of his crime resolution successes. His big worry, though, was that maybe this time the cops would figure it out first.

2

The Letter M

THE DAY AFTER HIS ARTICLE appeared on the front page
OF the morning paper, Samuel was once again in the medical examiner's office going over the evidence. He was seated
with Turtle Face in the conference room, the one with the
real skeleton from India and the examiner's rogue's gallery,
photographs of him with famous and infamous San Francisco
politicos and members of the criminal attorney's bar. Samuel's
favorite was the one of the examiner with the attorney Earl
Rogers and the writer Jack London. Each man had an arm
around another man's shoulder, and it was obvious that neither
Rogers nor London was feeling any pain.

Samuel and the examiner studied the photos of the piece
of thigh, which had been taken from several angles.

"No doubt someone used a saw, right?" asked Samuel.

"Yeah. You can tell by the serrated marks here," said the
examiner, pointing to the meaty part. "And you can actually
see them on the thigh bone itself."

"That means there must be other body parts lying around
the city," said Samuel.

"Could be, or it could be they've already been disposed
of and we'll never get more than we have right now," said the
examiner. "We just have to keep our eyes open."

Samuel picked up a photograph of the burlap. The rough material had been spread out and turned inside out. It was bloodstained and had been cut irregularly. Near the top where it was cut, there appeared the better part of what looked like the capital letter M. "This is interesting. It was probably part of a sack that held something else, don't you think?"

"Yeah," said Turtle Face, as he stood up and walked over to Samuel. He smoothed the sleeve of his white medical jacket and pointed at the burlap. "The question is what? We found some flakes on it that we've got under the microscope right now. Our working assumption is that it held pinto beans before it held the young man's thigh."

"You can tell it was a male's?"

"The victim came from south of the border and he was a man in his early twenties. We can also tell that the body part was washed with San Francisco water before it was frozen because it has residuals of Hetch Hetchy chemicals in its makeup."

"What are those white things on the sack?" asked Samuel.

"Hairs. We still haven't figured out if they're human or animal. In either case, the sack was in the company of someone or something that had white hair. My hunch is that it was an animal."

"I'm almost sure that's the letter M on the sack," said Samuel as he took the fabric in his hands. "Any idea where it came from?" He stretched the burlap and brought it up near his face for a close-up view.

"None, so far. I'm turning the solution to that problem over to you. Let's say somewhere in the world some producer, whose name starts with the letter M, shipped a sack full of beans—let's stick with beans for now—to San Francisco, or at least to the Bay Area. So whoever chopped this guy into pieces got his hands on the sack and cut it up to use for this nefarious purpose."

"Did you get any footprints?"

"There are too many to count. The body part was dumped in the trashcan, but everybody who came out of the building who had something to throw away made a contribution. I doubt if we'll ever be able to connect footprints to a criminal suspect."

"Did you find anything else that looks interesting?" asked Samuel.

"You've got the list, but it's confidential. Any one of those things may turn out to be an important clue. For right now, they're just items that fell out of the trash can or were in the vicinity."

"Okay, Chief, I'll begin my search and keep you posted," said Samuel. As he left the examiner's colorful conference room, he rattled the skeleton for good luck.

*　　*　　*

Samuel went to Chinatown and had a dim sum lunch at Chop Suey Louie's, his longtime restaurant hangout near his flat. Now run by Louie's widow and one of their daughters, there had only been a couple of changes since Louie's death a couple of years ago. The place still had its twelve tables with blue oilcloth covers, but the fish tank that had been shattered by an assassin's bullets had been replaced by an even larger one and was filled with several new and brightly colored tropical fish. As he sat at his usual place at the counter, Samuel reminisced with the widow about his friend Louie and the bets they made on Forty-Niners games. After lunch he jumped on the Hyde Street cable car and rode it down to the Powell and Market Street turnaround, listening to the rhythmic clanging of its bell as it approached each stop. He then went back to his office to type up his notes and make a few phone calls. In the late afternoon Samuel walked back to same cable car turnaround and caught the Hyde Street line going the other way, towards Fisherman's Warf, and rode it up to Nob Hill, where he got off in front of Camelot.

As he walked through the front door, Samuel saw Melba daydreaming at the oak Round Table (he always thought of it in capital letters) just inside the front door. There was a clear view of the park across the street and of the bay beyond. The wind was blowing briskly south and the water was filled with sailboats moving towards the Bay Bridge.

Melba was dressed in a bright yellow blouse, black and white checkered slacks, red socks and black Capezios, none of which quite belonged together fashion-wise, but that didn't appear to concern her. She was drinking a beer and smoking a Lucky Strike cigarette. Excalibur, the flea-bitten mutt, was at her feet. When Samuel came in the dog jumped to his feet, licking the reporter's hands and shaking all over. Samuel pulled a treat from his wrinkled khaki sport coat pocket and the dog wolfed it down, looking to him for more.

Samuel sat down in an empty chair next to Melba and exhaled heavily.

"Give me the news," demanded Melba.

"The big news is that the burlap sack probably had pinto beans in it before someone stuck part of a young Latin man's leg in it."

"That narrows it down," said Melba. "A lot of Latinos eat pinto beans, and most of them live in the Mission, so you'll start looking there, right?"

"On the button. To think that I came here to ask you that very question, and you gave me the answer before I even asked."

"I didn't spend all those years in the Mission twiddling my thumbs. Bring a phone book over here and I'll help you compile a list."

Samuel went to the back of the bar by the hors d'oeuvre table. Excalibur tried to follow him but Melba held him in check. He took a phone book from the mahogany booth and brought it back to the Round Table.

"Want a drink?" she asked.

"Naw, it's too early. What are we looking for?"

"First thing you do is look for places that begin with the letter M and that sell bulk food."

"Do you think that a food market in a place like the Mission would actually have its own imprint on a burlap sack?" he asked.

"Jesus Christ, Samuel. How the hell do I know? But you do the obvious things first. If we find one, that makes your job that much easier, doesn't it? And if you're that lucky, then you only have to find out who bought the beans from the store with the name that starts with the letter M and the case is solved. Am I right?"

Samuel nodded his head and smiled. "Something tells me it's not that simple. Maybe I'll have that drink after all."

"Scotch on the rocks," Melba yelled over her shoulder. "And give the poor bastard a double. He's been working too hard." She laughed, tugging on Samuel's coat sleeve. "After you've had a little juice we'll look at the phone book."

When the drink came, Samuel took a pull and sat back in the oak chair, looking out the window at two freighters going in opposite directions, one heading north towards the Golden Gate and the other passing under the Bay Bridge before it headed down the bay toward the San Francisco Naval Shipyard at Hunter's Point. The scene reminded him of his relationship with Blanche—how could two people going in opposite directions ever get together? While he pondered his thoughts, Melba set the phone book in her lap.

"When does Blanche get back?" he asked, feigning a casualness he didn't feel.

"The snow's pretty good at Tahoe right now, so I'd bet she won't be back until the end of the month."

He nodded his head slowly and took another pull.

"She's always just out of your reach, isn't she?"

Samuel didn't answer. He concentrated on the freighters until he could no longer keep both of them in his sight. "I'm sorry. Where were we?"

Melba smiled and pulled the telephone book from her lap to the top of the table. Together they perused the Yellow Pages until they found three food markets in San Francisco's Mission District that started with the letter M. Samuel wrote the names and addresses in his notebook and downed another drink before walking out the door and heading to Chop Suey Louie's for his evening meal.

The next day Samuel began pounding the pavement in the Mission. The markets were spread out over a wide distance, and the first two on the list had no brand name connected with their sale of beans and made no gross sales. It was after two when he reached the third market, Mi Rancho Market on Twentieth Street and Shotwell, just off Mission Street. It had a two-foot red brick base that ran along the base of the building except where there were doors. The rest of the façade was painted terracotta. A sign near the roofline read Mi Rancho Market, which was spelled out in red against a mustard-colored background. There were two entrances: glass double doors for customers and a reinforced steel door for deliveries.

It was a busy place and, based on someone's careful study of patrons' buying habits, the aisles were crammed with dry goods and colorfully labeled canned items, most of which came from Mexico and other parts of Central and South America. One aisle was devoted to the freshest produce Samuel had seen anywhere outside Chinatown. It made him think that people from other places must know something that Americans had forgotten—the magic of fresh food. Fresh bread, Mexican pan dulces and tortillas came from the in-house bakery and were stored in protected glass shelves near the bakery itself. Their aromas permeated the store. There was also a butcher shop that equaled any Samuel had seen anywhere. He checked on the prices of the mounds of fresh meat in the sloped windows and calculated that if this market were not so far from his flat in Chinatown, it would be cheaper for him to buy its high quality meat and cook it in his flat instead of wasting his money in the pathetic holes where he ate his daily meals.

The man behind the meat counter was stocky and had blondish-gray wavy hair. He wore a spotless white apron and spoke very good Spanish to the customers he was serving, even though he didn't look Latin.

"What's your secret to finding good-looking meat at such reasonable prices?" asked Samuel, hoping the man spoke English.

"I'm the secret," said the smiling butcher in accented but perfect English. "Come and buy from me and I'll give you special deals."

"Do you have a card or something? How can I get hold of you?"

"You call Mi Rancho Market and you ask for Pavao. I'll take care of you."

"Thank you, I may do that," said Samuel. He wrote the butcher's name in his notebook next to the phone number of the market.

The shop was cooled by the slow rotation of overhead fans, which circulated and mixed the aromas of spices and combinations of yet undiscovered foods from lands foreign to his senses, including the smell of the fresh tortillas that were being made in one corner of the store.

Samuel's thoughts were interrupted when he noticed sacks of pinto beans stacked in one of the aisles, the store's logo stamped on the front of each burlap bag. He was sure the M was similar to the one on the piece of cloth that was in the medical examiner's office. Samuel's reaction was visceral, but he knew he had to settle down. This was only the beginning. Now he had to find out how the sack ended up in a trash can with a body part in it. He knew before even starting his inquiries that it wouldn't be easy.

He approached an attractive young woman wearing a white apron who stood behind the checkout counter. She was a little over five feet tall, had short-cropped black hair and black eyes. Before he could say a word, she flashed a warm smile, showing her perfect white teeth.

"May I help you, sir?" she asked with a slight accent.

"Yes, thanks. My name is Samuel Hamilton. I work for the morning paper."

"Most of our employees don't read English and the rest of us are too busy to read the newspaper, if that is what you are selling."

"No, no. I didn't mean it that way," said Samuel. "I'm a reporter with the morning paper and I'm working on a story." He wasn't sure how much he wanted to disclose about the gruesome murder he was investigating, so he continued cautiously. "I'm looking into a story that involves a burlap sack with the letter M on it."

"What kind of a story?" quizzed the woman, her smiled dissipating.

"Someone found a burlap sack with a partial M on it, and I'm trying to find out where it came from and who owned it."

"We sell a lot of things in burlap sacks to organizations all over the Bay Area. We buy in bulk, and part of the reason we buy from certain growers is that they put our imprint on the individual sacks. What was in your sack?"

"Pinto beans," said Samuel, thinking that her English diction and vocabulary were impressive and unexpected, especially for someone who tended to Latins in a food market in the Mission.

"All our pinto beans come from Mexico. We buy more than five hundred sacks a year and send them all over the place."

"Do you also sell sacks to individuals?"

"No, not since I've been here. Institutions buy them in lots of twenty to get a special discount."

"Will you give me the names of all the institutions, in, say, San Francisco?"

She thrust her head back and squinted at him suspiciously. "You're asking a lot for someone I've just met, Mr. Hamilton."

Samuel blushed. "I'm sorry. What is your name?"

"I'm Rosa María Rodríguez."

"Can I assume that you're the owner of this market?"

"I'm one of the owners."

Samuel paused for a moment, not sure what he was going to say next, but it just came out. "I'm going to be honest with you, Mrs. Rodríguez," said Samuel, eyeing her wedding ring. "I'm trying to get information for a story I'm writing about a murder."

Her eyes opened wide. "You don't think we had anything to do with a murder, do you?"

"Absolutely not." Reluctant as he was to say more, Samuel knew he had to tell her what he was after; he had a hunch she would help him. "Here's what happened…." Samuel told her as much as he could about the crime, emphasizing that the body part was found in a part of a sack that looked like it had the capital letter M on it.

The Ugly Dwarf

"And you're sure it came from here?" she asked skeptically.

"Pretty sure, with the evidence that I've seen. But right now, I need to know where it went from here and who cut it up. If you sell five hundred sacks of beans a year, who knows when and to whom you might have sold the sack I'm talking about. But I have to start somewhere and I'm here. Can I buy a soft drink?"

"Of course. They're back there, nice and cold."

He went to the rear of the store and brought back the drink, which she opened. He drank it down as she waited on a couple of the customers who had been standing behind him. When he finished the drink, he returned to the counter and put down his dime.

"Will you help me?"

"I'll have to think about it."

"What can I do to convince you right now?" he asked.

"No, this is one of our traits. Gringos can't appreciate the Mexican way. If I trust you, I'll help you. Come back in a few days and I'll give you an answer." She smiled politely, but he could tell by her look that she was in charge.

"Excuse me," she said. "There's still a line of people behind you."

She motioned to the first woman in the line of people patiently waiting behind him. "*Sí, señora. Pase adelante.*"

3

Dusty Schwartz

TWO YEARS BEFORE THE grim discovery in the burlap sack, Dusty Schwartz entered the San Antonio Charismatic Catholic Church on Army Street in the Mission District. He had curly black hair, wide-set blue eyes and a pleasant face. He was also a dwarf—he had a large head and very short, bowed legs. Dusty was there because he wanted to become an evangelical preacher, and he'd heard that the best lay preacher on the Bay Area circuit was Antonio Leiva, who gave sermons at San Antonio's on Wednesday evenings.

Dusty arrived just before 7 p.m. to find the church packed with Latin workers and their families. To one side of the altar, two musicians pounded out gospel music on guitars, and a prompter egged on the crowd. The foot stomping and singing raised the noise to a level so intense that Dusty had to put his hands over his ears.

He climbed up and stood on a pew at the rear of the church, almost the last seat in the house, as Mr. Leiva took his place at the elevated podium. A tall man with erect posture, the preacher had dyed black hair and was dressed in a black tailored suit and white shirt. He was a compelling figure without even saying a word. Once he began to speak, his deep voice showed him to be a natural orator; it carried to every corner of the church without the aid of a microphone, capturing the undivided attention of his audience—including Dusty, who was Mexican on his mother's side and thus fluent in Spanish.

Mr. Leiva began by explaining the importance of faith in God, giving examples of the perils facing the non-believer, and as he continued his sermon his voice increased in volume and power. Once he had established the importance of faith, he moved on to the miracles that, according to him, believers could experience on an almost daily basis. As the speaker's sermon edged toward its finale, his voice thundered throughout the church, his hands gesticulating and his arms waving as he explained to the worshipers that the heavens would open up and they could be whisked upward to stand by God's side. Such was the force of his speech that the people responded with an almost hysterical pounding of their feet on the floor.

Dusty was both fascinated and jealous. Mostly jealous: He knew he'd come into the presence of his master, and he needed to know how the man did it. He decided he would attend as many of Mr. Leiva's sermons as he could.

After the preacher wound it up, the foot stomping and the string of hallelujahs continued unabated, helped along by the guitar player, who started up again as soon as the deacon left the pulpit. Finally, when it was time for donations, the music ended and volunteers holding baskets fanned out throughout the church.

It was then that Dusty saw the attractive young woman. She was tall and well dressed, her black hair pulled straight back. As she drew closer, he saw that she had an oval face and an inviting smile. His first thought, as she moved her basket from one pew to the next, was that she would be an exciting conquest for him. When the basket came to him, he noticed that it was full-to-overflowing, even though the audience was comprised of simple working people. It was obvious they were showing their affection and appreciation for the performance they had just witnessed.

He was still standing on the bench as she approached. He handed her the full basket, making sure she saw him deposit a ten-dollar bill. *"Perdóneme, señorita,"* he said in Spanish. "Are you related to the preacher?"

"Sí," she said. *"Es mi padre."* He's my father.

"¿Como se llama?" asked Dusty, trying to further the conquest fantasy that he'd already conjured up in his mind.

"My name is Marisol Lciva, she said. I'm helping my father out tonight as the priest and the other deacon are sick.".

"My name is Dusty Schwartz. I was very impressed with your father's sermon and would like to hear more. Where and when does he preach?"

"He's very popular and goes to many different churches, giving sermons just like he did here tonight. If you'd like to know where and when he's going to preach, call me at this number next week and I'll give you his schedule." She handed him a card.

Dusty looked at the card. It read "Janak Marachak, Attorney at Law" and included an address and phone number. Under the attorney's name Marisol had written her own. "You work for an attorney?"

"Yes, I do."

"Is he a criminal attorney? I work for the San Francisco Police Department."

She was surprised to hear that a dwarf worked with the police, but her expression didn't change. "No, no. He represents people injured by chemical exposure."

She smiled again and moved on. Dusty watched her graceful moves as she extended the donation basket to the people standing at the rear of the church. He would definitely have to see more of her.

*   *   *

The Ugly Dwarf

Dusty worked hard for the next year. During the day he was a property clerk for the San Francisco Police Department, but in the evenings he dedicated himself to the Universal Church of Physic Unfoldment, which he had founded on Mission Street. He started it in a rented building with funds he had inherited from his wealthy physician father. He didn't have much luck persuading anyone to listen to his sermons or donate to his church, but by providing food in the evenings after the service, he got the down-and-outers to sit through his Bible thumping. Afterward, Dusty mingled with the small crowd and tried to get them to join his church. He was not successful. His biggest disappointment, though, was that no pretty girls showed up.

Dusty continued to attend Mr. Galo's services when he could, especially on the weekend, and dedicated himself to copying the deacon's techniques. But nothing he tried worked.

Then he met Dominique, and everything changed.

4

Dominique the Dominatrix

DUSTY HAD ANOTHER OBSESSION besides religion. It was sex. He'd been hearing about Dominique the dominatrix for months, but she was so popular he had to wait in line. On the Monday of his appointment, he walked from his Mission apartment on Bartlett to Seventeenth Street, then down to Folsom. Seventeenth marked the start of the Mexican part of the Mission. It had once been an Irish neighborhood, but times had changed. As Dusty walked, he looked in the windows of the small businesses that had cropped up, which sold everything from furniture to shoes, much of which originated south of the border. He was happy to see a number of shoe stores featuring Mexican brand names in their windows. It reminded him of growing up in Juarez, just across the border from El Paso, Texas.

Dominique's building was an ordinary San Francisco set of flats with bay windows, a paint job that had seen better days, and an entryway cluttered with single sheets of newspapers and other trash blown in by the swirling wind that kicked up in the evenings. Since Dusty wasn't one of her regulars, he hadn't been able to get a late-night weekend appointment, so he'd had to settle for a six o'clock time slot on the one day of the week when his church was closed. The session was going to cost him thirty dollars, which he thought was a lot of money to pay someone to beat him up, but he'd heard from others that she was worth it. As he explained to the cops at work, before Dominique would accept him as a client, he'd had to sign an agreement that any injuries he sustained would be incurred solely at his own risk. No signature, no session.

He nervously rang the doorbell and waited for door to spring open. He couldn't see much other than the outline of stairs through the dirty lace curtain that covered the glass portion of the front door. Finally, after the fourth ring, the door creaked open, and he stepped into the dim light of the apartment's stairwell. Lush, well-cared-for plants extended all the way up the dark stairway.

When he got to the top, there was even less light than on the stairs, except for dim spotlights illuminating what appeared to be shrunken heads in recessed frames spread around three of the walls of the living room. In one of the doorways he made out the frame of a gigantic woman. She had on a G-string and a black leather bikini bra; her long hair was pulled back and held in place with a bright orange semicircular Spanish comb, the only vibrant color on her. She stood on six-inch stiletto boots that came up to her knees and she had a bullwhip in her left hand, which she snapped so close to his face that he jumped back.

Organ music played on a record player in the background. Dusty tried to brush aside the clouds of sweet-smelling incense smoke that engulfed the room.

"Hello, I'm Dusty," he said shakily. "I have a six o'clock appointment." Then he noticed a horrible burn scar covering the left side of her face.

When she saw him staring at her she cracked the whip again, several times. "Shut up, I know who you are," she snarled. "Never look at my face again. This isn't a beauty contest, and if it were, you wouldn't even win the booby prize, you ugly fucking dwarf. Just take off your clothes and keep looking at the floor. I'll make sure you get yours."

Dusty, not sure how to react, laughed. He was hypnotized. His heart began to beat faster with anticipation. He didn't know if he was afraid or overly excited, but either way he wasn't happy being reminded of what he looked like. He took off his clothes self-consciously, filled with the biting sense of shame that had followed him since childhood. He had seldom taken his clothes off in front of a woman since he'd become sexually active as a teenager. He preferred to have sex fully robed.

"Get on your knees and crawl into the torture chamber," the woman ordered, and cracked the whip above his naked body. He obeyed, entering an even darker room, which he supposed was a bedroom of the second story apartment.

She followed with a flashlight, pointing to the irons on the back wall of the room.

"Clamp yourself in those," she demanded in a low voice.

"Not that way, stupid!" she yelled as he moved to comply. "Face the wall!"

Once he was in the irons, her tone became even rougher.

"Well, well, you fucking little rat, have you come here to have some fun? I'll show you what fun is all about."

She got down on her knees beside him and began to masturbate him slowly, wearing an expression of disgust.

"What an ugly schlong you have," she sneered. "Very appropriate for such an ugly fucking dwarf!"

He was ready to come, but she wouldn't let him. He knew he was at her mercy.

"What a cock! It makes me want to puke. And if I do," she whispered menacingly, "you will pay, you little piece of shit!"

She took a strand of beads from a night table next to the chamber of horrors and dipped it in a bowl of lotion.

"Spread your legs, ugly," she ordered, and introduced the

strand into his rectum, "The whip is waiting for you…the whip is waiting for you."

She had one hand on the end of the strand and one hand on his penis. She squeezed harder and stroked faster. She then yanked the beads out and he screamed and came like he never had before in his life. His body convulsed for several seconds and he tingled all over.

"That was fantastic," he gasped.

Her tone got rougher still. "You haven't seen nothing yet, you worthless dwarf." Then she got up and left the room.

When Dominique returned, she unlocked his right wrist from its shackle and had him turn toward her. She held a hookah in one hand and a large Rolfing stick with more than three feet of foam rubber on the end in the other. It was wrapped tightly and looked like a medieval sword.

"I brought you some pot, little ugly. Have a couple of tokes off this."

He took the hookah in his free hand and inhaled. The dope went right to his head.

"Ooh, this is good stuff," he told her.

"Yeah, ugly, it comes from Vietnam. They grow good shit over there. Now turn around and jack off," she ordered. "Now you're going to get it, you mother-fucking dwarf," she yelled, and began beating him with the Rolfing stick. The harder she hit him the more excited he became, until he was ready to come again.

The statuesque dominatrix slapped him hard on the face and ordered, "Let go, ugly! Let go!" Dusty came again and slumped to the floor, his left arm still in irons.

* * *

After the session was over and Dusty was fully dressed, he sat in the dimly lit living room shaking so hard that his teeth chattered. The dominatrix entered and kneeled in front of him so that they were on the same level. "Now that you've had your horns clipped, we need to talk. Let's go into my study."

She grabbed him by the hand and pulled him up. Even in her stocking feet, Dominique almost two feet taller than he was. She pushed him to a door at the back of the flat, unlocked it and switched on a light. Dusty was startled. The room had the cartoonish aspect of a temple. It had recessed lighting and ethnic artwork from Mexico, Central America and Mesoamerica covered the walls. Copies of pre-Columbian statues on elevated platforms were placed strategically throughout the room.

"All these clay figures are gods from Latin American civilizations," she explained to her confused guest. "They must be included in any religious ceremony in which our people participate."

"Are you from south of the border?" he asked.

"You're fooled by the name Dominique. Do I look French to you? That's for marketing purposes. My real name is Dominga and I was born in Mexico."

On the ceiling were several wire loops that contained dried herbs and medicinal plants. The smell was pungent.

"What is this?" he inquired.

"This is my study and my meditation and healing room. This is where I do my real work."

"I don't understand," said Dusty, intimidated by the sudden change in her attitude. She was dead serious now, and almost gentle.

"I told you I know who you are. If I didn't, you would never have gotten an appointment with me. You work at the police department during the day and at night you struggle to get your church off the ground—when you're not out whoring around.

"Beating the crap out of guys is how I make a living right

now," the dominatrix continued, "but my passion and my gift is my spiritual practice and healing, which takes place here."

"This looks more like a witch's den than a spiritual retreat," said Dusty, who'd regained his composure. "It reminds me of the curanderos—you know, the healers' shops my mother used to take me to when I was a child. The man would do his mumbo-jumbo over me to assure her that I would grow to be at least taller than she was. Look how well it worked!" He laughed.

"Your mother was a dwarf, too?"

"How do you think I got this way?" he asked, clearly uncomfortable with the subject.

"You're Mexican?"

"Half Mexican, on my mother's side."

"You lived in Mexico?'

"That's where she was from and Juarez is where she worked."

"What kind of work did she do?"

"She was in the service business."

"I see," said a surprised Dominique. "I've heard of the dwarf culture in Juarez. Is it true that there was a whorehouse with two hundred dwarfs there?"

"I don't want to talk about it," replied Dusty. "What about you? Are you some kind of a witch?"

Dominique didn't like to be put off, but she knew that sooner or later the dwarf would have to confide in her, so she let his brush-off about his origins go for the time being. "Let's just say that I'm a practitioner of the occult. That's my calling. A William L. Gordon, Doctor of Divinity, trained me. You may have heard of him. He wrote *The Infinite Plan*."

"Doesn't ring a bell," shrugged Dusty.

She got up and went to one of the several bookcases in the room and returned with a small volume. A white Persian cat got up from a basket in the corner, meandered over and rubbed himself against her leg. She handed Dusty the tome and scratched the cat's back. "Here's a copy of his book."

The dwarf leafed through the pages and read the following passage to himself:

All is system; because of system, the Cosmos functions accurately; without system, nothing can be harmonious. Everything that builds in any way another thing is associated with it harmoniously, and becomes a part of its system. Man among other creations also possesses a system; he forms the nucleus of his own system. The remainder of his system consists of his possessions, friends, acquaintances, all things which he claims as his, and all things which he controls. The system he attracts and holds to himself by a ray which his physical body generates, and which we will call the Possessive Ray. The physical body generates the Possessive Ray which is projected by thought or concentration upon the possessed or desired object. The longer the concentration the greater is the energy expended: therefore, the greater is the cost in energy expended on the desired or possessed article.

He handed the book back to her. "I may be able to use that idea," he said. "What did you do for him?"

"At first, I was his pupil, then I became his assistant. And, for a year, I was his partner and traveled around the Southwest with him and his family, helping him preach his concept of spirituality. Unfortunately, he died in 1943, so I lost his guidance. Since then, I've had to learn the ropes on my own."

"Why are you telling me all this?" asked Dusty.

"Because I've been to your storefront operation and watched you try and convince those poor lost bastards to join your church."

"You've seen me in operation?" asked Dusty, surprised.

"I have, and you're doing it all wrong. You're overloading them with irrelevant crap. No one gives a shit about the facts and figures of sin and redemption. What you need to sell is the chance to get to Heaven on Earth—through you. Take Dr. Gordon's book and read it," she said, handing the book back to him. "And remember the cardinal rule that I will tell you now. You need to perform—to put on a show. You need to have a few simple themes that you pound into them. You need to show that you understand their losses, their suffering. They're immigrants who've left everything behind. All they've found in this society is a few dollars. Don't you see? They're disconnected from their roots. They're suffering from the loss of country, the loss of family, even the loss of church. You can become their spiritual father and replace all their lost institutions. You can do it if you play your cards right, just as Dr. Gordon did in his Infinite Plan tent."

"What do you mean by spiritual father?"

"Just what I said. You become the center of their universe and take the place of all their saints."

"The closest I ever got to feeling powerful was when I was a kid and I joined the circus for a couple of summers. I was a barker. I stood outside the sideshow and convinced people to come in and have a look at all the freaks."

"Then I'm surprised you're as dull as you are. If you open the floodgates, a lot of desperate people will follow you. But you have to give them hope. You have to show them that you've suffered. And being a dwarf makes you a natural for that. You won't even have to pretend, I bet. Just let them know that you understand their pain. If you can't or won't, you're fucked. The Universal Church of Psychic Unfoldment won't last another month."

"I don't see Mr. Leiva making that kind of a pitch," said Dusty.

"He doesn't have to. He has the Catholic Church on his side. It's all preordained for him. He just adds extra oratory and a little music. Your job is more complicated. The kind of people you want are those who are asking whether they should leave the comfort of the Catholic Church and come with you to greener pastures. If you can convince them, I guarantee that you will have a bigger payoff."

Dusty opened his eyes wide. "Do you mean a financial payoff?"

"Of course. They'll give up their rent and grocery money if you ease their pain a little and get them to believe you offer a solution to their misery."

"You're giving me a lot to think about," said Dusty. "But I'm not sure I know how to put all this into operation."

"That's not a problem. I'm going to help you. Here's what I suggest. First, read Dr. Gordon's book; then invest in some new clothes. What did you wear when you worked as a barker at the circus?"

"A cape and a top hat."

"Good. Bring back the cape. I'll have to think about the top hat. But buy a tuxedo, so when you're dressed up you'll look like a big shot."

"What makes you think all that will work?"

"Trust me. Give it three weeks. If you don't see a big difference, I'll withdraw."

Dusty laughed as he thought to himself: if I trusted her enough to beat the shit out of me, I should trust her enough to give me some input on my floundering career as a preacher.

"I'm not finished," she said. She got up, went to the closet and brought back a canvas, which she unrolled onto the floor. It was a painting measuring about ten feet in length and seven feet in height. She explained the meaning of the painting and told him how to use it in his sermons.

"You think this show will bring in enough money to keep me afloat? Right now, I don't think the people would even show up if I didn't offer them food."

"I can almost guarantee that the food you give them will be the frosting on the cake. They'll be knocking down your doors to get in. And some will be young, attractive women who need your guidance."

Dusty perked up when he heard that young women would show up. So far, he hadn't seen any lookers. "That might be the payoff," he said, trying not to act too excited. Then he became suspicious. "What do *you* want for helping me with all this?"

"I'd like to practice my healing, too. I can get clients from your followers just like I did with Dr. Gordon, and maybe, just maybe, I won't have to crack my whip in the other part of my flat."

They agreed they would meet again to talk within the next few days. Dusty left that night exhausted and sore, but also relieved and hopeful. He had a rolled canvas under his arm and a book by an author he'd never heard of. He went home, tacked the canvas up on his living room wall and started reading *The Infinite Plan*. It took him several days to figure out what the doctor of divinity was saying, but after he finished the book he acknowledged that maybe Dominique and Dr. Gordon were his real teachers and he'd been going about things the wrong way. It was worth a try and, in any case, he had nothing to lose.

5

Melba to the Rescue

WHEN SAMUEL HADN'T HEARD from Rosa María after several days, he headed over to Camelot to ask for help. It was early afternoon and Melba and Excalibur were at their usual places at the Round Table.

"The prodigal returns," greeted Melba, putting down her glass of beer and blowing the smoke from a Lucky Strike out of the side of her mouth.

"I've been busy," said the reporter, patting the over-excited dog on the top of its head and slipping him his usual treat. "But I've run into problems in the Mission and I need your help."

"It's a war zone for guys like you. I bet you didn't get to first base."

"That's not entirely true," said Samuel defensively, and told her what he'd learned so far at the Mi Rancho Market. "Now I can't get her to answer my calls," he complained.

"Rosa María Rodríguez?" asked Melba.

"Yeah, that's her. Do you know her? Can you help me get information?"

"I know her well. But whether I can get her to help is another matter. What is it you want?"

"How do you know her?"

"I'll tell you later. Knock off the crap and tell me what you want from her."

"I want her customer list. The one that names everyone who has bought a sack of pinto beans from her in the last two years."

"That's doesn't sound like such a big deal. Let me give her a call." Melba got up, tugging on her gaudy white slacks with black polka dots, which she wore with a bright red blouse.

"Where are you going dressed like that?" laughed Samuel.

"None of your goddamned business. And who are you to comment on fashion?" She smirked and disappeared into her office behind the horseshoe bar. She returned several minutes later, smiling. "It's all taken care of."

"What do you mean?" asked Samuel.

"She'll talk to you. She invited us to dinner at her house tomorrow night. She wanted Blanche to come, too, but I explained she was still in Tahoe.

Samuel was surprised and happy. "How did you manage that?" he asked.

"I'll explain everything later," said Melba coyly. "Be here at six-thirty tomorrow and I'll drive."

"You talk to Blanche," he said, figuring there was a better chance of her coming if the invitation came from Mama. Then he groaned. "And can't we take a taxi?"

From the get-go, Samuel regretted getting into Melba's 1949 two-door Ford sedan. A cigarette dangling from her lips, she swerved erratically up California Street to Gough, where she turned and headed south to Valencia Street. From there she made a right turn up to Dolores and whisked a left past Mission Dolores, the oldest surviving structure in San

Francisco. Two more hill climbs brought them to Liberty Street, which overlooked the green expanse of Dolores Park and Mission High School, as well as the bell towers of the Mission itself. Looking east, Samuel could see the buildings of downtown San Francisco lit up and the outline of the Bay Bridge beyond. Just when he thought he might lose his lunch, Melba climbed one last hill and pulled up in front of Rosa María's house, hitting the curb as she parked. Amazingly, the ash on her cigarette, now over two inches long, was still intact. She rolled down the window and flicked it out, exhaling the smoke into the evening air.

Samuel let out a huge sigh of relief. "Shouldn't you wear glasses when you drive, Melba?" he asked when he'd regained his composure.

"Yeah, I forgot them. What the hell are you complaining about? You're here in one piece, aren't you? And it didn't cost you a dime."

They stood in the archway that led to the front door of the Rodríguez home. Melba was better dressed than the day before. She had on a green dress with a flower pattern that gave her the fresh look of a box of detergent, and her blue-gray hair was neatly coiffed.

Just as Melba was about to ring the bell for the second time, a small boy of about seven opened the door, a big smile on his dimpled face. He was neatly dressed in slacks and a starched white shirt, his too-long tie tucked into his pants. Samuel thought he looked on the skinny side. "Hi, I'm Marco. Welcome to our home."

"I'm Melba. We know each other. This is Samuel. He's a friend of mine."

The boy extended his hand. "Nice to meet you, Samuel. Please come upstairs. My mom's waiting for you."

Rosa María stood at the top of the stairs in a red satin dress and a white apron. A girl, three or four years younger than Marco, peered out from behind Rosa's apron. She had long braids and wore a blue velvet dress with what looked like a white embroidered breast piece. "This is Ina," said the hostess. "She can be shy around people she doesn't know."

The girl tried to disappear behind the apron, but Rosa María grabbed her hand and pulled her out. "Say hello to our guests."

Samuel and Melba extended their hands to the girl. Blushing, she shook them one at a time, her eyes glued to her shoes.

"Welcome to our home, Mr. Hamilton. My husband Alfonso will be here shortly. I hope you like Mexican food. I know Melba does. She's been here many times."

"Really," said Samuel. "I had no idea you two knew each other so well." He wanted to pursue the matter, but was swept out onto the back porch where he found freshly made hors d'oeuvres on a wooden table overlooking a spectacular vista of downtown San Francisco and the bay. Plates of refried beans, guacamole, and hot and medium salsas surrounded a large bowl of deep-fried tortilla chips. Samuel wasn't used to gourmet food, but he could tell that Rosa María knew what she was doing.

"What are those green cubes that bowl?" asked Samuel.

"Those are nopales. You would call them cactus. Mexican people eat them as a treat."

"You must write cookbooks," he said, munching on the crisp chips, which he'd loaded up with guacamole.

"Would you like a drink, Melba?" Rosa María asked.

"Just a beer."

"How about you, Mr. Hamilton?"

"I'll have a Scotch on the rocks."

"Oh, come on, Mr. Hamilton, be adventurous. Try something south of the border."

"Like what?" asked Samuel.

"Like a straight shot of our tequila with a lime chaser."

"Why not?" said Samuel, giving in to her suggestion.

"Coming right up," said a voice from the kitchen. It belonged to a Mexican man about Samuel's height who appeared in the doorway. He was Alfonso Rodríguez, Rosa María's husband. He wore a mustache and an easy smile. Samuel could tell he was a worked in the service industry just by observing his generous movements. Alfonso disappeared into the kitchen and returned with a bottle of tequila, two shot glasses, a lime cut into quarters and a bottle of beer. "I'm bringing you a Mexican beer, Melba. We just started carrying it at the market. Tell me if you like it." Samuel looked at the label, which read "Corona" in blue Old English script.

Melba poured a portion into a glass, squeezed lime into the beer and took a pull. She licked the foam off her lips and nodded approval.

Samuel wasn't sure what to do.

"Lick the back of your hand, sprinkle some salt on it and lick it again," said Alfonso, showing him how. "Then down the shot, just like this." Once again, Alfonso demonstrated his technique. "After that, suck on the lime."

Samuel complied and made a sour face. But he quickly caught on and soon was asking for another.

"Now you'll be grateful that I'm driving, buster, laughed Melba. "You won't be able to walk straight after a couple more of those."

"I knew there was a reason I trusted my life to you," laughed Samuel, downing another shot.

"How is Sofia, Melba?" asked Alfonso.

"Doing fine," said Melba.

"You know the Garcias?" asked Samuel. Sofia was the widow of Rafael Garcia, Melba's former employee who was killed in prison.

"Of course," said Rosa María. "When Rafael went to

prison, the family started shopping at our market and Melba paid the bill. After he was killed, his wife, Sofia, and his mother became Melba's partners at the bar. They preferred to continue to charge their groceries at Mi Rancho and have Melba pay for them monthly out of their share of the profits. So that's the way we work it."

"I'm beginning to see the connection between you two," said Samuel.

Marco and Ina passed the plates of hors d'oeuvres around for the guests to nibble on. "Don't eat too much," Rosa María warned. We're going to have a good dinner."

After a few minutes, she called them into the dining room. Although several sets of fancy porcelain dishes packed a china cabinet against one wall, the French-style oval table was set with colorful Mexican ceramic plates and soup bowls that matched the placemats and napkins.

Alfonso sat at the head of the table with his wife at his right, near the kitchen so she could get up and check on the meal and the serving girl as needed. The guests and the children sat along the sides of the table. The young boy, Marco, participated in the conversation with ease and charm, but his sister concentrated on the food, never saying a word.

When the serving girl came in and filled the bowls, Rosa María described what they were eating. "The soup is *sopa de flor de calabaza* and is made from the flowers of the squash," she said. "Enjoy!"

Alfonso poured a white wine with a label—Wente Brothers Grey Riesling— Samuel had never seen. "The wine is very tasty," he said after taking a sip. "I've never heard of it before."

"We're very lucky," said Alfonso. "It's a local wine, made locally in Livermore, and there's plenty of it."

"Rafael Garcia was a good friend of mine," said Samuel, changing the subject.

"That's what Melba told me," said Rosa María. "It's because

of what she's done for the Garcias that I decided to help you. And your friendship with Rafael didn't hurt, either."

"That's good news," said Samuel.

"But that will have to wait until after dinner. Right now, it's time for the main course."

"And what might that be?" asked Melba.

"I've prepared *enchiladas de camaron*. Shrimp enchiladas." As the serving girl put plates of rolled corn tortillas filled with chopped shrimp and melted cheese, all topped by a crème sauce, in front of the guests, Samuel finally connected the mouth-watering aromas he'd picked up when he first entered the house. Then came a salad plate of romaine lettuce, jicama and slices of orange.

"A picture of this food belongs in a magazine," said Melba.

"Too good for that," said Samuel. He instantly forgot all the rules of etiquette he'd ever been taught and, without waiting, cut into the enchiladas with his fork. And when he'd finished what he had on his plate, he asked for more. Then, still savoring the taste of the wine and the delicate dish he'd just eaten, he raised his crystal glass: "To the chef," he said. "I've never eaten better in my life." Even the children joined in the toast, giggling as they mimicked the adults.

"I hope you saved room for dessert," said Rosa María.

Samuel's face contorted in dismay, but he said nothing.

When the table was cleared, the serving girl brought out a vanilla flan with cut strawberries on top, and glasses of *agua fresca de mandarina*. Samuel poked at his flan, but couldn't find room for more than a nibble and a sip of the juice.

"Do you think you could write down that recipe for me? asked Samuel. "I'd like to try it out someday?"

"Are you kidding?" laughed Melba. "You can't even boil water."

Everyone laughed except Samuel, who turned red.

The Ugly Dwarf

When dinner was over, Rosa María excused herself and summoned the children. In her absence, Samuel and Alfonso sipped Kahlua from brandy snifters, and Melba drank another Mexican beer.

"Seen any good movies lately, Alfonso?" asked Samuel.

"Frankly we're still celebrating the Academy Awards of two years ago, when the Latinos won all the Oscars," said Alfonso.

"You mean *West Side Story* as best picture and Rita Moreno as best supporting actress?" said Samuel.

"Yes, sir," said Alfonso.

"Yeah, that was pretty impressive," replied Samuel.

"How about Sophia Loren as best actress," interjected Melba. "What a broad."

"The flick she won it for, *Two Women,* wasn't so bad either," said Samuel.

They all lifted their glasses and toasted Hollywood, laughing. "Sometimes they get it right," said Alfonso.

After about twenty minutes, Rosa María returned with two sheets of paper in her hands. "Sorry, I had to read the kids their bedtime story."

"Alfonso and I made a list of all the companies we sell sacks of pinto beans to in San Francisco, Mr. Hamilton," she said, handing him one of the pieces of paper. "We're surprised there are so many. We didn't realize that business was so good. You'll see the names, addresses and phone numbers, as well as the number of sacks we provided each company through June of last year. Good luck, and if you need any more help, let us know.

She laughed as she handed him the second sheet of paper. "And here's the recipe for the shrimp enchiladas. I hope you will make them for Blanche."

Even though Samuel was stuffed, he read through the recipe, Melba looking over his shoulder.

Shrimp Enchiladas

Ingredients:
2 lbs. lg. shrimp peeled and deveined
2 tbs. corn oil
6 green onions, diced
4 med. garlic cloves, finely diced
1 small serrano pepper, finely chopped
2 tbs. chopped cilantro
1 tsp. red pepper flakes
1 tbs. butter
1 jar "crema agria Mexicana," 25 oz.
1½ cups chicken broth
¼ tsp. garlic salt
¼ tsp. pepper
Salt to taste
1 Mexican fresco cheese
1 Mexican anejo cheese
¼ cup Parmesan cheese
1 dz. corn tortillas

Preparation:
Shrimp:
In a heavy pan heat corn oil to smoking point, add shrimp, green onions, garlic, serrano pepper, garlic salt, reg. salt and pepper. Turn shrimp with spatula for 3 minutes or until pink. Remove from heat and add cilantro. Place in bowl. Let cool and chop shrimp into medium size pieces.

Sauce:
Place one third of the shrimp in a blender with chicken sauce and cream. Blend until smooth. In the pan where shrimp was cooked, add butter, shrimp and cream mixture and warm at very low heat until it thickens. (Maintain low heat and mix with spoon

The Ugly Dwarf

or it will curdle.) Season with salt and remove from heat.

To assemble:
Butter a Pyrex dish that holds one dozen enchiladas and have ready. Grate the cheeses and mix. Warm tortillas to soften and add a little sauce to bottom of Pyrex. Submerge each tortilla in sauce, fill with reserved diced shrimp and cheese, then roll and place in Pyrex. Repeat with remaining tortillas until Pyrex is filled. Spoon the rest of sauce on top of enchiladas. Add cheese evenly on top and bake in preheated 400-degree oven for 12-15 minutes.

Serve with chopped green onions as garnish

Can be accompanied with romaine lettuce salad with jicama, cucumber and orange segments.

6

Shaking the Passion Fruit Tree

THE BLEND OF AROMAS FROM Rosa María's feast still lingered
in Samuel's nostrils the next morning when he went to the
medical examiner's office with the list of addresses she'd given
him. Turtle Face greeted him with his usual faint smile and
pointed to a seat on the other side of his cluttered desk.

"I got a list of all the places Mi Rancho Market sold pinto
beans to last year," said Samuel.

"I'm sure Homicide will be glad to hear it," the examiner
said impatiently.

"Does that mean you're out of the loop?" asked Samuel, a
perplexed look on his face.

"I was never in it. My job is forensics. Their job is to solve
murders."

"Is there anyone in particular I should contact over there?"
asked the reporter, disappointed to lose his inside connection.

"Yeah, the new guy, Bernardi. Bruno Bernardi."

"You're kidding!" said Samuel, wide-eyed.

"Why would I kid you? He was just hired. He worked in
Richmond for years. In fact, I've helped him on several cases.
Old what's-his-name kicked the bucket—a heart attack, so
it happened pretty fast. They needed someone who could hit
the ground running and Bernardi was available. That's all I

know."

"I know him well. I just worked on a case with him."

"He's a straight shooter, which is more than I can say for some of the dipshits around here," said the examiner.

"Where can I reach him?"

"What did I just say?" growled Turtle Face. "He's in Homicide for Christ's sake."

The examiner got up hurriedly, as if he'd wasted enough time, and ushered the reporter to the door, anxious to get back to his own work.

* * *

Samuel walked the short distance to 850 Bryant Street, which was the location of the new Criminal Courts building. In addition to housing the District Attorney's office, the building was home to the main office of the San Francisco Police Department. The building was gray and rectangular, and lacked the charm of the department's old Kearny Street location, which featured arched windows that overlooked the bay. Now, the only view from the department's upper floors was of the 101 Freeway.

Samuel took the elevator up to Homicide. "Bernardi, please," he told the receptionist.

"Sorry, sir. He won't be back until two."

"Are you sure?"

"Look, Mister, I'm just a clerk. The big boys do what they want to do. I just write down what they tell me."

Samuel put his hands up, palms facing her. "Okay, okay. Just trying to save time."

"Come back at two then."

"Can you at least tell him that Samuel Hamilton came by to see him?"

Without looking up, she wrote something on a message

pad in front of her.

Samuel took the hint and left. He went to the basement coffee shop and worked on the list that Rosa María had given him, separating the company names into their respective Bay Area regions: the East Bay, San Jose and, finally, the Mission, where he wanted to concentrate his efforts.

At two he rode the elevator back to the homicide floor. When the door opened, he saw Bruno Bernardi standing at the reception desk. His stocky five-foot-eight-inch frame hadn't changed a bit; neither had his cropped salt and pepper brown hair or his slightly flattened nose, which gave him a rugged appearance that he otherwise didn't project.

Bernardi looked at Samuel. "When I heard you were looking for me and would be here at two, I decided to wait right here until you came."

"Still wearing brown suits, even in San Francisco." Samuel extended his hand, an enormous smile on his face. "What a surprise to find you here in the homicide bureau."

"It was time for a change, with the divorce and all. When the opening came up here, it seemed like the right thing to do."

"Did Marisol have anything to do with you making the change?"

Bernardi blushed. "Come into my office, Samuel." He put his arm around the reporter's shoulder and they walked down the hall to his cubbyhole.

Samuel recognized the same photographs on the wall he'd seen when he'd visited the detective in Richmond; he particularly remembered the one of the large family gathering at the picnic celebrating his grandfather's hundredth birthday.

Bernardi took off his suit jacket and his shoulder holster and hung them up on the coat rack in the corner behind his desk. He sat down in his shirtsleeves and suspenders, glancing out at the view from his office window. Cars zipped back and forth along the 101 Freeway, which ran east and west, right next to the Hall of Justice, with the office buildings of the Financial District visible in the distance.

"Is this a social call?" Bernardi asked. "I saw your name on one of the new cases they gave me."

"That's why I'm here. I have information that may lead to some evidence." Samuel explained how he'd gotten the list of names and addresses for the companies that had bought the beans in San Francisco the previous year.

"You found out where the sack came from?" asked Bernardi.

"I found out where it came from originally, but so far that's been the easy part."

"Was the sack made last year?" asked Bernardi.

"I don't think we'll ever know when it was made," said Samuel. "The real question is whether or not we can figure out if it was transferred directly from any of the companies that I have on this list to the person who committed the crime." He pulled out the two sheets of paper, one that Rosa María had given him and another he had prepared that separated the addresses into geographical areas to make the investigation easier.

"Since the dead guy was from south of the border, I figure that the ones in the Mission are the most plausible," said Samuel.

"Does that mean you're going to help me with this case?"

"That's the idea," said the reporter. "It worked pretty good for us in Contra Costa, didn't it?"

"I'm not complaining," said Bernardi. "I've got my hands full. They turned fifty files over to me. I need someone I can trust to cover my back on some of this stuff. So far, I don't have much on this case. Fill me in."

He and Samuel spent the next hour going over all the evidence in the file and everything else Samuel had learned since the moment he got the phone call from Melba.

"Let's say you find out where the sack came from. That doesn't solve the case, does it?" asked Bernardi.

"No, it doesn't," said Samuel. "But it's a start."

"Okay, I'm with you on that. How about you take the buyers in the Mission and I'll put someone on the rest of the city. If you find something of interest, we can go and take a look. Just keep me posted and don't publish anything in the newspaper without talking to me first. Is that a deal?"

"That's a deal," said Samuel, smiling.

Bernardi pushed the file to the side of his desk, pulled at his suspenders and rocked back in his brown leather swivel chair. "It wouldn't hurt if you could fill me in on who and what to watch out for in the department. Also, who's Melba?"

"You've asked two questions," responded Samuel. "Explaining who Melba is—that's easy. I'll take you to Camelot some day after work and introduce you to her. Your first question is more complicated. There are a lot of sleaze balls in the SFPD, and some of them are dangerous. I'll have to think about who you should stay away from, and I'll have to ask a few questions around town before I answer that one."

*   *   *

The next day Samuel was back pounding the pavement in the Mission district. Most of the places he inquired at were either restaurants or Catholic Church schools that served lunches to their students. The last place he visited was also a church that served meals to its parishioners.

This one, however, wasn't like the others. It was a storefront operation with plate glass windows that were covered with black drapes. The sign above the front door measured approximately four by seven feet and featured a white background with purple lettering outlined in black. It read "The

The Ugly Dwarf

Universal Church of Psychic Unfoldment," with words in written underneath in Spanish that Samuel didn't understand. On the door near the knob was a small sign in English, which read: "Deliveries please go to the rear." Underneath was a second sign, in Spanish, which he assumed said the same thing.

He went around to the back alley looking for the delivery entrance and found a door with the church's name on it. It led to a kitchen, where five people were working in a cramped space. A plump Latin man with a round face and black hair approached him. *"Nadie habla inglés aquí señor. ¿Si quieres hablar con el pastor regrese a las cinco y media?"*

Samuel didn't understand anything the man said except *"cinco,"* which he knew meant five. But that was also the number of employees he counted in the kitchen. He put up five fingers and said *"Cinco?"*

"Sí, señor, esta tarde a las cinco y media."

"This afternoon at five?"

"No. A las cinco y media."

*"Media..,*okay, five-thirty, I got ya," said Samuel, nodding his head as he left.

*   *   *

Samuel didn't feel like wandering around and knocking on any more doors, so he returned to his office and called Marisol Leiva. She was sorting the day's mail at her secretarial desk in the law offices of his friend Janak Marachak. As the phone rang, the wind from an open window blew a letter off her desk.

"Hello, Samuel, haven't heard from you in a while."

"That's true. I've been in hibernation. But I have a new problem to bother you with. I'm looking at a church in the Mission and the people there only speak Spanish, as far as I can tell. So I want to know if you'll accompany me there this afternoon and act as my translator? I need to talk to the cooks and to the pastor."

"What church are you talking about?" she asked.

"It's a storefront on Mission Street called The Universal Church of Psychic Unfoldment."

"I know something about it. Let me check my calendar."

Marisol put the phone down and glanced through her Day Timer before grabbing the phone again. "I'll be glad to go with you. I'd like to see what they are doing there." She got up and went around the desk to pick up the piece of paper that the wind had blown off when she first answered the phone. "What's your interest in it, Samuel? You're not religious. I remember how you struggled during my father's sermons at the church in Stockton last year."

"I don't remember much about the sermons. I just remember that Bernardi couldn't take his eyes off of you. But it hasn't got anything to do with religion. I'm trying to find out if a sack of pinto beans came from there."

"What?"

"Never mind. I'll explain when I see you. Can you meet me in front of the church after work?"

"What's the address?"

Samuel gave her the number, and they agreed they'd meet there as soon after five as she could get there from downtown.

When Marisol arrived, Samuel was pacing back and forth in front of the building. The black drapes were now open and he'd been able to see inside the mysterious place. There were several rows of folding chairs with an aisle down the middle, directly in front of the door. At the end of the aisle was an elevated platform with a podium. Attached to the ceiling directly above were several spotlights, each focused on a different area. A bunched black curtain in front of the lights was raised to the ceiling, giving the platform the appearance of a theatrical stage.

Samuel greeted Marisol with a hug. "I see that Bernardi's made a new home for himself in the San Francisco Police Department," he said, teasing her.

"I know you two have talked about some case," she answered, trying not to give away too much.

"No mystery in that," said Samuel. "You two are obviously an item, and I congratulate myself for introducing you. You owe me big time for that, Marisol."

"Not so fast, my friend. His divorce isn't final yet and you know the rule about not dating people until they've been divorced for at least six months."

"I don't think that rule applies here, trust me. Did he tell you about the case we're working on?"

"Nothing. He only mentioned that he'd run into you."

Samuel tried to explain enough of what he'd learned so that she could follow his reasons for dragging her down there on such short notice.

"So why are we here?" she asked.

"According to Rosa María Rodríguez, this is one of the places that bought sacks of pinto beans from Mi Rancho Market."

"I've met the man who runs this church," said Marisol. "He was at one of my father's sermons a couple of years ago. And I've heard about him since then from my father."

"Oh, really. What did you hear?"

"You'd better see for yourself. I understand he puts on quite a show."

"Come back to the kitchen with me. That's where I need help." Samuel took her arm and escorted her to the back. They parted a black curtain in the rear of the space next to the stage and entered the cramped kitchen. There was hardly room for the five people already there, much less for Samuel and Marisol.

"Mi amigo, que no habla español tiene algunas preguntas," explained Marisol.

The man with the round face answered her in Spanish. "Your friend came earlier and I told him to come back when the pastor was here."

Marisol responded, again in Spanish. "Right now I don't think we need the pastor. His question is for you. What do you do with the empty pinto bean sacks after all the beans have been used?"

"That's all he wants to know?" asked the man. "Come, I'll show you."

He took them into the alley where Samuel had entered the kitchen earlier. Next to the kitchen entrance was a padlocked double steel door resting at a forty-five-degree angle from the sidewalk. He unlocked the padlock on the bar across the doors, opened up the slabs of steel and hooked them on iron rings. This uncovered a stairway that led to a door at the bottom.

The man descended, opened the basement door and switched on a light, inviting them to follow. Inside were shelves stacked floor-to-ceiling with canned food. The room was twice the size of the kitchen and had one light that hung from a single cord in its center. Ten sacks of pinto beans were in a corner. The one on top had the name Mi Rancho Market printed on it. Next to the full sacks was a small pile of folded empty ones.

"Is this where he puts all the empty sacks?" asked Samuel.

The man nodded when Marisol repeated the question in Spanish.

"Who has access to the storeroom?"

"My kitchen staff, if I open the door for them," Marisol translated.

"Anyone else?"

"Not that I know of," he answered. "But as you saw coming down here, the key is tied to this long piece of wood and it hangs on a hook in the kitchen."

"Has he noticed any sacks missing from the pile here?" asked Samuel.

"He hasn't," answered Marisol.

"What does he do with them?"

"We give them back to Mi Rancho when they bring us more beans."

"Can I come back and take a photograph of this place?" asked Samuel.

"You need to ask the boss," Marisol translated. "He's probably here by now."

They all went back up the basement stairs, through the kitchen and into the storefront. The place had begun to fill up. There were a number of Latinos sitting together in groups, many of the women dressed in the vibrant colors of their native countries. The front two rows were filled with noisy young teenage girls.

Samuel and Marisol saw a dwarf dressed in blue jeans and cowboy boots talking to a large woman who looked like a giant next to him.

"Who's that?" asked Samuel.

Marisol laughed. "That's Dominique the dominatrix. She's attached to his church. I hear she wears two hats."

Samuel didn't know whether to continue the line of inquiry about the strange woman or to focus on the dwarf.

"The little man is Dusty Schwartz. He's the preacher and owner of the church. The dominatrix is his spiritual adviser."

Samuel laughed. "You're kidding."

"I'm not kidding, but keep your voice down. They might hear you."

Dusty had his back to them and was immersed in conversation with the dominatrix, who saw them approaching and alerted the dwarf to their imminent arrival. Samuel worried that she'd seen him and Marisol laughing at them, but it was too late to avoid the encounter.

Dusty turned slowly and smiled as soon as he saw Marisol. *"Hola, amiga,"* he said to her.

"Hello, Mr. Schwartz. I'd like you to meet Samuel Hamilton from the morning paper. He's heard a lot about you and would like to do a story on you and your church."

Dusty gave an "aw shucks" response, but his blue eyes zeroed in on Samuel for a once-over. The dwarf wanted to see what he was up against. "Be glad to talk with you, sir," he smiled. "But it'll have to be after my sermon. We're almost ready to start."

"Of course," said Samuel. "I'm anxious to see the show." He and Marisol exchanged glances, but neither said anything. The reporter watched as the bow-legged dwarf climbed the stairs to the stage and disappeared behind one of the side curtains.

As soon as Marisol, Dusty and Samuel began talking, Dominique retired into the background. When the preacher was out of sight, Samuel turned to watch Dominique walk towards another closed black curtain, this one located in a far corner of the space, away from the kitchen. In front of the curtain were five chairs occupied by three young men, who appeared to be under twenty, and two women, probably in their forties. They would remain seated there during the ceremony to ensure they wouldn't lose their place for their audience with Dominique if they weren't received before the preaching started.

Once installed behind the curtain, Dominique opened it slightly and beckoned to the person seated in the first chair.

"What's that all about?" asked Samuel.

"My father says she's a witch. She sells spells and potions to the poor."

"Are you sure about that?"

"Yes, I'm sure. Many people believe in all kinds of magic, and she's supposed to be a master at casting spells."

"You mean she practices black magic."

"That's what it's called."

"Isn't that illegal?"

"Only if she gets caught," answered Marisol.

"Why don't you report her?"

"Because someone else would quickly take her place and she doesn't do any harm, really. The people won't listen when it comes to changing the old ways."

"What's wrong with her face?" asked Samuel.

"I heard she was burned," said Marisol.

By now there were no empty seats, and Samuel could smell cooked beans and freshly made tortillas. He shook his head; there was too much going on. He tried to focus on one thing at a time. "The smell of all that food really makes me hungry."

"That's part of the strategy," said Marisol. "The smell of the food entices the people to stay until the sermon is over and the donations are collected. Then they get something to eat."

"Where?"

"Right here. See those tables up against the walls? I bet they set them up for food right after Schwartz is through with his sermon."

"Pretty clever. It compensates for having a dwarf for a preacher, wouldn't you say?"

"Wait 'til you hear him," answered Marisol, "You won't think he's so weird."

A group of six musicians dressed in mariachi regalia—big sombreros included—took the stage and proceeded to play Mexican rancheras. The crowd quickly turned festive.

Samuel thought how different this was from the two gospel music performers he'd heard when he attended the service conducted by Mr. Leiva, Marisol's father, at the Catholic

Church outside Stockton the year before. This was more like a boisterous carnival than a religious gathering. When the musicians stopped playing there was clapping, whistling and calls for more, but at that point Schwartz came out from behind a black side curtain.

All spotlights converged on the dwarf, who was dressed in a tuxedo, a black cape with red velvet lining and a top hat. Mad cheering accompanied his approach to the podium. The teenage girls in the first two rows screamed as if he were a matinee idol. Schwartz disappeared from view for an instant; then, climbing atop two Coke boxes, the upper part of his little body appeared above the podium. He waved his top hat solemnly in all directions, the bright lining of his cape gleaming in the spotlights. His dark curly hair glistened with Brilliantine and his blue eyes sparkled with the excitement of the power he wielded. Samuel had to admit that he looked majestic.

As soon as Schwartz began to speak in his deep-throated voice, his Spanish melodic and educated, the crowd silenced. He had an actor's sense of timing—he made use of long pauses, his voice soft and slow—and he nailed each person in place with his hypnotic eyes. Samuel, who was entranced, ignored Marisol's nudges as she attempted to bring him back to reality. The reporter couldn't make much sense of Schwartz's words, but like nearly everybody else he soon surrendered to the preacher's dramatic cadence. Schwartz made point after point, his voice getting louder, faster and more forceful, but the meaning of his sermon was growing more and more obscure. As Marisol translated, Samuel recognized some themes that he remembered from Mr. Leiva's sermons, but it seemed this man was giving himself a bigger role in the grand scheme of things than Galo ever did. No. Samuel corrected himself, it wasn't a just grand scheme: the dwarf called it The Infinite Plan.

King of the Bottom

Schwartz told the congregation he had lessons to teach and that those who followed him would experience miracles. He said his mission was to watch out for the well being of each and every person in the room, for they were the beloved lambs of his flock, and he would guide them through the darkness. Yes, the forest was dark and deep and full of perils, but he knew the way. He had been chosen as the guide—he was God's new apostle. The Infinite Plan could not be understood—like all things heavenly, it was incomprehensible—but he had been given divine instruction, he had studied at the source. He was different. Couldn't they see that God had made him different? Only he knew what The Infinite Plan was, and only he had the key that would unlock it for them.

Schwartz then launched into a rant—or so it seemed to Samuel—about the mind, God, the physical world, his role as an apostle, and something about a "possessive ray" that the reporter couldn't quite grasp. It seemed that what the preacher was really trying to perfect was described in The Infinite Plan as the Possessive Ray. In the beginning he wanted to use it to control everyone, but as Marisol explained to Samuel later, he got sidetracked and ended up using it just to try and get control over his sexual conquests. The preacher continued yammering, but Samuel stopped trying to follow. He felt dizzy and confused, and he realized that he was not the only one: the atmosphere was dangerously charged and the emotional crescendo in the room had reached an almost unbearable intensity. He noticed, however, that Marisol was the only person in the congregation immune to Schwartz's palaver. Samuel thought that she'd probably cultivated a thick skin listening to her father's sermons. In fact, it was more than that, as Samuel later discovered. Marisol knew just how sick the dwarf was.

Schwartz pulled a cord and a canvas dropped away from the ceiling in front of the musicians to expose a Renaissance painting some ten feet in length and seven feet tall. All spotlights were focused on it, save for the one that remained on him. Schwartz extended his short arms to draw everyone within a metaphysical embrace and began an explanation of the two central figures in the painting: one was Christ, God's principal prophet on Earth in Biblical times; the other was his future apostle, shown seated next to a moneychanger. The crowd could see that the artist had focused the light on the mysterious chosen one.

The Reverend was now at the apex of his eloquence. He was shouting, pounding the podium and waving his arms wildly in the air. "See how Christ is enticing his future apostle away from the moneychanger! He is calling him into God's service! What does this mean? The moneychanger represents greed, selfishness and apathy. Christ is telling you that you have to forget worldly things and follow The Infinite Plan. How will you do that? Trust me, I will guide you. Follow me!" By then the congregants were on their feet—most noticeably the teenage girls—clapping and yelling "*Salvador! Salvador!*" Savior! Savior! The musicians filed out from behind the painting and blasted out a flamboyant hymn. Samuel thought his head was going to explode with all the noise.

Suddenly an older woman near Samuel fainted. Before he could reach out to help her, Marisol grabbed him by the sleeve. "Don't even think of interfering!" she shouted above the noise. A man in the next row tumbled into the center aisle and, with a scream of ecstasy, dropped to the floor, convulsing and foaming at the mouth. Another woman followed, and within seconds several people were writhing on the ground, their limbs flailing in all directions. The reporter fell back in his chair in disbelief. Marisol patted his shoulder and smiled knowingly.

Donation baskets flew down the aisles to the accompaniment of blasts from the trumpet and more chanting of "*Salvador! Salvador!*" They were quickly filled to overflowing, and Samuel calculated that Schwartz was bringing in a pretty good haul from a group of such poor people.

The service ended with a fanfare from the musicians. The dwarf descended from the boxes, put on his top hat and, with a twirl of his cape, disappeared behind the side curtain. The crowd's mood suddenly changed. The formerly hysterical parishioners calmly climbed back to their feet, the musicians segued into popular rancheras, and people moved out of the way to make way for the placement of tables and the folding of chairs so the feast could begin.

Not everyone moved toward the tables, however. Samuel noted that three teenage girls from the front row quickly climbed the steps of the platform and followed the dwarf. In addition, the five chairs in front of Dominique's curtain remained occupied; when one person got up to enter her domain, the others slid down to the next chair in the row and another client quickly filled the vacant seat.

Marisol and Samuel stood in the middle of the floor watching the tables and seats being moved all around them. "I wouldn't have believed it, if I hadn't seen it," the reporter said. "It's hard to imagine that people would follow this guy."

"He's charismatic, all right. My father could learn a thing or two from him."

"I wonder where he got that painting," asked Samuel. "It's obviously European and pretty old. A little out of place in this environment."

"I think it's pretty clever," said Marisol. "It gives the impression that he is part of the Catholic Church, and it gives him a connection to the Bible, both of which are important to his preaching. In any event, since you're going to see him shortly, you can ask him."

Samuel nodded his head and tugged Marisol's sleeve. "Who's the guy in the electric blue suit, the one with the hair hat?"

"That's Michael Harmony, an attorney. He's come here to

pass out business cards to the church members. He tried the same thing with my father, but he was run off."

"Is that legal?"

"You've got to be kidding! My hunch is that the pastor says it's okay. I bet the dwarf gets a piece of the action."

"How'd you figure that out?" asked Samuel.

"When I told Janak that Mr. Harmony approached my father, Janak told me that a lot of attorneys hang around organizations like this just to hustle injury cases; if the leadership allows them to prey on the members, they get a payoff.

"I bet if you introduce yourself and tell him you're from the morning paper he'll leave rather than talk to you."

*   *   *

As the crowd devoured the food and the mariachi band played in the background, the preacher appeared from behind the black side curtain. He'd changed back into his blue jeans and cowboy boots. He searched the room from the platform and beckoned to Samuel once they'd made eye contact.

Samuel climbed the stairs and looked down at the man as he shook his hand. "Thanks for taking the time to talk with me. Should I call you Reverend?"

Dusty laughed. It was genuine and full of self-congratulation. "No need for that. Just call me Dusty. But if you print something about me, then call me by my appropriate title. I'll leave the accolades to you."

Samuel thought the response was affected but he tried not to smirk. He realized that he had to look as if he took the man seriously if he wanted to get information. "Where can we talk, Reverend?"

"Come back to my dressing room and office. It's about the only place I get any privacy around here."

Samuel followed him to a solid wood door with triple

deadbolt locks in it. Dusty took out a keychain, unlocked all three and waved his hand for the reporter to enter. Inside was a half-open drop-leaf table pushed up against the wall. Next to it was a record player on a stand, with long-playing records stacked side by side beneath it. Against the other wall was a single bed that appeared to have seen recent use, Samuel thought, remembering the teenaged girls who had gone backstage with the dwarf. The blanket was pulled back, and on top of the pillow was a rag doll with black hair made from wool threads. On the night table next to the bed Samuel saw the tip of a package of condoms poking out from beneath a newspaper. The donation baskets were stacked in the corner, still brimming with the recent take, waiting to be counted. A strange smell hung in the room.

"Pardon the mess," said Dusty. "We usually wait until the people leave, then we count the money behind locked doors so we can deposit it in the night slot at the bank before one of us goes home."

"Who's we?" asked Samuel.

"Dominique, the healer. She's my assistant."

"Really? What does she do?"

"As I said, she's my assistant. She handles the books."

"Does she have her own church here?" asked Samuel.

"No, no. She does have clientele who seek her advice. You probably saw them sitting outside her consultation area"

"What do people consult her about?"

"Spiritual things, Mr. Hamilton. If you want specifics, you'll have to ask her."

"Fair enough. Let's talk about you. But first, what's that smell?"

"Probably the result of an incense cleaning by Dominique," Dusty answered vaguely.

"How did you get this organization up and running? And so efficiently I might add."

Dusty gave a lengthy explanation of how he started his church, emphasizing his own achievements and leaving out any mention of Dominique's role in its development. He described his long-standing calling to be a preacher and how he had finally achieved his dream. "Being a little man helps. Once I convince people that God works through a person like me, they surrender, since they see that they're not as deformed as I am, so clearly God can work through them, too."

"What do they ask of you?"

"Life is a painful process, Mr. Hamilton. Mostly they are looking for reassurance, for someone who will understand and share their pain."

"How do you do that?"

"I take their pain inside and I try not to shed the tears that are welling up inside me, it hurts so much. Then I embrace them and tell them to go in peace."

"What do you do when you encounter evil in a person?"

"That's a good question and a hard one to answer. It happens more often than you think. I have to find a way to exorcise the evil, and I get Dominique to help me with that person and with the process. But sometimes the darkness is so intense that I have to bathe myself in an aura of light and, afterward, Dominique cleanses me."

"How does she do that?"

"Ah, that's her secret. You'll have to ask her that question."

"I guess I'll have to interview her as well."

Samuel was taking notes as fast as he could, trying to figure out if he could broach the subject of the pinto bean sacks, but he couldn't find an opening. "There was a large group of overexcited girls in the front row during your sermon, and after it was over, three of them came backstage."

"Yes, they came for guidance. I spent a few minutes with them and explained how they should follow my spiritual teachings. I then asked them to check in with me often so I can evaluate their progress."

"I see," said Samuel, eyeing the disheveled bed and the strange doll on the pillow. "Did you see them all together or one at a time?"

"All together," Dusty sighed. "I didn't have time to solve their individual spiritual problems, so I listened to them collectively and told them to go home and pray, and to come back and see me on Sunday."

I bet, Samuel thought. He knew where he wanted to go next—it was to the pinto bean sack, but if he did and the dwarf had something to hide, he'd shut down. "Would you mind if I interviewed your assistant to get some more background on you for my story?"

"It's okay with me, but you need to check with her, if she's still here," said the dwarf, getting up from the stool in front of his makeup table. Samuel caught Dusty's reflection in the theatre-like mirror, which was surrounded by miniature bulbs.

"Where did you get that painting? It's old and beautiful. Looks Italian."

"That's another question for Dominique. She loaned it to me."

"Thanks for spending time with me, Reverend," said Samuel, once again emphasizing the dwarf's self-imposed title. "I'll make sure the article comes out on a Sunday and I'll send you a copy."

"Anytime… Give me your name again?" said Dusty, feigning absentmindedness.

"It's Samuel. Samuel Hamilton. Here's my card, just in case you think of something you might want to add."

*   *   *

Samuel walked back out onto the stage and into the now

almost-empty space. Marisol was seated on one of the folding chairs talking to a bald fat man dressed in a checkered sports coat. As the reporter approached, she got up and turned towards him. "This is Art McFadden," she gestured. "He's Mr. Harmony's investigator."

"I'm Samuel Hamilton," said the reporter, extending his hand, which the fat man engulfed in his clammy mitt.

"Glad ta meet ya," the man said solicitously. "Any friend of Marisol's is a friend of mine."

"You work for Mr. Harmony, do you?

"Sure do. Among other things."

"What exactly do you do for him?"

"Mostly public relations."

"What does that mean?"

"I make sure he has clients. Then I take care of them." The fat man hesitated. "Look, I'd like to spend more time with you, but I gotta talk to the preacher." He headed towards the Reverend's dressing room.

"What's that guy's story?" asked Samuel as he watched the fat man labor up the steps to the platform.

"He's Michael Harmony's paymaster," said Marisol. "He's the one who gets the business and keeps the providers happy. He's no doubt on his way to the dwarf's dressing room right now to make a payoff. If I were you, I'd spend some time with him. Everything is for sale with Fatso, so you'll find out most of what you want to know about what goes on here."

Dominique walked out from behind the black curtain. She was dressed in black and wore her stiletto-heeled boots, which made her almost six feet tall. A large gold pendant hung from her neck. She was imposing looking, even with the scar on her face.

The Ugly Dwarf

"Busy night, huh?" asked Samuel.

"Yes. They have so many problems and we have so little time. Who are you, may I ask?"

"My name is Samuel Hamilton. I'm from the morning paper. I just interviewed the Reverend Schwartz for a story I'm doing about his church. He told me you were his assistant. Can I ask you some questions?"

"I'd be glad to oblige you, Mr. Hamilton, but right this minute I'm pretty tired and I still have a lot of work to do around here. Here's my card. Call me later in the week and we'll have a chat."

"Okay Miss…"—Samuel looked at the card—"…Dominique, but I hope it can be as soon as possible. I can't finish writing the article without your input."

"Call me tomorrow."

*　　*　　*

It was after ten o'clock when Samuel and Marisol left the Universal Church of Psychic Unfoldment. When they were around the corner, Samuel shook his head. "I was really surprised about all the under-the-table business that was going on so openly. This preacher-man is wrapped pretty tight. If he's trying to protect his empire, if that's what you call it, he isn't doing a very good job of it. He's being very careless letting everyone know he's having sex with underage girls. He can get in a lot of trouble for that."

"Someone would have to complain first," said Marisol. "You saw those girls screaming down there in the front row. They're star-struck, and the union representatives aren't going to complain as long as they get their payoffs."

"But he can't keep them all happy all the time. It's a jealousy thing. Sooner or later, it's going to mean trouble."

"Maybe, but that's all in the future. Let's talk about the

reason you came here in the first place. Did you find out anything about your sack?"

"There wasn't an opening. Actually I was afraid to ask him. I'll have to figure out another approach, like using the fat man as you suggested."

A few hours later, after the money had been counted and Dominique left to deposit the cash in the night deposit slot of the bank, Dusty sat down amidst the clutter of his dressing room office and turned on the record player. Out came the voice of Victoria De Los Angeles. Her operatic timbre filled the room with a medley of songs contained on the long-playing disc. When she launched into *La Paloma*, Dusty hurled himself on top of his sex-stained bed sheets, buried his head in one of the pillows and began to sob.

7

Which Road to Travel?

BERNARDI SAT AT THE ROUND TABLE drinking a glass of red wine and watching the middle-aged woman with blue-gray hair seated opposite him greet customers as they entered the bar. She sipped from a glass of beer and, after crushing her cigarette out in the ashtray full of butts on the table beside her, immediately lit another. She waved it in the air, smiling occasionally or nodding her head in recognition of a patron. The mangy mutt at her feet didn't move, but watched every movement that went by. Bernardi figured that she and her dog knew just about everyone who came in.

It was just past six o'clock and the park across the street was nearly deserted. The sun reflected off the downtown buildings to the east, and boats came and went under the Bay Bridge beyond.

Samuel was late. When he walked in, the dog jumped up and wagged his tailless bottom. The reporter rushed up to Bernardi and slapped him on the back. "Sorry. Just running behind schedule." He then went over to the dog, which stood on its hind legs and licked his hands. The reporter groped in his pocket but quickly realized that he didn't have anything to offer. He gave Melba a forlorn look but she just shrugged her shoulders. Excalibur didn't understand that there was nothing for him and continued pawing at Samuel's pant leg.

Samuel finally moved away and motioned to the lieutenant to approach, grabbing the sleeve of his dull brown suit jacket and extending his other hand toward Melba. "Melba, this is Bruno Bernardi. He's the new homicide detective I've been telling you about."

"I already figured out who he was. No such thing as a cop in disguise. I didn't want to say nothing 'cause I didn't want him to feel scrutinized." She laughed.

"Melba's the one to come to when you really want to know what's cooking in San Francisco," said Samuel.

"Good to finally meet you, Melba. I feel like I already know ya."

"Don't be too sure about that, Mr. Detective. There's so much bullshit flying around this city 'bout me that most people don't know what to believe. I like it that way."

Bernardi smiled. "I've only heard good things, Melba, only good things."

"Yeah, sure. You flatterers are all the same. You must have taken lessons from Samuel." She laughed again, lit another Lucky Strike and took a sip of her beer.

"Thanks for coming, Bruno," Samuel said. "I wanted you two to meet. I also need a favor, Melba. Bruno wanted to know who he should watch out for in the San Francisco Police Department, and I decided there was no better person to ask than you."

Melba looked around the moderately crowded bar, blew smoke out through her nose and crushed out her cigarette. Then she motioned for the two men to come closer. They both sat down, one on each side of her. Samuel reached down and scratched the earless side of Excalibur's head.

"You're here because Charlie MacAteer died, Mr. Bernardi. He was one of homicide's best and a real prince of a person. A lot of guys envied him." She gave the lieutenant the once-over, as if to satisfy herself that her appraisal of him was correct. She made sure that he was looking directly at her. "The rumor on the street is that you're even better. There are a few wannabes in the department who fought to take his place as the top dog, but the brass knew what they were doing. You're a big problem for some of those bureaucratic bastards, though. Just keep your eyes and ears open. The best always trump the mediocre. And you'll know instinctively who not to trust in homicide.

"Stay alert. After you've cracked a couple of big ones, they'll relax and you'll be in. It just takes time in grade. Make the rounds to all the local bars in all the precincts, so the bartenders and the owners know who you are. Once they trust you, you'll get a lot of information that will make your job easier. After a while, they'll start giving you credit for solving crimes that you didn't even know were committed." She lit another cigarette and drank what was left in her beer glass, signaling to the bartender that she needed another drink.

"Isn't there anyone in particular he should watch out for?" implored Samuel, all but ringing his hands.

Melba cocked her head to the side, dismissing the inquiry. "I know you're thinking about Maurice Sandovich, Samuel, 'cause you've dealt with him before.

"Just for your information, Bruno, he's in Chinatown vice. He's had his ups and downs, but like I told Samuel, he's small potatoes, and for a few bucks, he'll get you all or most of the information you need from Chinatown. But you fellas are trying to find out about something that we all think happened in the Mission." She stubbed out her cigarette and put down her empty beer glass, since the new one hadn't yet arrived.

"The most important cop in the Mission is Captain Doyle O'Shaughnessy, a tough old Irish bastard who knows his stuff. He runs the Mission District with an iron hand and doesn't take shit from nobody. He knows about you already and he knows about your case. Ordinarily he'd tell you to go fuck yourself because you're new on the force, but he also knows that the crime probably happened in the Mission on his watch, and he's not happy about it, so he'll open up to you for all the help he can get. Usually, if it's not murder, he finds out who did it and he pushes 'em out of the Mission so that his yard looks clean. You pay O'Shaughnessy a visit real soon. You know where to find him?"

"At the station house, right?"

"Bullshit. Go to Bruno's restaurant in the Mission any day from noon to 3 p.m. That's where he hangs out with his buddies the union bosses. Kind of funny, Lieutenant, you can tell people your family owns the place." She laughed again.

"That's where Art McFadden told me to meet him," said Samuel.

"Art who?" asked Bernardi.

"I'll tell you about him later," said Samuel.

"That fat-ass ambulance chaser. He lives at Bruno's. You know why?" Melba smirked.

"It must be City Hall, the main base," said Samuel. "You said even the top cop hangs out there."

"You've got it right, pal. That's where the action is in the Mission. You tell that fat bastard hello for me and ask him when he's going to pay me for delivering the Ragland case to him."

"Jesus, Melba, you're well connected. What do you know about the dwarf preacher, Dusty Schwartz?"

"Not much, so far. He's not my patron yet. But after you and Detective Bernardi talk, you fill me in."

"Okay, will do," said Samuel. He picked up his drink and motioned for Bernardi to follow him. They went to a table at the back of the bar by the mahogany phone booth and sat down, Samuel with his Scotch on the rocks and Bernardi with his glass of red wine.

Samuel explained how he'd traced one of the sales of the

pinto bean sacks to the Universal Church of Psychic Unfoldment. He then told Bernardi about the dwarf preacher, his
establishment and his performance, and about Dominique,
the spiritualist, whom Marisol believed to be a witch. Then he
told him about Michael Harmony and his ambulance chaser,
Art McFadden. His last words were about the dwarf's sexual
appetites.

"We may have to use the sexual thing in a pinch if we
can't prove anything else," said Bernardi. "But overall, that's a
pretty good day's work."

"Yeah, my head is still spinning. Now the problem."

"What's the problem?" asked Bernardi, taking a sip of the
cheap Chianti Melba's bartender had served him.

"Which road to travel first?"

Bernardi thought it over. "I see what you mean. You've
got three directions to go and they all lead to different places.
In addition to that, I have some confidential information that
complicates everything."

Samuel's tired eyes brightened. "What's that?" he asked,
licking his dry lips.

"They found another body part in the bay. It's a section of
an arm with a surgically repaired break, just above the elbow.
It was a pretty bad one, too."

"When did this happen?" asked Samuel, pulling his notebook out of his coat pocket.

Bernardi put his hand out, palm down. "Hold it, my friend.
I said this was confidential."

"For how long?" asked Samuel, his eyelids returning to
their drooping position.

"That's a good question. We want the perpetrator to keep
giving us body parts, so we need public acknowledgement that
we're receiving them. At the same time, we don't want to scare
him or her away. We need to get the news out in the most in-
nocuous way possible."

Samuel got the not-so-subtle restriction that Bernardi was imposing on him but ignored it for the moment. He knew the detective needed him to help catch whoever was behind the crime.

"Do you think a woman could have done this?" Samuel asked.

"Let's say 'them' instead of 'him' or 'her.' Maybe it's a team."

"So, for how long am I under wraps on the specifics?"

"Let's say we hold everything else for three days. I meet with the medical examiner tomorrow, and I'll know more after that."

"Can I come along?"

"It'll be off the record, right?"

"I'll only publish what you guys want me to."

"Okay, tomorrow at 10 a.m. at his office. Now, let's get back to your dilemma."

Samuel took a last swig of his Scotch and got up to get another drink. "Want a refill, Lieutenant?"

Bernardi hesitated. "Sure, it's still early enough for me to have another glass before dinner." He was now totally relaxed.

Samuel returned with the drinks, sat down and stirred his with his finger. "I got distracted. I don't have any hard evidence that the sack containing the body part came from the church, so I'm just going on a hunch. But there's a lot of sorting out that needs to be done about all the stuff that's going on in one place." He ticked them off on his fingers. "There's the dwarf. There's the spiritualist. And there's the ambulance chaser who works for the big hair-hat attorney, Michael Harmony. We need to know more about all of them and their connection to one another.

"Let me check out the fat guy and the spiritualist. If you approach them as a cop, they'll panic. Since Schwartz either works for the San Francisco Police Department or did, you can get a lot of background on him. Maybe even from Maurice Sandovich—that is, if the runt hasn't already compromised him for a few bucks. Since O'Shaughnessy is supposed to be on your side, find out what you can from him. From what Melba said, he'll be very happy to meet you, especially if he thinks you're cleaning up a mess that he'll get credit for."

"Okay," said Bernardi, "just be careful not to do anything to step on O'Shaughnessy's toes while you're at Bruno's. No doubt he has connections there that won't stand up to public scrutiny, and if you meddle too much, they'll all clam up, maybe even on his orders."

"Are you saying the Captain's crooked?"

"Not at all. I'm just saying that in police work, miracle workers cast a wide net. He sounds like one of them, so he's bound to have a lot of unsavory connections."

"In other words," said Samuel, "I don't talk with McFadden about getting cases from the SFPD."

"Yeah, and don't talk to him about whatever else you sense might turn him off from giving you inside information. Besides, we don't care who's paying who for cases right now. We want to know where the sack came from.

"But I think you're right to question the spiritualist because the victim is Latin—the church is filled with Latins and she's Latin."

"Great," said Samuel, and they clinked glasses.

"Cin-cin," said Bernardi. They drank what was left in their glasses. Samuel went to the restroom and when he got back, Bernardi was gone.

On his way out the door, Melba snagged him.

"I like your new detective with the worn-out brown suit. Within a year he'll be a hit in San Francisco 'cause he's smart and a people person."

"Yeah, I think so," said Samuel. "Is Blanche around?"

Melba smiled and took a sip of her beer. "I already told you, she's in Tahoe. She won't be back 'til next week. You can wait that long, can't you?"

Samuel nodded sheepishly and looked at the floor as he scratched the dog's back.

"Now tell me what you were talking about back there," Melba commanded.

*　　*　　*

Samuel and Bernardi met the next day in the medical examiner's office. Turtle Face, dressed in his customary white lab coat, was his usual grumpy self, but the myriad songs coming from the long-playing record quietly playing on the phonograph in the background eventually soothed his disposition. Samuel knew better than to leaf through anything on the examiner's desk. Turtle Face had an eagle eye for any displacement, and the reporter had previously been chastised for picking something up and putting it back down in a slightly different position.

"Gentlemen, I see you've already made friends, and in such a short time," he said observantly.

"Barney, this is Bruno Bernardi," said Samuel. "I think I already told you we worked together on another case."

"Yeah, you did. Hello, Detective Bernardi. I'm sure you remember I helped your man MacDonald on a couple of complicated cases a few years ago."

"I sure do, Mr. McLeod. I never forget a favor; more important, I respect and appreciate competence. You were so right about the issues you analyzed for us, and we got convictions in both cases."

A look of pleasure almost broke through the medical examiner's stoic countenance but he quickly got himself under control. "You've come here to discuss a part of an arm that was found floating in the bay. Ordinarily, I would be reluctant to have this conversation with Mr. Hamilton present, but because he's been involved since the beginning of this case and he's kept his word—even though he's a reporter—I'm inclined to let him sit in. As long as both of you agree that everything said here today is off the record."

"I've had the same kind of experience with Mr. Hamilton and also found him reliable," said Bernardi.

Turtle Face inclined his head. "So, we're off the record?" The reporter and detective nodded their agreement.

"Okay, let's get to it," he said. "Follow me." He picked up a large envelope from a slot behind his desk and the three of them walked down the corridor to the morgue. The examiner opened the door of a freezer compartment and pulled out a plastic bag, which was tagged with a Doe name and a number. The bag contained two body parts: the thigh they'd already seen, and an elbow connected to part of an upper arm.

"We may be lucky with this piece of evidence," said Turtle Face, pulling out an X-ray from the envelope he'd carried from his office. He laid the envelope on the table and slapped the X-ray film in the light box on the table. "This is part of the same body as the thigh we found in China Basin. He was a young Latin male. But look at this. You see the fracture line above the elbow? That represents a pretty severe break that was surgically repaired, and the repair was not done in the U.S. It's Mexican. We can tell by the technique. So we can conclude that whoever the young man was, he broke his arm in Mexico, or at least had it repaired there."

"How can you tell that?" asked Samuel.

"By the way it was fixed."

"Meaning?" asked Samuel.

"That doctors do things differently in Mexico than they do here."

"Any way to tell how long he's been dead?' asked

Bernardi.

"No way to tell. We were lucky, though. A fisherman cast his line off a pier South of Market and came up with it. It was still partially frozen."

"Was it close to China Basin?" asked Samuel.

"Closer to China Basin than it was to the Golden Gate. I'd guess that wherever it was thrown in the bay, the current carried it south, but not too far, based on the condition it was in when the fisherman pulled it out of the water."

Turtle Face pulled the X-ray off of the light box and inserted it back in its envelope. "That's all we know."

"Can you tell if the same saw was used to cut the arm up?" asked Samuel.

"Oh, I forgot to add that. Sure, the same type of equipment was used. It has the same serrated marks on both ends that the thigh bone had."

"Now we have to figure out who's missing," said Bernardi.

"Giving a face to this young man would help a lot," said Turtle Face. "But whoever's doing this is too clever to give us a print or a head. You can kiss those clues goodbye."

"In Melba's words," said Samuel, "it's the least we can do."

"What?" grumbled Turtle Face.

"Give the victim of this crime a face," said Samuel.

"That's up to you boys," said the examiner.

Bruno's restaurant was on the 2300 block of Mission Street. It was a place where those in positions of working class power did their business in a city filled with snobbish and pretentious downtown watering holes where they weren't welcome and where they wouldn't go anyway. Bruno's took on its lofty position soon after it opened in 1940. Its reputation as an important working class hangout came as a result of the growing influence of the labor movement after it won the longshoreman's strike in the 1930s; the restaurant's stature only increased with the rise of labor's power during World War II. By 1963, the restaurant was past its physical prime, but the shabbiness it exhibited around the edges fit in well with its image as the appointed gathering place for those whose job it was to represent the interests of the San Francisco's underdog wage earners in San Francisco.

Samuel had tried to make a reservation to have lunch with Art McFadden for the next day, but found he couldn't get in. He telephoned the man to give him the news and was told not to worry, to just show up and they'd be taken care of, regardless of the day. Samuel took him at his word. The next day he took the Mission Street electric trolley and got off at Twenty-Third and Mission. He walked the half block to Bruno's, passing along the way a Mexican shoe store; a medical clinic whose plate-glass windows featured a photo of a doctor holding a stethoscope and descriptions of various exams written in Spanish, their prices next to them; and two shops selling dresses for girls' first communions, which was clearly a big thing in the Latin community. There was also a market offering fresh fruits and vegetables in crammed-to-overflowing stands on the sidewalk. Samuel thought the neighborhood looked thriving and prosperous.

When Samuel entered the run-down establishment a little before one, the bar was packed. Union officials from most of San Francisco's labor organizations were pushed up against the bar, where they mixed with politicians and plainclothes police officers—even a few high-ranking ones in uniform. There was so much smoke hanging in the air around the bar that all Samuel had to do was to take a deep breath in order to satisfy any real or imaginary craving for a cigarette that still lingered in his psyche.

He spotted Art McFadden, dressed in the same checkered sports coat he'd been wearing at the church a few nights before, at the end of the bar. He was chewing on a stogie and talking with a man the reporter didn't recognize. Samuel muscled his way through the crowd to get to him.

When McFadden saw Samuel, he took the cigar out of his mouth, gulped down his Bourbon on the rocks and slapped Samuel on the back, all in one motion, before introducing him to his companion, who was the head of the Laborers Union. Samuel nodded in greeting, but there was so much noise and smoke in the bar that it was impossible to hear much of any conversation, let alone recognize anyone.

"You're right on time," McFadden chortled.

Samuel guessed what he was getting at. "Not easy to get through the crowd, as you can see."

McFadden slipped the maître'd a couple of dollars and the two were ushered to a table far enough away from the din of the crowd so that they could hear each other. Before they sat down, McFadden told the maître'd to have the waiter bring him another Bourbon on the rocks. "What's your pleasure, Samuel?"

"Scotch on the rocks," yelled the reporter before realizing he didn't have to yell anymore.

The men sat down. The beefy Irishman was gregarious and easy to talk to, and from what Samuel had seen so far, he was well connected in the world of the workingman.

"I haven't seen you around much," McFadden said. "Are you a newcomer to the paper?"

"I became a reporter about a year and a half ago," explained Samuel. "And before that, I didn't get around much. How about you?"

McFadden laughed. "An Irishman always has a home in this town. As you can see, there are plenty of us."

Samuel didn't want to waste any more time, but he also didn't want to tread on dangerous ground, so he decided to wait for the right moment before asking too many pointed questions. In the meantime, McFadden did most of the work for him.

"Let's have a few drinks and learn something about each other," said McFadden. "I like to know who I'm dealing with."

"That's fair. I'd also like to know more about you."

They drank their drinks, each ordering two more, while consuming plates of Petrale sole sautéed in butter with a side of scalloped potatoes. During the meal, friends and acquaintances of McFadden's stopped by the table to say hello or to ask him to spend a minute with them after his lunch.

"Seems like you know everybody in this joint," said Samuel, noticing that the Irishman was more relaxed after they'd both had a couple of drinks.

"This is one of the places I conduct business. It's where I make most of my deals."

"What's your relationship with The Universal Church of Psychic Unfoldment?" Samuel finally asked, watching a giant cockroach lumber up the wall next to their table. He didn't bother to squash it, figuring there were plenty more to take its place.

"It's a source of cases for my boss, Michael Harmony," answered McFadden. "One of San Francisco's finest attorneys."

"The Reverend recommends his parishioners to your boss's firm?"

"He sure does, and plenty of them."

"And what's the quid pro quo?" asked Samuel.

"I knew you were going to ask me that, and I'm not at liberty to tell you," said McFadden.

"I promise I won't put anything you tell me in print. Just give it to me on background so I understand how it works."

"You're a reporter, aren't you?"

"I sure am."

"And you know it's illegal to solicit and pay for cases, don't you?"

"I've heard that." Samuel smiled.

"What do you think the D.A. would do if he found out that people in this city were buying cases in the Mission?"

"Probably nothing, if it were among Irishmen," said Samuel. They both laughed. "There are a lot worse things going on in this town than helping people get representation."

McFadden let out a big belly laugh that caught the attention of the patrons at the tables around them. "You're pretty good, Samuel. I'll have to remember that line. But seriously, what do you think would happen if that kind of information got around?"

"Obviously, there'd be a lot of finger-pointing by attorneys who weren't getting the business," said Samuel. "But I'm not interested in that specific information for publication purposes. I'm interested in what goes on there, that's all."

"Okay, okay. As long as it don't go beyond us, I'll let you in on how it works. But you gotta promise."

"I promise," said Samuel, laying a twenty-dollar bill on the table. McFadden's meaty hand scooped it up and stuffed in his lapel pocket.

"The Reverend gives me the cases of his injured parishioners. He tells them that God wants them to come to me for help."

"What does he get from you in return?"

"Pussy," said McFadden with a straight face. Then he laughed. "The dwarf likes to fuck young pussy, so I go out like a pimp and find him young girls to attend his services. The rest is easy. He has a way with the young ones. But no money changes hands. It's a sweet deal."

"How you do you get them to do that?"

"Never you mind," chuckled McFadden. "I just do."

"Do any of the girls ever come back to you and complain?"

"What do you mean, that they didn't get enough of the dwarf?" McFadden roared with laughter, slapping his hand down on the table. "No, sir. Not once in the six months we've been working together."

"Tell me something about the dwarf that I can use for my article?"

"Hell, that's easy. He's a straight shooter, a man of his word. He's also a shrewd operator; he knows the meaning of a buck, which helps when you're basically running a charity."

"Do you think he's trying to milk the charity? I mean, for money?"

"Yeah, but mainly he enjoys the power. It makes him feel like a big shot. But he knows how to make money, and from the looks of the show he puts on, he's making a lot. Aside from the girls, I know I pay him well."

"But I can't use that part of his operation to show his money-making skills."

"That's true, but you can say he's a good businessman."

"By saying what?"

"That he packs 'em in and collects a lot of money."

"Since we're sharing secrets, can I ask you something in confidence?" Samuel inquired, wondering if he would be doing the right thing by broaching the subject of the pinto bean sack.

"Go right ahead, young man," said the Irishman, wide-eyed in anticipation of selling more inside information.

Samuel considered the man's eagerness and thought better of asking his original question. "What's with the beautiful Renaissance painting that he uses as prop?"

"I asked him the same thing. He said he got it from Dominique. That's all I know."

"What about Dominique? What do you think of her?"

"I know her in her other business, if you get what I mean."

"Yeah. I heard that guys pay money for her to beat the shit out of them."

Samuel laughed and McFadden roared. "Can you imagine buying magic from that broad, thinking the whole time that all she really wants to do is shove something up your ass?" said McFadden. "Actually, though, she's a pretty savvy businessperson, too. She's the one who put me on to the dwarf. She told me that a little pussy went a long way with him, and she was right." He roared with laughter again.

Samuel figured he'd gotten as much as he was going to get from the Irishman without tipping his hand about what he really wanted. "You've been a big help to me, Mr. McFadden," he said, calling to the waiter for the check.

McFadden waved him off. "Call me Art, Samuel, and the lunch is on Mr. Harmony. I'll tell him he's made a friend at the morning paper."

"Thank him for me. And tell him it's always good to have friends in high places." They laughed again and shook hands.

On his way back to his apartment from the Mission— Samuel took the bus to Fifth and Market and then hitched a ride up Powell on the Hyde Street cable car—he thought about the screaming young girls in the front row of the church service he'd attended and wondered if they had anything to do with the crime he was investigating. But the timing was wrong. In any case, he'd had too much to drink to make any sense out of it. He hoped he'd remember everything in the morning.

8

Octavio and Ramiro

Two days after his lunch with McFadden at Bruno's, Samuel was all set to keep his appointment with Dominique. He had dropped by Camelot the night before to tell Melba all the latest and to schmooze with Blanche, who was finally back in town and tending the horseshoe bar. He'd asked after Excalibur, but Melba told him the pooch was having a flea bath and a "do," so he turned all of his attention to Blanche. "My friend Bernardi, the homicide detective, wants to invite us to an Italian restaurant in North Beach so you can meet his girlfriend Marisol."

"That sounds like fun," replied Blanche. "Can he make it for a Tuesday night? That's my only day off when I'm in the city."

"I'll make sure it's on a Tuesday."

Samuel thought Blanche looked radiant, especially since she'd accepted another opportunity to explore San Francisco with him. He admired her blonde hair, which was pulled back in a ponytail and held in place with a black rubber band, and took in her vivid blue eyes. Studying her, however, he wasn't so sure her complexion looked as healthy as usual. "You look awfully flushed today. Are you okay?"

"Of course," she smiled. "I just ran all the way here from

home and my pulse hasn't returned to normal yet; it takes exactly twenty-four minutes." She smiled and winked. "Now that you don't smoke, why don't you come running me with sometime?"

"I tried that once in Golden Gate Park, remember?"

"You cheated, you took the bus."

"How did you know?"

She winked again. "Easy. When you came into Betty's Diner after the run, you didn't have a hair out of place and your face was its usual putty color, like right now, not bright red."

His mind was working on a quick response when Melba yelled from the front of the bar by the Round Table. "Phone call, Samuel. It's Rosa María." Blanche handed him an extension from behind the bar.

"Hello, Mrs. Rodríguez, this is Samuel. How are you?" His forehead creased in puzzlement. Other than his dinner at her house with Melba, when she had given him the list of purchasers of pinto bean sacks, he really didn't know her.

"The children have news for you, Mr. Hamilton. Can you come to the store?"

"When?" he asked.

"They get home from school around three o'clock. Shall we say at four tomorrow? It's about a friend of theirs. I'd rather have them tell you so I don't end up getting it all mixed up."

"Okay. I'll be there. You're on Twentieth and Shotwell, right?"

"That's correct. See you tomorrow."

Samuel ordered another Scotch and went through his notebook for a couple of minutes. He asked Blanche if he could borrow the phone again. He dialed a couple of numbers before finally connecting with Dominique. "I need to postpone my interview with you for another day," he explained. They agreed on a new date and he hung up.

"A lot going on?" asked Blanche.

"Yeah, everything seems to happen at once. But Mrs. Rodríguez says that her kids have something important to tell me."

"Why don't you call her Rosa María?"

"I don't know her well enough."

"She sounds formal, but she's really down to earth."

"I went to her house with your mom. She invited you, too, but you weren't in town."

"I heard. Who's Dominique?" Blanche looked away, trying not to be obvious.

Samuel's hopes shot up. Could she be jealous that he was talking with another woman who was unknown to her? Watching her face for a reaction, he explained who Dominique was and how she was connected with the dwarf preacher. He added that people said she was actually a witch.

"What do you mean, a witch? Magic potions and all that kind of stuff?"

"Black magic, they tell me."

"Isn't doing that mumbo jumbo stuff illegal?"

"I've heard that too. But I'm not so concerned with what she does with her 'mumbo jumbo' as you call it, but rather what information she can provide."

"What kind of information? Are you looking for a love potion?" She giggled.

Samuel blushed. He actually had thought about asking Dominique for something like that. "Would it do any good?"

"Don't be silly. I'm teasing you."

"I figured," he said, wiping the water beads off his glass with a finger before taking one last pull on his drink.

* * *

The two children bounded into Mi Ranch Market from

school the next day while Samuel was chatting with Rosa María. They seemed happy to see him and greeted him politely, Marco shaking his hand, while Ina, still shy, sought refuge behind Rosa María. They each had a snack and a glass of milk in the small area behind the counter that was used as an office and hidden from public view. Rosa María offered Samuel a soft drink or a cup of coffee, but he declined.

"Tell Mr. Hamilton what you told me yesterday," she instructed them after they were fed and had settled down. She left the door ajar in case she needed to attend to a customer.

"Our job is to help our parents at the store after school and on the weekends," explained Marco.

"We make friends with some of our customers," interrupted Ina.

"We especially like Octavio and his cousin Ramiro," said Marco. "They come into the store together to buy their food for the week, usually on a Saturday."

"Where are they from?" asked Samuel.

"They're both from Mexico," said Ina. "And they don't speak English, at least not to us."

"About six months ago, they stopped coming in. We just thought that they went back to Mexico," said Marco. "But last Saturday, Ramiro came in alone. He looked really sad. I asked him where his cousin was."

Ina, not to be outdone, interrupted. "He said his cousin had disappeared."

Samuel, who was busy taking notes, looked up, first at Rosa María and then at the two children, "Disappeared?"

"That's what Ramiro said," they answered at the same time.

"How old is Octavio?" asked Samuel.

Both children looked at him blankly.

"I would say in his early twenties," said Rosa María.

"What does he look like?"

"Short and skinny, like most recent immigrants from Mexico. He is very handsome, but also tough, if you know what I mean."

"Not exactly," Samuel answered, trying to get a mental picture of Octavio.

"He had that street-smart look about him, like a person who knows how to take care of himself. That's why I was hesitant to call you, but the kids convinced me that he wouldn't just wander off."

"How can I get a hold of Ramiro?"

"I have an address and a phone number," said Rosa María, handing him a piece of paper. "Remember, he doesn't speak English, so you have to have a translator. But, first, you have to convince him you won't report him to the *Migra*, to immigration; he is illegal, of course. But I can help you with that. I'll call him and let him know who you are and tell him that you may be able to help him find his cousin. Unfortunately, I can't go there with you, because of the kids and the market."

"I can get a translator," said Samuel. "When can I talk with him?"

"I'll try and get hold of him this evening and let you know. It will probably have to be after he finishes work or on the weekend. Should I contact you through Melba?"

"No. Here are my phone numbers at work and at home. Tell him it's better on the weekend. You'll let me know when?"

"I will," she said.

Samuel smiled at her with appreciation. "Thanks for your help, kids. What you've told me may be very important. If it turns out that way, I'll put both of your names in the newspaper."

Both children got very excited. "Next to the funnies?" asked Marco.

Samuel got it. "Sure, Marco, next to the funnies."

*　　*　　*

Samuel contacted Marisol and told her what he'd learned and got her to agree to accompany him and act as his translator. When Rosa María phoned Samuel and told him that Ramiro was willing to meet with him, she gave Samuel the name of a Mexican restaurant where the young man would feel comfortable, and then confirmed that he would be there.

It was almost noon on Saturday when a young Mexican man walked up to the plate glass window of the out-of-the-way Mexican restaurant on Twenty-Sixth Street, just off Valencia Street. He stared inside and then went to the doorway, where he hesitated. He was a shy boy who looked to be no more than twenty years old. He was around five-foot-five, at the most, and skinny. He had an angular face, cinnamon-colored skin and brown eyes that showed both fear and sadness.

Samuel was eating tacos, enjoying the smell of refried beans on his plate and the coolness of his Mexican beer. Marisol looked up from her salad and beckoned to the young man, who was slow to acknowledge her invitation. He looked around furtively, as if to make sure that he wasn't being sucked into a trap and to assure himself that there was no one behind him. Samuel didn't move a muscle. He watched the young man, taking mental notes so he could identify him should Ramiro decide to leave before talking to them. Finally, Ramiro entered the restaurant and approached the table. He introduced himself and sat down.

Marisol spoke to him for several minutes in Spanish and he began to relax, although he declined her invitation to order something to eat. Samuel pushed aside his cleaned plate and empty bottle of beer, and asked Marisol to find out why the young man was so jumpy.

"He says that ever since his cousin disappeared six months

ago, he's been afraid. At first, he thought the *Migra* got Octavio, but as of last week, no one in his village, which is outside Mazatlán, had seen or heard from his cousin, so he was not deported. He says it is very scary when someone you're used to seeing every day just goes away without saying anything to anybody."

Samuel wanted to know when he left home and why he and his cousin had come here. Again, Marisol and Ramiro spoke in Spanish.

"He says they left over two years ago. They came for the same reasons all the men in their village do—to work so they could save money to buy land for ranching and to build a house."

When asked to give a physical description of his cousin Octavio, Ramiro gave the same one that Rosa María had given. He didn't describe him as street smart or tough, though, so Samuel asked to hear more about Octavio's character.

"Was he mixed up with a gang or with drugs?"

"No. He was a very hard worker. He wanted to save money so he could marry his girlfriend and take her home with him, but she changed her mind about marrying him and leaving San Francisco."

"Why?" asked Samuel.

"She became very involved in a church they went to. She liked the preacher a lot. Octavio was jealous and wanted to get her away from San Francisco. He even went to the pastor and told him to stay away from his girlfriend."

Samuel and Marisol stared at each other in disbelief.

"Are you talking about The Universal Church of Psychic Unfoldment?" Marisol asked Ramiro.

"Yes. Sara Obregon, his girlfriend, went to that church two or three times a week, so he started going there, too. That's where Octavio got the idea that something was going on with the preacher. But the preacher's bodyguards blocked him from coming into the church. This made him more angry."

"What did Sara say about all this?" asked Samuel.

"By then she was getting sick and weak, so she went to see the witch at the church. Then Octavio and Sara had a big fight about the preacher, and he asked her to go back to Mexico with him and forget about the preacher."

Samuel shook his head. "Did I understand what he just said? They fought about the preacher?"

"Yes," answered Marisol. She continued to translate. "She said she wasn't interested in the preacher but had to get something straightened out with him. Then Octavio disappeared; later, so did she."

"She disappeared, too?" asked Samuel, shaking his head and squinting. "Have him say more about that."

"After Octavio was gone, Ramiro asked Sara where he was. She looked very upset about something. She said she didn't know where he was and she didn't care. She said she had her own problems."

"Ask him what her problems were?"

"She wouldn't talk about what was bothering her. He didn't know her that well anyway. Then she disappeared, too."

"How long after Octavio was gone?" asked Samuel, his mind flashing back to the screaming young girls in the front row of the church. Once again he wondered if they were somehow connected to the crime he was investigating.

Ramiro scratched his head and stared out the window. Samuel could see that reliving the experience of his cousin's disappearance was taking a toll on him. The boy clenched his fists and slammed them down on the table. Then, calming down, he asked, "*¿Me puede dar un vaso de agua?*"

"Of course," Marisol answered and summoned the waiter to bring him water. "Samuel, do you want anything?"

The reporter turned a page of his notebook and shook his head. The waiter brought the water and Ramiro drank before continuing. "I'd say it was around a week after Octavio was gone that she disappeared," he told Marisol.

"Did Ramiro talk to the preacher or to Dominique about his cousin?" asked Samuel.

Ramiro wiped a furtive tear from his eye and looked down at the table. "Yes, he did, and neither one would admit that they knew anything. Ramiro got mad and told Dominique that he knew that she'd given something to Sara but he didn't know what. Dominique got angry and said it wasn't true. Then she said she couldn't talk about her clients, and she wouldn't even admit that Sara had come to see her. But Ramiro knew that wasn't true because he saw her go into her office at the church. When Ramiro tried to approach the preacher, the bodyguards prevented him from speaking to the dwarf. That's when he gave up. He stopped going to the church and decided to wait, hoping that Octavio would return."

"Does he know what Dominique gave Sara?" asked Samuel.

"No, but he thought it made her sick."

"That's too bad," said Samuel. "What about her family? Did you contact them?"

"Yes, I did," answered Ramiro. "They come from a different part of Mexico, from Guaymas. It's up the coast from Mazatlán. I thought maybe they had gone there together, but her family checked with relatives who are still there, and they haven't heard from Sara, either."

"Did he or anybody from Sara's family report them to the police as missing?" Samuel asked.

"Are you kidding? They're all illegal. None of us trust the police."

"Can you tell me anything else that you think is important about either disappearance?"

"I went with Sara's family to visit Saint Dominic's Church on Bush Street and we prayed at the shrine of Saint Jude," he told Marisol.

"What's the significance of that?" asked Samuel.

"Saint Jude is the champion of lost causes," Marisol answered. "There's only one church in San Francisco with a statue of him. Everyone who is Catholic knows it's there. When all else fails, we go and pray to him to help us find a loved one or solve an unsolvable problem. If they went that far, they must have been pretty desperate."

"Would you go to Saint Jude or to Dominique?" Samuel asked Marisol.

She rolled her eyes.

Samuel asked for a short break and had another beer, while Ramiro drank a soda and Marisol sipped a coffee. Then they talked some more. By the time they'd finished, Samuel had plenty to report back to Bernardi. But his head was spinning with too many details, and he couldn't yet put them all together. He needed time to think and to check things out.

9

Some Surprising Developments

SAMUEL HAD ONE MORE THING to do before he met with Bernardi. He figured that Marisol would fill the detective in on what they'd learned from Ramiro. He would find out what the witch knew, if anything, about the pinto bean sack that contained the body part, and whether or not it had any connection to the church. He'd learned a lot more since he'd originally set up the meeting with Dominique, and now he had to decide how to broach the information Ramiro had provided about the girl's visit to her, including the magic potion. He had to find a way of approaching those subjects without having her clam up. Part of his problem was that he'd agreed to wear two hats: he was both investigating a murder and doing his job as a newspaper reporter.

Using the article about the preacher as his pretext, he rescheduled his appointment with Dominique, arranging to meet her at her flat. According to her, she no longer received clients with spiritual requests there, since she could take care of them at the church. Her flat was reserved for her other services. Although Samuel knew about those other services, he wasn't interested in that side of her life; he needed information.

The outside of the Dominique's building, located at Seventeenth and Folsom, was in need of a paint job and trash was strewn all over the sidewalk. As he rang the bell, he figured she lived in a dump. He changed his mind, however, when the door slowly swung open and he walked up the dimly lit but well-decorated stairwell. He was even more impressed when he reached the top. Dominique met him dressed in stylish slacks and a silk blouse. She ushered him into the living room, where he immediately noticed the recessed lighted frames in the walls, which held what looked like shrunken heads.

"You have very unusual taste," said Samuel.

"I like to collect ethnic things from all over the world. Hopefully, seeing them makes people stop and think about other cultures."

"I've never seen anything like the collection you have here."

"It's taken a lifetime," she said with a self-assured complacency. "Come in, please. Have a seat."

Samuel sat down and tried not to stare at the shrunken heads, but his eyes kept returning to them.

"They take a little getting used to. Would you rather go to my study?"

"That might be less distracting."

She got up, unlocked the door behind her and turned on several light switches. When Samuel walked in, he found himself standing beneath a garland of herbs that hung from the ceiling. Overwhelmed by the smell, he struggled to not sneeze. Several statutes that appeared to be of pagan gods decorated the room, all lit from above by spotlights.

"This is even more spectacular than the other room," he said.

"Do you recognize any of the goddesses?" she asked. "This is Xochiquetzal; she's the Aztec goddess of flowers and love."

Samuel looked at the complicated clay figure, which wore a large feather headpiece and an ornate costume.

"She's a very positive figure in Mexican society, especially among the poor. The one on the other side is the Aztec goddess of birth, Tlacolteutl."

Samuel observed a figure squatting, a small baby's head coming out from between its spread legs.

"This is my retreat. Here is where I used to receive most of my clients who wanted spiritual help; that is, until I got so busy at the church."

"And the other part of your flat?"

"That was for other services that I'm sure you've heard about, Mr. Hamilton." She smiled mischievously. "But, frankly, I haven't had the time or the inclination to work that part of my business since I started seeing so many people at Reverend Schwartz's church. I realize now that I'm a healer; that's my real calling.

"I admit that I know about your other business, but I'm not here to talk about that. I'm writing a story about the Reverend. Tell me how you two got together. Fill me in on how the church works. It seems to me that you have a lot to say about what goes on there."

Dominique didn't take kindly to his suggestion that she helped run the church; Samuel noted her annoyance in the elevated pitch of her voice and in the way she rubbed the palms of her hands on her slacks as if to wipe away nervous sweat. But she didn't say anything. Instead, she provided him with a lengthy explanation of how she'd been the assistant to a William L. Gordon, a "doctor of divinity," and of how she'd helped the Reverend Schwartz adapt Gordon's teachings to the storefront church.

After about ten minutes, Dominique gave him a penetrating glance and abruptly changed the subject. "You've written in your newspaper about a body part that was found in a trash can. From what your articles say, you continue to investigate that story. Or do I have you confused with someone else?"

"Yes, that's right. I'm investigating that incident. But"—he lied—"that's not why I'm here."

"You're sure you don't think I had something to do with that?" she asked suspiciously, sitting up in her chair.

"Yes, I'm sure," he lied again.

Dominique moved to the edge of her chair. "Tell me about that story. It sounds awful. From what you wrote, the victim is a young Latin male. I'm curious, since I live in the Mission, and we see so many young Latin men in our neighborhood and in our church."

Samuel jumped at her lead, knowing that Octavio had been a client of hers. "You haven't noticed anyone missing from the church, have you?"

"Mr. Hamilton," she parried, "you have to understand that we deal with a migrant population. They come and they go. One day we're giving guidance to someone, and the next day he or she is gone."

"So what you're saying is that you're not aware that anyone's missing."

At that moment a white Persian cat strolled into the room, went to Dominique and rubbed its body against her leg.

"This is Puma," said Dominique, ignoring his question. "She's my companion,"

The cat stared at Samuel, then scurried away and jumped into a basket in the corner. Samuel noticed that the basket was lined with a burlap material, and that there were traces of red lettering printed on the end that stuck out. He was about to get back to his questions but thought better of pursuing them. First he had to consult with Bernardi. At the same time, Samuel knew he couldn't just get up and leave. He needed to exit gracefully, so he spent a few minutes exploring what exactly Dominique did for the Reverend Schwartz.

"The Reverend told me that when he felt overwhelmed by too much evil, he'd turn to you for a cleansing. I asked him how that worked and he said I'd have to talk to you."

"Sorry, Mr. Hamilton, I'm not at liberty to discuss how I treat my clients. I will only confirm that Reverend Schwartz is a client of mine and that I see him professionally when he asks for my guidance."

"But he gave me permission to ask you," said Samuel, wondering what cleansing the dominatrix provided the preacher. He realized, however, that he wasn't going to get any more information out of her.

"I have another question, and that's about the painting the Reverend uses in his sermon. He said you loaned it to him."

"Yes, it's mine."

"Where did you get it? It looks like it was painted by an old master."

"That's a long story, which I won't go into now. Let's just say that the Reverend has certainly made the most of it."

Samuel asked a few more perfunctory questions and then excused himself, trying not to appear in a hurry as he left the apartment.

He stopped at a phone booth and called Bernardi. The detective wasn't in, so he made an appointment with the receptionist to see him the next morning at eight.

* * *

Samuel arrived at Bernardi's office in the Hall of Justice a half an hour late the next morning. He was red-faced and appeared frustrated. Bernardi, however, was unperturbed by Samuel's tardiness; he had piles of files—some on his desk, some on the floor—that needed his attention, and waiting gave him an opportunity to tackle some of them.

"You must have had a rough night," the detective commented, sipping his now-cold coffee and swallowing the last of his sugar doughnut. Then, completing his daily ritual, he brushed his hands together, wiping away any granules of sugar that clung to his fingertips.

Samuel sat down in one of the two chairs opposite Bernardi's desk. "I got off to a bad start this morning. There's so much going on in my head that I left my wallet and my pocket change at home."

"What's the problem, friend? I heard all about your visit with Ramiro from Marisol. And the receptionist told me you had something real important to tell me. I hope you've come across something that will be a bigger breakthrough than what you learned about Octavio and his missing girlfriend."

"I found out something else besides that and, for the moment, it puts looking for them on hold," said Samuel.

"Really? Bernardi leaned against his desk in anticipation. "I'm waiting,"

"Dominique, the witch, has a white cat."

Bernardi stared at him. "So what?"

"Don't you remember that when the body part was first found, there were white animal hairs on the sack?"

Bernardi bolted to his feet and slapped his forehead as if he'd just awakened from a dream. "Shit, Samuel, you're right."

"That's not all. The white cat sleeps in a basket in the corner of her flat and the basket is lined with, guess what?"

"Don't have a clue," answered Bernardi.

"A burlap sack with red printing on it, just like the one the body part was wrapped in.

Bernardi squinted. "Are you sure?"

"I didn't go over and pull the sack out of the basket because I didn't want her to know what I'd seen, but I'm certain. What do we do now?"

Bernardi sat down, leaned back in his chair and thought for a moment. "Let's go to the medical examiner's office and take another look at the sack, the white hairs and the arm. Once I see the evidence again and add your discovery to the picture, we'll figure out what to do."

*   *   *

After they'd gone over the evidence again, Bernardi scratched his head and bit his lower lip. "I bet the witch doesn't understand the significance of what you saw in her apartment. The only people who know about the animal hair on the sack are you, the medical examiner, and me. Besides, if she thought that her cat might provide a clue for all this, she wouldn't have invited you there for the interview."

"I'm not quite following you," said Samuel. "Aren't we after evidence that links someone to the sack? Doesn't the cat hair do that?"

"I want to go into Dominique's flat and get the evidence, but before we do that I'd like to know more about Sara. Let's talk to her family first. Ramiro told you that she lived with them."

"Why do you want to talk to Sara's family?" asked Samuel.

"If there's anything left of what Dominique gave Sara, and we can figure out its chemical compound, then we can add those ingredients to our search warrant list."

"Are you saying you think there was another murder and it was Sara?"

"I'm not saying anything; I'm just trying to build a case. And the way I do that is to get as much evidence as I can before I start pointing fingers.

"We'll get a sworn statement first from each of them, based on Sara's status as a missing person."

*   *   *

When Marisol tried to set up an appointment with Sara's

parents, however, she ran into a stone wall. Even though the family had been searching desperately for the girl since her disappearance and were anxious for just about any help they could get, they didn't want to accept it from the police, who had an often-antagonistic relationship with the Latin community. They refused to cooperate even when approached in Spanish. Marisol and her preacher father, Mr. Leiva, paid a personal visit to their home in a last-ditch effort, but they still wouldn't budge. Finally, based on the information Samuel and Marisol had obtained from Ramiro, Bernardi was able to get a search warrant, arguing that there might be evidence in the home that could be used to connect a defendant to a possible homicide.

The Obregons lived on Army Street, in the Mission District, just a few doors down from the Catholic Church where Mr. Leiva preached his sermons. It was a small, run-down home located behind a larger house, which was equally rundown. Both had siding missing from their exteriors and looked pretty shabby. Samuel suspected that the owner was simply collecting rent on the smaller property, hoping that it would eventually appreciate in value. That was cheaper than improving the structure and pricing it out of the market for the class of tenant he was currently able to attract.

Bernardi, Samuel, a court reporter and an official interpreter arrived with the sheriff, who served the writ. Standing on the rickety porch, Samuel observed as a woman in her early forties answered the door and listened to the interpreter explain that her house was going to be searched by the police for evidence. Maybe she had been a looker in her younger days, but she'd put on weight over the years, and her unkempt hair was dull and her face was puffy. She wore a white denim apron with patches of red and green sewn on with matching thread. Cooking smells—cumin, chipotle chili and oregano—drifted out the open door from the kitchen at the rear of the house and a radio played ranchera music in the background.

Once all the introductions had been made—the inter-preter was careful not to mention that Bernardi was from Homicide so as not to frighten the woman more than she already was—the group moved inside. As Sara's mother called out for her husband to join them, a boy of around ten years of age peeked through the curtain separating the living room from the rest of the house. A girl in her early teens appeared a moment later, pushing the boy aside as she came through the curtain. A frail-looking Mexican man with bags under his eyes and a sad look on his face followed the girl. He stared at the floor, avoiding all eye contact with the five men. Mrs. Obregon reluctantly introduced the trio as her husband, Car-los, and her daughter and son. She explained that Carlos had taken Sara's disappearance very hard, as the girl was the eldest and his favorite. So hard, in fact, she told the interpreter, that he hadn't gone back to work as a laborer since their daughter vanished six month earlier.

Bernardi explained to them that the law allowed him to take official statements from all of them about Sara. He asked for a photograph of the missing girl, and the mother pointed to a large framed picture on the mantle of the fireplace. Look-ing at the photograph, Samuel and Bernardi were surprised to see a young woman with movie-star good looks.

"She was so beautiful, my Sara!" The woman smiled sadly. "When I was her age I looked like her. But look at me now! We had that taken when she graduated from Mission High. She was the first person in either of our families to graduate from any school. We had so many hopes for her."

In the face of the detective's gentle manner, Samuel could see that the woman was beginning to relax.

"I'm sorry to have to ask you these questions, Ma'am," said Bernardi softly through the interpreter. "How old is your daughter?"

"Nineteen."

"Was she working?"

"She was going to City College. Actually, she was doing very well in school and was excited about it. That is, until she started going out with Octavio and they got tangled up with that awful church."

"I'll get to that in a minute," said Bernardi. "You didn't like Octavio, is that what you're saying?"

"At first I did, but they started going to that church on Mission Street and then they fought all the time."

"Did Sara tell you what they were fighting about?"

"It was something about the church, but she wouldn't tell me."

The other daughter, who bore almost no resemblance to the girl in the picture, piped up in English. "Octavio was jealous, I know that much, but she would not tell me why."

Samuel was busy taking notes, taking care not to insert himself into the conversation so his name wouldn't appear in any recorded statement. At this point, however, he leaned over and whispered something to Bernardi.

"Did Octavio ever hit her?" asked the detective.

They all shook their heads. "She would have punched him out if he'd done that," exclaimed her younger sister. "And she would have told me that!"

"Did she ever mention a woman named Dominique from the church?"

"I'm sorry," said the interpreter. "Can you repeat the question?"

Bernardi repeated it.

"Yes," said the sister. "She talked about her and even went to see her."

"What for?" asked the lieutenant.

"Dominique is a *curandera*, a healer. She gave her some medicine because Sara was getting sick and throwing up."

"What did you think was wrong with her?"

"I didn't know, so I was happy when she went to see the healer."

Samuel again whispered something to Bernardi, who shook his head.

"Do you have any of that medicine here in the house?" he asked.

"I will have to look for it in her room," the mother said to the interpreter.

"Do you mind if I come with you?" asked the detective.

"No, come this way," the woman responded, having now completely surrendered to Bernardi's charm. "She shares a room with her sister."

Mrs. Obregon pushed through the curtain and the group followed her down the hallway. The hardwood floor was painted dark brown and the walls beige. She opened a door on one side of the hallway to expose a tidy room with two bureaus and twin beds, both neatly made up. "This is the girls' room," she explained.

"Is this her bathroom?" Bernardi asked, seeing that the room was accessible from the girls' bedroom.

"This is the only bathroom we have."

"Do you mind if I look through it?"

"You are welcome," she answered.

Bernardi opened the compartment above the sink but found only toothbrushes and toothpaste. There was no medicine of any kind. The cabinet below the sink contained a half-full box of sanitary napkins and some toilet paper. "Do these belong to Sara?"

The sister blushed. "We both used them for that time of the month."

Bernardi returned to the bedroom and looked at the bureaus. "Which one is Sara's?" he asked. The sister pointed. He opened the top drawer and rummaged through, finding the usual things that a woman wears: panties, bras and stockings, all neatly folded in piles. The other drawers held several pairs of jeans, sweaters and folded T-shirts. As he was looking through the T-shirts, however, Bernardi saw a small manila envelope. He called the mother over. "Do you know what that is?"

"I have no idea."

"Do either you or your daughter have tweezers to pluck your eyebrows?" he asked.

The girl opened the top drawer of the other dresser and produced a pair of tweezers. Bernardi used them to pick up the manila envelope, nudging it open with the plastic bag he held in his other hand. There was nothing in the envelope, but it retained a strange odor. "Do you recognize the smell, Mrs. Obregon?"

She furrowed her brow and thought for a few seconds. "No. It smells like medicine, though."

Samuel had stopped taking notes and was observing the proceedings with great interest. He leaned over and smelled the envelope. "It doesn't ring a bell with me either," he whispered to Bernardi.

Bernardi pushed the envelope into the plastic bag and closed the flap, securing it with a rubber band that was attached. "May I take this with me?"

"Is that really necessary?

"It's official police business," he explained. Then, pointing to the closet: "Is half of that closet filled with her clothes?"

"More than half," announced Sara's sister with a shrug.

The remainder of the search produced nothing of interest. The mother found a good snapshot of Sara that she gave to the detective so he wouldn't take the family's cherished photograph from the mantle.

"What do you think?" Samuel asked Bernardi when they were outside.

"Let's see if there are any traces of anything in the envelope. I have my suspicions," said the detective, "and they're probably the same as yours."

*　*　*

Captain Doyle O'Shaughnessy stepped out from behind the protective partition of the Mission District police station to greet Homicide Detective Bruno Bernardi, meeting him by the booking desk. He was in full uniform, minus his hat, and was smoking a Chesterfield. At over six-feet-two-inches tall, O'Shaughnessy towered half a foot over Bernardi, and he weighed more than two hundred pounds. He had red curly hair, freckled skin and blue eyes, and if there were any doubt about his Irish heritage, his old-country brogue dispelled it immediately. He extended his big freckled hand to Bernardi's much smaller one, though their hands met with equal firmness.

"It's about time we met, Lieutenant," O'Shaughnessy said, exhaling smoke through his nose. "I've heard good things about you."

"Likewise, I've heard good things about you."

"Is this a get-acquainted meeting, or do you have something specific you want from me?" asked the captain, flicking the cigarette onto the floor and stepping on it.

"Both. I intended to get here before now, but I have so many files on my desk that I haven't had a chance."

"Ole Charlie MacAteer was a great guy," said the captain, reminding Bernardi where his loyalties lay. "We're all sorry he's gone."

"Yeah, I know I have big shoes to fill," acknowledged Bernardi, a touch of humility in his voice. Melba had warned him that the going would not be easy for him in this part of town. "We have a situation here in the middle of your territory, and

I need your help."

O'Shaughnessy squinted. He didn't like hearing about trouble in his own backyard, especially from people outside the Mission. "Like what?"

"Murder, and maybe a double murder."

"This all happened in the Mission? How come I'm just hearing about it?"

Bernardi knew O'Shaughnessy was lying. He'd already been warned that the captain kept tabs on everything that went on in the Mission. "We're not sure where the first murder happened, and we're not sure there was a second one. We're just preparing for the worst. Let me tell you what I know."

Bernardi gave a detailed explanation of what he'd learned, from the discovery of the piece of thigh in the garbage can, to Samuel observing Dominique's cat cuddled in the basket lined with burlap—though he never mentioned the reporter's name or his involvement in the investigation.

"I've had my eye on that goddamned midget since he opened that phony church," said the captain. "And I know about that dominatrix slut who's working with him. For some reason, a lot of cops like to get the shit beat out of them by her, so they're giving her a free pass. At least having them both under the same roof makes it easier to keep an eye on them. And, don't forget, that that little bastard works for the SFPD. Don't think that I'm not reminded of that every day. I've looked the other way, since he's only cheating and screwing the greasers. We can live with that, don't you think?" O'Shaughnessy gave Bernardi a knowing wink.

Bernardi stared straight ahead and didn't say a word, though he was insulted by the captain's use of the word greaser. Marisol was Latin.

"I know about the little man and the girls, but I'll be honest with you. We haven't had any complaints from anybody about that. What you tell me about the missing girl may be what we need to shut the little prick down."

They were still standing by the booking desk, since the captain hadn't invited Bernardi to come back to his office. The detective was aware of the captain's hostility towards him, and he was trying to be as diplomatic as he could and still get his job done.

"With all due respect, Captain, if you shut him down, we may lose the trail we're following."

"What are you suggesting?" asked the Captain, irritated at being challenged.

"I'm not sure. I think we need concrete evidence before we accuse anyone. And if we show our hand against either of these people now, our leads will dry up."

"So you're telling me that right now you don't want a search warrant for the woman's apartment, even though that would give us the burlap with the cat hairs on it."

"I want it, but not yet. I have someone working on the case who may have some insight on what to do next."

"Who's that?" asked the captain impatiently.

"I'm not at liberty to tell you that right now."

"All right, goddamn it." O'Shaughnessy pulled himself up to his full height and looked down at Bernardi, his face bright red. "When you're ready to share information with a fellow police officer, we'll renew this conversation." He turned abruptly and went back through the protective door.

Bernardi nodded, waved, waited for the door to slam, and then slowly walked out. He didn't trust the captain enough to let him in on how much the reporter was involved. He and Samuel would have to figure out what to do next without his help. Melba was right. He'd run into roadblocks set up by his fellow policemen.

10

Going Where the Leads Take Him

ASSISTANT U.S. ATTORNEY Charles Perkins opened the door to his office and peered out into the reception area. "Is that you, Samuel Hamilton? I haven't heard from you since I gave you the inside dope on those stories you wrote about all those crooks in Chinatown." He laughed sarcastically. "And if I know anything," said the sallow-skinned young man, his straw-blond hair hanging in a limp clump over one eye, "you wouldn't be here now if you didn't want something from me." He gave the reporter a stern look and extended his hand. "How the hell are you?" But Samuel could tell Perkins wasn't interested in his answer.

"Come on in," said Perkins, moving to one side while still holding the door. The office hadn't changed much; it was still littered with papers piled in every available space. Boxes of case files were spread across the floor, some that the attorney was working on, others that had been ready to go to the file room for years but that still hadn't been removed, including a few that had been there the last time Samuel visited.

Charles Perkins had a chiseled look and cultivated an appearance of great authority, but the reporter knew him to be a petty egoist who had a bad habit of pointing his index finger at whoever he was talking to and pontificating with a condescending air of indifference, always eager to be the center of attention. Samuel had gone to university with Perkins, and had convinced the assistant U.S. attorney to help him on his first case back when Samuel was still an ad salesman for the morning paper.

Perkins was right. Samuel needed his help again, and that was the only reason he was there. And the reporter knew Perkins would help him; he just didn't know what price the man would extract as payment for it. Still, given that he could provide the self-centered attorney with newspaper coverage in return for information, Samuel was in a better bargaining position than before.

"Okay, what is it now?" Perkins asked.

"Don't you want to B.S. a while?" responded the reporter. "We haven't seen each other for over a year."

"Come on, Samuel, it's me you're talking to," said the attorney, smirking. He still wore the cheap Cable Car three-piece suit and off-color white shirt that Samuel remembered from before, along with the same gold-plated cuff links. Perkins brushed his hair out of his eyes and sat down at his desk, which was piled high with papers. He directed Samuel to the chair on the other side.

"All right. I do need your help. I need a contact with the U.S. Border Patrol in Nogales, Arizona. But it has to be someone who has access to U.S. immigration files and who will open them up to me."

"Oh, the beggar wants to be the chooser, huh?" Perkins sneered. "First, you'd better tell me the story." He put his feet up on his desk.

Samuel spent the next two and half hours telling Perkins what he knew and why he needed specific information that he felt only the U.S. Attorney could provide. When he finished, Perkins sat lost in thought, his hands spread out on top of the desk. After a few moments, he went over to a filing cabinet in one corner of his office. Opening the second drawer, he rummaged in the mass of papers and pulled out a file. He set it down on top of one of the many piles on his already crowded desk, mumbling incoherently to himself. "Here it is!" he finally announced. "You're lucky I have such a good memory!"

Perkins scurried around the mess in his office, looking for a pad to write on. Pulling one from a briefcase on the floor, he scribbled a name and some numbers. "Here's the Border Patrol officer you want to talk with in Nogales, Arizona. You'd better check to make sure he's still there. Here are some phone numbers. If he's not there, they'll tell you where to find him. Remind him that he worked with me on the Simona case, and that he said when it was over he owed me a favor. Anything else?"

Samuel thought that whoever the poor bastard was, he must not have known who he was dealing with when he made a promise like that to Perkins.

"Is that all?" Perkins was getting impatient.

"There's one more thing." Samuel decided to push his luck a bit more. "At the church I told you about there is a beautiful old painting. I think it's Italian." He described it for Perkins. "It just seems to me that it's too valuable to be in a dump like that. Is it possible it's stolen?"

"Anything's possible," said Perkins. "We have a small staff in Washington, D.C., that works on tracking down stolen European art that ended up in the United States during and after the war. If you want me to look into it, I'll need a photograph of the painting."

"I've got my hands full right now trying to identify the dead young man, whose parts are lying on a tray at the morgue. But as soon as I come up for air I'll get you the photo. Thanks for all your help. I'll be in touch."

Samuel shook the limp hand extended to him, surprised that Perkins had given him so much information with so little hassle. He wondered if the attorney was just shining him on, or if he had changed. Then, on his way out the door, Samuel smiled, suddenly aware of the strength of his position as a reporter: Perkins had figured out what the power of the press could do for his image.

*　*　*

A few days later, Samuel stood at the front desk of the U.S. Border Patrol office in Nogales, Arizona. He asked to see Officer Duane Cameron and, after a few minutes, a stocky young man with a suntanned face and a crew cut came out of a door marked "Employees Only." He wore the dark green uniform of the border patrol, complete with a pressed-pleated shirt and sergeant stripes on his sleeves. Samuel was surprised to note softness in the man's face, since he'd heard a lot of bad things about U.S. Border Patrol officers.

"Thanks for taking my calls and for locating the file" said Samuel. "I really appreciate you taking time to meet with me."

"Good morning, Mr. Hamilton." The officer smiled as they shook hands. "Did you get a good night's sleep? I bet you noticed how vacant the city was last night when you arrived and, in comparison, how vibrant it was this morning."

"Yes, I did. Coming in on the puddle jumper from Tucson last night, I saw this big, sprawling city. The lights went on for miles. But when I got to the hotel and looked out the window, the streets were empty."

"That's because most of the people who work here live in the much bigger city on the Mexican side of the border. They're only welcome in the U.S. to work, and they have to be back on their own side by nightfall. The gringos don't want them mixing into the fabric of their social life over here."

"I heard from Ramiro that this was a pretty rough place for young Mexicans trying to cross the border," said Samuel.

"Yes, that's putting it mildly. But most of the time, it doesn't go that far. He and his cousin just ended up in the wrong place, is all. We'll talk about it. Come in and have a cup of Arizona coffee."

Samuel followed the officer through the door marked "Employees Only." They walked down a long corridor and into what must have been an interrogation room. It contained a round table made of worn-out hardwood and four flimsy green folding chairs. A large window separated the room from the corridor, but it had no glass—just green wire mesh—so whatever went on inside the room could be witnessed from the outside.

"I remember those boys," said Cameron. "I ran into them three years ago. Octavio was only sixteen at the time; his cousin, a little younger. They were scared out of their wits."

"I heard some of it," said Samuel. "Some guy chased them out of a restaurant with a meat cleaver."

"Yeah, not a great comment on the class of citizen we have around here."

"What happened?" asked Samuel.

"The two boys were hitchhiking north to Tucson, but no one picked them up. Their uncle had told them they could eat really good wherever truckers ate, so they went into the first truck stop they saw. They thought they would be welcome because there was a sign by the front door of a man wrapped in a serape and wearing a big sombrero on his head, a dog lying next to him.

"As soon as they sat down at the counter, the waitress ran into the kitchen. Out stormed a man swinging a meat cleaver, and he chased them from the restaurant. The owner then called us and reported two illegal aliens trying to patronize his establishment. When I got to the truck stop, he told me it was just like the sign under the sleeping man said: 'NO DOGS OR MEXICANS ALLOWED.'" The border patrolman shook his head in disbelief. "Obviously, those boys couldn't read English.

"I picked them up as they were running down the highway, heading south. I took a pellet pistol from Octavio and transported both of them back here. We took mug shots, fingerprinted them, and made a record of Octavio's left upper arm tattoo, which was of the Virgin of Guadalupe, as you can see from the file. That was all I knew of them until I got your phone call. What happened after they left here?"

"They felt it wasn't safe to travel on this side of the border, so they decided to take the bus to Tijuana," said Samuel. "They started the journey at night, and on the way, the bus overturned on Mexican Highway 2 near Sonoita. Octavio needed medical attention, so they ended up staying there for more than a month. I found the town on the map, just across the border from Lukesville, Arizona. I need to go there and see if I can find any evidence of what happened to them."

"By the time they reach Nogales, most kids have come a long way and they're usually pretty weak," said Cameron. "Some of them shouldn't keep going. It's a miracle that more aren't killed. If you're going to Sonoita now, at least you've come at the right time of the year. It's still not too hot and it's a pretty drive through the Organ Pipe Cactus National Monument."

Samuel told Cameron that his only experience with hot weather had been as a youth on the plains of Nebraska, where there was a lot of humidity, so he didn't know much about the searing temperatures of the Sonoran desert. "I'm lucky that on my first trip I have the good fortune to come when the temperature is bearable. I have a couple of more requests. Can I have that extra photo of Octavio and a copy of your file?"

The officer thought for a moment. "I'm not supposed to release information from these files. But since Charles Perkins sent you, and I owe him a favor, I'll do it."

Samuel thanked him. He then pulled out a road map of Arizona and spread it on the table. "Will you please direct me to Sonoita?"

The officer showed him the quickest route, estimating that it would take him between four and five hours. Then he made a copy of the file and handed it to the reporter, along with the photo of Octavio.

As Samuel headed out the door, the patrol officer patted him on the back. "Good luck, Mr. Hamilton. I hope you get the rest of the information you need. It helps those families down in Mexico to at least know what's happened to their loved ones."

The reporter nodded as he shook the officer's hand, wondering how long a Good Samaritan like Cameron would last in the Border Patrol.

*　　*　　*

Samuel crossed the U.S.-Mexican border into Sonoita five hours after leaving Nogales. He drove the few blocks to number 16 Calle Augustín de Iturbide, where Ramiro told him the clinic that had treated Octavio was located. He didn't find what he expected. He saw a building with a large sign on top that read *Fabrica de Tortillas Ana María*. The background was a faded blue and the white letters so washed out that the underlying metal showed through in many places. It looked as if the slightest wind would cause it to collapse into the street.

He parked his rented car by what was left of the curb and got out. There was no sidewalk, just the red dirt of the desert. He tried the door of the address he'd been given, but it was locked, and no one responded when he pounded on it. He checked his watch. It was after 7 p.m.

He went next door to a small restaurant, which had five brightly painted tables arranged randomly on a cement floor.

The Ugly Dwarf

Two of the tables were occupied: one with men in work clothes and the other with a couple and two children. A plump woman sat by a green oilcloth curtain that led to the rear of the establishment. Above her head was an opening with a wooden plank on which rested two steaming plates; looking through the opening, Samuel could see two people toiling in what looked like a makeshift kitchen. Against one of the walls was a blackboard on which was scribbled the day's menu: *menudo 5 pesos, chile verde 6.50, tamales de pollo, dos por 3 pesos*. Samuel was hungry. He didn't know what *menudo* was, so he pointed to the *chile verde* and asked for a *Dos Equis* beer. He thought about smoking a cigarette, even though he had struggled mightily to quit a couple of years before, but the desire quickly passed with the thought and smell of the food.

"*¿Pago con dinero americano?*" he said, reading from the phrase book in his hand.

The woman smiled. "*Sí, señor, sí se puede. Sientese.*" She swept her hand toward one of the three unoccupied tables.

Samuel sat down and sipped at the beer that a young boy had quickly brought to his table. He could smell the *tomatillos* even before the plate of *chile verde* was put in front of him. The boy also put down a basket of corn tortillas wrapped in what looked like a dishtowel, but there was no silverware. Samuel made a motion with his hands that he at least wanted a spoon, and the boy went behind the counter and brought one back, along with a knife and fork and a piece of white paper to use as a napkin.

After a few minutes, when he had almost finished the *chile verde*, Samuel spoke to the old woman, "*¿Clinica?*" he asked, and pointed to the building next door.

The woman nodded.

"What time does it open?" he asked, pointing to his watch.

"*A las ocho de la mañana,*" the woman answered, and put up

eight fingers.

Samuel nodded his understanding of what she was saying. He realized it wouldn't do any good to rush, and since he had no place to go, he decided to try something new from the menu. *"Menudo, por favor."*

The young boy brought what turned out to be tripe soup, and Samuel slurped it down almost as fast as he had the *chile verde*.

"¿Hotel?" he inquired of the old woman.

She gestured and pointed down the street. *"Flamingo."*

At eight the next morning, Samuel opened the door to the clinic. The waiting room bustled with activity and all the seats were filled. A young woman in a white uniform sat behind the reception desk. Samuel approached her.

"Do you speak English?" he asked.

"Yes, sir."

Relieved, Samuel smiled. "May I please speak to señora Nereyda Lopez Niebles?"

"She's not here right now," said the receptionist, who had no noticeable accent. "Can I help you?"

"I had an appointment with her for this morning."

"I'm sorry, sir, she's not here."

"When can I see her?"

"I can't tell you that, sir, come back tomorrow."

"You said you could help me. I'm here to look at the medical records of Octavio Huerta."

"Only señorita Lopez can authorize you to see medical records. Come back tomorrow."

"Are you serious? I came all the way here from San Francisco, and I had an appointment with señora Lopez for this morning."

The Ugly Dwarf

"I already told you she's not here. Come back tomorrow." Furious, Samuel slammed the door as he left. What the hell am I going to do now, he thought. I've come all the way out here on a wild goose chase. This woman promised me she would be here and that she would talk to me.

He went back to his hotel and called Marisol who had helped him set up the appointment. While Marisol was trying to run down his contact, Samuel went on a sightseeing tour of the desert, followed by lunch at the city's only upscale restaurant. In the afternoon, he called Marisol again. There had been a mix up, she told him. The woman would see him the next day. Samuel got up early the next morning and went back to the clinic, arriving just as it opened.

The same young woman greeted him. "I took your advice," he said. "I've come back to try and see señora Lopez again."

"I will see if she's in. Who may I say is calling?"

"Tell her it's Samuel Hamilton from San Francisco. I am inquiring about a patient of hers named Octavio Huerta."

She was back within a couple of minutes. "Come this way." Opening the swinging double doors behind her desk, she ushered Samuel down a corridor to a large dormitory-like room with at least thirty cots, all occupied by bandaged men in various stages of health. Standing in the midst of the cots was a tall woman who looked to be in her early thirties. She had angular cheekbones and cinnamon-colored skin, and was dressed in a nurse's uniform, complete with a starched white cap and a stethoscope around her neck. She was attending to a man with a cast that covered his leg from top to bottom; the leg was elevated and held in place by a wire that hung from a ceiling beam.

When Samuel approached, she stopped what she was doing and smiled warmly. "Hello, I'm Nereyda Lopez Niebles. You wish to speak with me?"

"Yes," he said, surprised that she, too, spoke perfect

English. "I'm Samuel Hamilton from the morning paper in San Francisco, California. I thought we had an appointment for yesterday?"

"Something came up, and I had to go to Arizona," she said, as if breaking appointments were a normal part of her each day. She made no attempt to apologize, and Samuel realized he didn't have any leverage anyway. She had something he needed.

"I've come to see if you can help me obtain the medical records of Octavio Huerta. He was a patient of yours about three years ago."

Her face was a blank. "We see a lot of people. Give me a few minutes and I'll look him up." She finished making her rounds and went into what looked like an office at the end of the dormitory. She came back a few minutes later with a file in her hands. "Yes, I remember him," she said, warming up now that he had put a human face on what he wanted. "He was so young. He had a badly broken arm that was surgically repaired by one of our volunteer doctors."

Samuel smiled. His journey had paid off. "Can you give me his X-rays?"

She removed her stethoscope with a graceful movement of her slender arm and held it in one hand. "In Mexico the rules are more relaxed than in the States, Mr. Hamilton, but you still have to have a valid reason to see another person's medical records."

"I'll explain. As your records probably confirm, he and his cousin were on a Mexican bus that overturned about fifty miles from here while it was on its way to Tijuana. Octavio was badly injured and was brought here by ambulance."

Samuel detailed the boys' journey after they left Sonoita and how they ended up in San Francisco. "Ramiro, his cousin, told me that Octavio disappeared a few months ago. That helped us zero in on him as a possible victim of a crime because we know that an unidentified Latin male killed in San Francisco had a broken arm that was surgically repaired."

Nereyda turned pale. "Are you sure the body you have is his?"

"I'm sorry, I haven't made myself clear. I guess I'm trying not to shock you. We don't have a body, just a part of a thigh and a part of an arm with a surgical scar and a plate. That's why we need the X-rays."

Nereyda shook her head and moistened her lips. She said nothing for a moment, but he could tell she was mulling over his request. "I'll help you, Mr. Hamilton, but we don't have those records here. The orthopedic surgeon who operated on Octavio has his office in another location, near the hospital. It's on the other side of town."

Samuel drove her to the doctor's office and waited in the car. She quickly returned with a large envelope. Once they were back at the clinic, she took the X-rays out, placed them on an improvised light box and explained to Samuel what they were looking at. "This one shows the break, and this one shows how the doctor repaired it. I assume that's the one you want?"

"Yes. That's more than I expected to find. Thank you. Can I repay you with an invitation to lunch today or dinner this evening before I leave?"

Nereyda considered his offer. "Of course," she said. They arranged to meet that night at one of Sonoita's better restaurants.

Later, when Samuel and Nereyda were comfortably seated at their table overlooking the town square, Samuel inquired about her life. "How is it that you are so well-trained and that you speak such excellent English?"

"The answers are simple. I was born here. My family immigrated to Phoenix when I was a year old, so I grew up and was educated there, but we came here often. I saw how unfairly our people were treated at the public facilities in Phoenix, and I also learned that Sonoita is a way station to the north for many weary travelers. Because of their exhaustion and excitement at almost reaching their goal, or because of the greed of those who want to profit from getting them to the border the cheapest and easiest way possible, there have been a lot of bad injuries on the highway in this part of the country.

"There was no one to take them in or to pay for their treatment. A lot of them died because of it. That bothered me a lot, so I started a charitable organization. Originally, I ran it from Phoenix, but it quickly grew too big and I came here to run it. Mind you, I have many sympathetic contributors from North America—mostly from Arizona and even from California. We also have many medical professionals who come down here and help. Once the gringos started coming, the local professionals didn't want to be left out, so they also began to donate their time. That's how Octavio got such excellent treatment for such a serious injury."

"Are you married?" Samuel blurted out, turning red.

"Unfortunately, no. Men don't like strong women in this part of the world. But one never gives up hope." She smiled softly and looked at him directly.

Samuel felt awkward. His hands were clammy and he rubbed his palms on his khaki pants, which were now without pleats. He had a hard time imagining such a good-looking and talented woman not having a companion. He hadn't intended to get into her personal life—it just came out.

"All that you've said makes sense," he said, regaining his composure. I didn't expect to get as much help as you've given me."

"Do you think those X-rays confirm that Octavio is dead?" she asked, a pained expression on her face.

"I think so, but I'll have to let the medical examiner make that determination. But whatever I find out, I'll let you know. Can I have a phone number where I can reach you?" He tried very hard to keep his demeanor professional.

After they exchanged information, Samuel found it difficult to pry himself away both from Sonoita and Nereyda.

On his way back to Tucson to catch his flight to San Francisco, he again drove through the Organ Pipe Cactus National Monument, enjoying the beauty of the giant saguaros and the absolute silence surrounding them. He thought a lot about Nereyda, her unpretentious beauty and her open heart, and wondered why he continued to pursue the recalcitrant Blanche when someone like the woman he'd just met would better suit his personality. On the long quiet drive, alone with his thoughts, he shrugged and acknowledged that a woman like her wouldn't be interested in a man like him.

11

Rounding 'em Up

A DAY AFTER HIS RETURN to San Francisco, Samuel went to Bernardi's office. The detective took him down the hall to the room where the search warrant evidence obtained from Dominique's flat and her church cubbyhole was stored. As soon as Bernardi opened the door, Samuel got a whiff of the herbs piled in the corner. The first things he saw were the many statues of the pagan goddesses he'd previously seen at her place. Tlacolteutl, Coatlicue, Xochiquetzal and the others were all squeezed together in another corner.

"Why did they confiscate all those statues?" he asked, covering his nose with his handkerchief.

"They may lead to evidence of a crime," smiled Bernardi.

Samuel put his handkerchief away and scratched his head. "Do those herbs you have piled up lead to anything, or is that just to show that you mean business?"

"We don't know yet. Aside from Dominique's and the girl's fingerprints, all we got from the envelope was the smell. But none of those herbs caused it." Bernardi picked up the doll. "And none of them match this smell either."

"Couldn't the toxicologist identify the chemical compounds from what was left in the envelope and on the doll?" asked Samuel, turning the rag dummy, black wool strands protruding from its head, over in his hands several times.

"Not from what we gave him."

"You mean identifying herbs may be more of an art than a science? Is that what you're saying?"

"It sure looks like it," said Bernardi.

"In that case, I have an idea how to find out what the names of those herbs are. Will you loan the envelope and doll to me for a day or two?"

"No. The evidence has to stay with me."

"I remember that being a problem in another case. It has to do with the chain of evidence, doesn't it? No problem, you can come with me. I remember this doll." Samuel sniffed its pungent odor. "I'm pretty sure I saw it, or one like it, in the preacher's dressing room. The place was full of the same smell. Since you found it at Dominique's, I bet it has something to do with voodoo. And look closely, it looks like it has human excretions on it."

"What do you think it is?" asked Bernardi.

"To me it looks like mucous or semen. I wouldn't be surprised if it was the preacher's."

"I thought it looked more like semen, and if you saw it in his dressing room that would make sense. But the medical examiner can't tell us conclusively and it's way beyond my expertise," said Bernardi. "And we don't have a police expert on black magic or herbs either, but those are certainly questions for Dominique."

"If this is the same doll, it's interesting that it was in the dwarf's dressing room and ended up in the witch's apartment," said Samuel. But maybe it was the other way around."

"What do you mean by that?" asked Bernardi.

"Maybe she gave it to the preacher, and when he was through with it, he gave it back."

"Maybe," nodded Bernardi. "I'll have to chew on that one."

"Think about it for a minute. She's the witch. She's the one who probably made the doll, not the preacher. He obviously used it and then returned it to her."

"Okay, I'll take that tack," said the lieutenant.

"What about the cat hairs and the sack?" asked Samuel.

Bernardi, who had been lost in his thoughts, came back to the present and smiled. "You're a great observer, Samuel," he said, giving the reporter a locker-room punch on the shoulder. "You're the one who spotted the cat hair, and it's a perfect match. Now, you've apparently connected the doll and its weird smell to the preacher. That's pretty good work."

"Was the cat's sack from the same material that the body part was wrapped in?"

"No, it was a whole sack from a different batch. If it'd been a match, we'd have our killer," said Bernardi. "But listen to this. There was a basket in her cubbyhole at the church that was also lined with a Mi Rancho sack, and it was covered with the same cat hair."

"From what you're saying, there was no match of that sack either, since it was a whole sack?"

"That's right, no match."

"I take it there was no home freezer with body parts in it?"

"No such luck," laughed the detective.

"Can I write this much of the story?" asked an excited Samuel.

"Not so fast. We have to interrogate Dominique first and hear what she has to say."

"When does that take place? And more importantly, can I listen in?"

"We can work that out," said Bernardi. "First, I have to arrange my thoughts so I can cover all our areas of concern."

"Let's talk about the preacher for a minute," said Samuel. "Since he had the doll with the same smell in his dressing room, why can't you get a search warrant?"

"If we can make the connection you just did, we can go after him, but you'll have to sign an affidavit. That will interfere with your cover as a reporter.

"Right now the evidence is mostly against her. We only have a suspicion that he was plugging the girl and, as you point out, messing around with the voodoo doll. What the hell do people use something like that for, anyway?"

Samuel didn't answer; he was busy looking for something in his notebook. When he found it, he spoke hurriedly, his eyes scanning the material in his notes. "We know from the X-rays that the body parts belong to Octavio, the girl's boyfriend."

"Those X-rays only prove the boy's dead, they don't give us a clue who killed him," said Bernardi.

"Let's see if I'm missing something," said Samuel, referring once again to his notes. "You have two parts of a dead body that belong to Octavio, and a missing girl who may be among the living or the dead. You know she was supposedly taking a mysterious herb that we can't identify, but you have its smell on an envelope with Dominique's and the girl's prints on it. And you have a rag doll that I'm sure has the same smell that was in the preacher's dressing room, and it's the same kind of doll he had on his bed. But you have to find out what causes the smell and what the herb is used for before you start asking questions or making accusations against anyone. The only other concrete thing you have is some cat hair that can be traced back to Dominique's flat and to the cat's cradle at her cubbyhole in the church."

"I'm afraid that's it for now," said the detective, running his hand through his short-cropped salt-and-pepper hair. "But once we can identify what was in the envelope and all over the doll, it's enough to start asking Dominique a lot of questions."

*   *   *

While Samuel waited for Bernardi at Mr. Song's Many Chinese Herbs shop, he and the albino proprietor exchanged pleasantries, with Mr. Song's niece acting as interpreter. Mr. Song was dressed in a gray silk Mandarin jacket embroidered with scenes of Chinese mountains. His niece, whom Samuel had long ago nicknamed Buckteeth, wore the same school uniform Samuel had always seen her in: a plaid skirt and a starched white shirt emblazoned with the pagoda logo of a nearby Baptist school on its front pocket.

As they stood at the black lacquer counter, which was about twenty-five feet from the entrance, Samuel saw that the walls were stacked with rows of the same earth-colored clay jars he remembered from his previous visits. The jars apparently still acted as a depository for both Mr. Song's herbs and the wealth of his clients.

Samuel and the albino were discussing what had gone on in Chinatown since they'd last seen each other when the bell above the front door tinkled and Bernardi walked in, carrying a briefcase under his arm. Even though Samuel had previously described Mr. Song to him, the detective was taken aback by his first look at the white-faced herbalist, whose pink eyes stared out at him through thick glasses. After a moment, though, Bernardi was hit by the powerful smell emanating from the garlands of herbs that were hanging on wires from the ceiling. He realized that Mr. Song and Dominique had something in common, and he understood why Samuel had invited him there. He quickly got hold of himself as the reporter introduced him to the sage.

Samuel turned to Buckteeth. "Explain to your uncle that the Lieutenant has two pieces of evidence with some kind of smell on them. No one can identify the substance that causes it, so I asked him to bring them here. I figured that Mr. Song knows more about what herbs smell like than any person alive."

Buckteeth laughed. "You mean the police don't know what plants cause these smells." The herbalist listened quietly to their exchange, his pale face expressionless.

"I'm afraid we don't," Bernardi agreed, placing his briefcase on the counter and removing two plastic bags. One held the manila envelope that he'd retrieved at Sara Obregon's house; the other contained the rag doll with the black wool hair that had been confiscated from Dominique's flat.

Mr. Song took the two objects and sniffed them. A faint smile came to his thin lips and laugh lines appeared at outer edge of his pink eyes.

"He says the doll has been doused with what you white devils call henbane. It's a species of the hyoscayamous plant."

"Wait a minute," said Samuel. "He knew that from one sniff?"

"It's all in the nose, Mr. Hamilton." The girl laughed.

"What is it used for?" asked Samuel.

As Buckteeth and the herbalist conversed in Chinese, Samuel and Bernardi examined the rows of small, locked boxes that covered the wall behind the black lacquer counter.

"It's what we Chinese call a love potion," Buckteeth said, turning back to face them. "It's an ancient way of getting someone to fall in love with the person who administers it. The usual way it's taken is by making a tea from the leaves and getting the other party to drink it. My uncle is not sure why the doll smells so strongly of it. But it must have been acquired from someone who knows about such things, and it's worth investigating what the doll was used for."

Samuel and Bernardi looked at each other and nodded their agreement. "What about the envelope?" asked Samuel.

"My uncle says it is *cao wu tou*, what you people call

aconite. It is used to end pregnancies."

"Can it be used for anything other than that?" asked Samuel

"It has many medicinal uses, especially if it is combined with other herbs; but alone, that's the most popular one."

"The first use of what you call aconite makes more sense to me than the other," said Bernardi. "I know where to go with that one." He and Samuel had thought from the beginning that the contents of the envelope were used to induce an abortion in Sara; the nausea her sister had described sounded like morning sickness. And if Dominique was involved in giving it to the girl, she could be in big trouble, since abortion, or even attempting it, was against the law in California. That would be an important bargaining chip in his interrogation of her.

*   *   *

"Do you understand why you're here, Miss Dominga?" asked Bernardi, looking directly at the woman.

"I'm not entirely clear on the reason, Lieutenant," she responded coquettishly, "but I'm sure you'll enlighten me. Please call me Dominique. That's my business name and that's what I go by."

Samuel stood behind an opaque two-way mirror in a cramped and soundproof observation space. A lone speaker carried the voices from the unventilated interrogation room. Bernardi sat next to a tape recorder on one side of a table, with two assistants at each end; Dominique was seated opposite Bernardi, facing Samuel, though she didn't know that only a wall separated them.

"You understand I'm going to ask you questions about items that we took from your flat and your place of business at The Church of Psychic Unfoldment," said Bernardi. "The interview will be recorded on this machine." He pointed to the tape recorder in the middle of the table, which also held four empty ashtrays.

"I see. I'm not sure I can add much, but I'll answer the best I can."

Bernardi had a notebook on the table in front of him and a pile of evidence to his right. The first item he picked up was a manila envelope. "Do you recognize this?"

"It's an envelope," she smiled.

Samuel thought she looked especially ugly in broad daylight. The scar on her face was much more obvious, even though she'd tried to hide it with makeup. She was dressed all in black, perhaps to enhance her power as a witch, or maybe to remind people she had other talents. Samuel imagined her with a whip in her hand, ready to dish out the punishment she was famous for in her night job.

"Isn't this an envelope you used to dispense herbs?"

"I have no way of knowing that unless you give me some kind of context," she replied.

"Let's approach it another way. You do sell herbal medicines to the public, don't you?"

"I sell herbs to my clients, yes."

"And one way you deliver the herbs is in manila envelopes, like the one I have in my hand, right?"

"Yes, I do use envelopes like that to give herbs to my clients."

"Did you give Sara Obregon medicine in this envelope?"

"The identities of my clients are confidential, Lieutenant."

"You don't understand," said Bernardi. "You're here because we found incriminating evidence in your flat and at the church that you helped create that may associate you with the commission of crimes. This envelope has your fingerprints on it, as well as those of Sara Obregon. So what's it going to be, Dominique, the truth or the slammer?"

Samuel, his nose pressed up against the two-way mirror, was listening so intently that he almost forgot where he was. He'd never seen Bernardi zero in on anybody the way he did the witch.

"Very well, Lieutenant. Since I have nothing to hide, I'll tell you about the transaction, but I reserve the right to protect my clients." She crossed her long legs and inched her skirt up above her knee.

"First, make sure that you answer my questions completely and without reservation, Ma'am," answered Bernardi, ignoring the come-on.

"I did have a meeting with Sara Obregon. She came to me because she was having episodes of nausea. I gave her some aconite and explained to her that if she mixed it with ginger or licorice it would probably solve her problem."

"Did you sell her the ginger and licorice, too?"

"No, sir. I don't carry those items. I told her to buy them in Chinatown."

As Bernardi wrote down her answer, Samuel, on the other side of the mirror, pounded his fist into his palm. Mr. Song had told them that aconite could be used for other conditions besides inducing abortions, including for nausea. There was no evidence of ginger or licorice in the envelope or in Sara's room. The fact that there were no chemical traces of the other items in the envelope should have bolstered their case against Dominique, but as he listened to her claim that she had put Sara in charge of adding the ingredients, Samuel felt their leverage against the witch slipping away. Without hearing from the girl directly, it was impossible to know if Dominique was lying.

Bernardi continued. "Let's talk about your cat."

"Puma?" Dominique's expression was quizzical. "She's a delight. What about her?"

"We found two different baskets for her, one in your flat

and another in your office at the church. Each basket was lined with a burlap sack from Mi Rancho Market."

"I like those sacks. They're perfect for making a comfortable bed for her."

"Where did you get them?"

"From the church kitchen. The cook uses a lot of pinto beans. You know, they're a staple of the Mexican diet, and most of our parishioners are from south of the border."

Bernardi didn't want to tip his hand by announcing that part of Octavio's body had been found in a piece of burlap sack with Puma's hair on it, so he had to be careful with his questions. "The sacks we confiscated—are they the only ones you used for your cat's cradles?"

"Now that you mention it," said Dominique, "I had to replace the one from the church twice. I complained to the Reverend and to the cook, but neither said they knew anything about it, and the cook gave me a new one each time."

"When did the first one disappear?"

Dominique put her hand on her furrowed brow and pondered for a moment, while Samuel cocked an ear and edged closer to the mirror. "The first one went missing five or six months ago. The second was taken a couple of weeks before you confiscated everything."

"You never found out who took them?"

"That's correct. There's a lot of traffic that passes through the church, so it could have been anybody. Those sacks aren't of great value, so I hadn't given it much thought until you brought it up."

"The ones we took were whole sacks. Did you ever cut any of them up and place them in the cat's cradles?"

"No, sir. The idea was to give Puma as comfortable a bed as possible."

Another dud. We need some kind of a break, thought Samuel, puckering his lips in exasperation. There was a dirty pitcher of water on the table in the room, an equally dirty glass beside it. He poured himself a drink, wishing he could grab Dominique by the neck and shake her, telling her to knock off the bullshit.

Bernardi picked up the doll and waved it back and forth, its black-wool mop of hair flopping wildly in the air. "What is this thing with the strong smell used for?" he asked.

Dominique squirmed in her chair and folded her arms. "It's a doll. You can tell by looking at it."

"We know that. What's it used for?" The detective tried not to show his impatience.

"I'm not at liberty to discuss that," said the dominatrix, sitting straight up in her chair with an air of self-assuredness.

"Do I have to go over it again, Ma'am? Either you start talking this over with me now," Bernardi lied, "or I lock you up until you're ready."

Dominique leaned back in her chair and smiled. "You can't bullshit me, Lieutenant. You can't lock me up and hope that I'll talk. You have to charge me with something or let me go. You know all about habeas corpus."

"Maybe, maybe not," said Bernardi. "But I can make life miserable for you, lady. And unless I get answers from you today, I guarantee you'll be sorry you ever met me."

"You're a very mild-mannered guy, but I believe you. So what's in it for me if I start talking about the doll and my relationship to it?"

Samuel laughed. She knew they had her on the voodoo charge.

"What do you want for telling the truth?" asked the detective.

"I don't want any criminal charges brought against me for my practices."

"As long as you don't bullshit me and tell me about the doll, I guarantee you won't get hit on the charge of practicing black magic." said Bernardi.

"I want it in writing," she replied.

As Bernardi and the two police detectives with him huddled outside the room, Samuel emerged from the observation room. "I think she's lying about the licorice and the ginger," he said. "Why give her a break on the doll?"

Bernardi beckoned to Samuel with his forefinger and they walked down the hall. "I don't want my colleagues to overhear us. Too many cooks spoil the broth kind of thing. Here's the problem. Without some kind of immunity, she's not going to talk. She weaseled her way out of the abortion threat, but she knows we have her on the black magic rap. If we give her immunity and she lies, we have her anyway."

"I see," said Samuel. "You give her a little and see where she takes you. If she lies, then you have her on two charges instead of one."

"Exactly," said Bernardi.

"But who's going to prove her a liar?" asked Samuel.

"You are. I know your reputation as a bloodhound, but she doesn't."

Samuel raised an eyebrow. "That's a pretty tall order with the few crumbs she's feeding us. I'll have to run this past Melba and see what she thinks."

"Maybe I'll come with you," said Bernardi, laughing.

"Melba would love that," said Samuel, slapping Bernardi on the shoulder. "It gives her a bigger stage from which to pontificate."

Bernardi and the two detectives then went down the hall to speak with the D.A. in charge of Octavio's murder case. They returned a few minutes later with a single, typed page, and the group reentered the interrogation room.

"All right, Miss Dominga, here's your immunity agreement." Bernardi handed her the document. She read it over and looked up at the detective.

"You understand, this is immunity from prosecution for practicing black magic in connection with dispensing the doll and the herbs, nothing else. And we want the name of the person you gave it to. That's part of the deal. As soon as you tell me who it is I'll write it in the agreement so there's no doubt about the immunity."

"Black magic is an all-inclusive term. It incorporates voodoo, right?"

Bernardi squinted. "I think the word is broad enough to include that."

"Write it in here by hand then," she demanded.

Bernardi gave her a slight smile, took a ballpoint pen out of the plastic insert in his shirt pocket and scribbled "voodoo" in the definition of black magic in the immunity clause. After he initialed the document, Dominique signed it.

"Since my client has disappeared, I'll tell you what I know," she said, sitting straight up in the chair. "Octavio was pining over Sara Obregon. But according to him, she ignored his advances. He came to me for help. I made him the doll with the black wool thread as hair to represent Sara. I doused it heavily with henbane, and told him to hold it and caress it several times a day. It was a way of keeping him in her thoughts with the power of his mind, kind of like osmosis."

Bernardi scribbled Octavio's name in the agreement to ensure that both parties understood that Dominique's immunity only extended to the doll and its recipient. As he took notes, Samuel studied Dominique's body language, curious to see if anything in her movements contradicted her words. He was puzzled as to why she sat up so straight in her chair as she recounted her story.

"What's henbane?" asked Bernardi.

"It's a love potion."

"A love potion? How's it administered?"

"Usually in a tea. I gave him a big bag of it and told him

to make a drink for her and to give it to her as many times as possible.

"Did he pay you for it?"

"Of course he paid me for it."

"How much?

"Thirty dollars."

"How long was it supposed to take to get results?"

"One never knows the answer to that. Sometimes it works with one application, sometimes it takes weeks, and sometimes it never works."

"What about this time?"

"I have no idea, they both disappeared."

"So why the doll, if the tea was supposed to do it?"

"The doll was insurance. I told him to make sure he stuck it in the herb several times a week so as to maintain the potency."

"How did the preacher end up with it?"

"He told me that Sara gave it to him after she took it away from Octavio. Apparently he was making a nuisance of himself with it, shaking it in her face all the time."

"I'm going to be candid with you, Dominique. We've been told there may have been something going on between Sara and the preacher. Some of my people think you gave it to the preacher to help him entice the girl, and for some reason he gave it back to you. We want to know the answer to both whys."

"That doesn't make any sense, Lieutenant. I already told you I made it for Octavio. He and the girl were having problems, and he wanted to woo her."

"If that's true, why would the girl give it to the preacher, and why did it have the preacher's semen on it?" Once again, Bernardi lied, hoping to surprise her into disclosing more information.

"You'll have to ask him that."

"What did he say about it?" asked Bernardi.

"I just told you what he said, Lieutenant."

Samuel muttered to himself. Sure, say anything to cover your ass, bitch, especially when the two principal witnesses who can contradict you have disappeared.

* * *

A week later, Bernardi and Captain O'Shaughnessy sat in the same interrogation room across from the dwarf preacher and a smartly dressed attorney named Hiram Goldberg, a heavyset man with curly black hair and jowls that hung over his starched white shirt. His briefcase matched the color of his hair and had his initials stamped in gold next to the handle for everyone to see and admire. He'd propped it on the table with the lid open so that it blocked Samuel's view of the preacher's face. Samuel guessed he'd done this on purpose, as the attorney was familiar with the way police interrogations worked and knew it was likely someone was behind the mirror. Even before that insult, Samuel wasn't happy to see the lawyer; he knew it meant the dwarf would clam up.

"Good morning, Mr. Goldberg," said Bernardi. "Thank you for coming. We're ready to ask your client, Mr. Schwartz, some questions about a pair of missing persons."

"My client, the Reverend Dusty Schwartz, is willing to cooperate with a reasonable police investigation," said the attorney, his meaningless answer uttered in a singsong tone as he pointed his finger at the group gathered on the other side of the table, a gold bracelet dangling from his pudgy wrist. "But right now, he asserts his Fifth Amendment right to remain silent.

"Your people stripped his church and his apartment of almost everything when you executed your search warrants. Now it's impossible for him to open his church or preach a sermon. So his question to you is when are you going to return the pots and pans to his church kitchen, his bed and makeup table to his dressing room, and the painting that hangs from his stage—not to mention the food that belongs in his storeroom? And I haven't even started on what's missing from his apartment." Goldberg spoke almost without taking a breath. "The truth is, Lieutenant, you've basically left this man naked and literally found nothing incriminating." He sat back and folded his arms with a self-satisfied smirk.

"We won't know if you're correct until we ask him some questions about some of the items we took from the church, Mr. Goldberg. And then we're prepared to return the things we took from his apartment."

"I've already told you, Lieutenant, on the advice of his attorney, Mr. Schwartz takes the Fifth. He says nothing. If you want to charge him with something, or even arrest him, be my guest. Otherwise, we're prepared to leave, and if his property isn't returned promptly, we'll file a motion with the Court and ask that the police department be sanctioned."

A restless O'Shaughnessy, a lit Chesterfield in his mouth, spread his arms on the table. He was hatless, but the brass on his uniform clearly emphasized his authority. "We think your client has been having sex with underage girls," he said in his Irish brogue. "And unless we get some cooperation from him about these missing persons, we'll keep his joint buttoned up tight." He stubbed his cigarette out in the ashtray in front of him.

Goldberg held his ground. "If you think you're helping the community by keeping his church closed, I've got news for you. You're letting groups of marginal people go hungry. I wouldn't be one bit surprised if the crime rate you're trying to control in the Mission just exploded. These people are desperate to eat, and some of them will resort to burglary or robbery in order to survive."

"You listen to me, Mr. Attorney," said the captain, pronouncing his words slowly and provocatively. "Your client ain't welcome in the Mission. He don't belong there. Tell him to move his church to the Tenderloin, where they're used to his kind of greaser vermin."

"You wanting him to go to another part of town isn't the same as having evidence against him, Captain," answered the lawyer. "So charge him or let him go, and give him back what he needs to open his church doors again."

"Like what?" asked Bernardi.

"Like his artwork and the pots and pans from the kitchen, so he can preach and feed the people."

"What do we get in return?"

"He'll agree not to sue you for business interruption," answered Goldberg.

"I thought he was running a church, not a business." The detective laughed at the empty threat.

During the course of the dialogue, Goldberg had closed his briefcase and Samuel was able to observe the dwarf's face. He studied Schwartz's expression closely to see if he could discern any reaction to what was going on. All he saw was sadness, which confused him. The man looked depressed.

"At some point we need to talk about your department giving this man, who's not been charged with any crime, his life back."

"That's a police commission and civil service matter," said Bernardi. "It's way outside my jurisdiction."

"That, Lieutenant," said Goldberg defiantly, "is going to cost the city, big time."

The pointless squabbling went on for another ten minutes until the preacher and his attorney left, followed by Captain O'Shaughnessy.

Samuel rushed into the interrogation room. "What do you make of all that?" he asked the detective.

"Which part?" asked Bernardi. "The stonewalling by the preacher or the racial slurs by the captain?"

"Both," replied Samuel.

"Not much," said Bernardi. "The captain's well known for his myopic view of the world, and we didn't find anything important in our search that would implicate the preacher in the disappearance of either Octavio or the girl."

"What about the sex thing with young girls?"

"A lot of condoms in his dressing room and a pile of unwashed sheets that still had evidence of pecker tracks—which doesn't make sense if you think about it."

"What do you mean it doesn't make sense?" asked Samuel.

"If he was using condoms every time he had sex, there wouldn't be pecker tracks."

"There must be a reason. We just have to figure it out. How about his masturbating on the doll, pretending it was Sara," said Samuel.

"A real possibility. Who do we get to testify to that?" Bernardi laughed. "Right now all we can show is that there's semen on the doll, but we can't prove whose it is."

Samuel shrugged. "What about the painting?"

"So far, nothing. I had it photographed and sent the photo to the assistant U.S. attorney, like you asked. But unless we hear from him real soon, we'll have to give everything back."

"This is a big disappointment," said Samuel. "I was sure you'd find something in his dressing room."

"We found a little of that henbane herb, certainly not enough to prove anything against him. If the witch is right, he can claim that the girl gave it to him along with the doll."

"What about the investigator, McFadden? Didn't he say that he provided the dwarf with young girls in exchange for injury cases?"

"He denied that when we questioned him," said Bernardi."

And in order to protect your cover, we didn't bring up your conversation with him. I have a man checking with some of the union people. But you know what happens when a man's livelihood is at stake. He buttons up real tight."

Bernardi tapped his ballpoint pen hard against the desk. "I can't believe everything just dried up," he said. "I thought we had 'em both. I have to stew on this for a day or two."

"It's going to take longer than that," said Samuel. "We're missing something important here. Let's take a break. Come to Camelot tonight and we'll talk it over with Melba."

12

Back to the Drawing Board?

SAMUEL AND BERNARDI WERE seated at the oak table at Camelot with Melba, who was blowing smoke from her Lucky Strike into the not-yet-stuffy interior of the bar, which was beginning to fill up with patrons. The men were filling Melba in on what each had learned about Octavio's death and Sara's disappearance.

"Well, you boys have been busy. Any more body parts show up?"

"Nope," said Samuel. "Whoever was getting rid of them must have learned some lessons from what's already been discovered."

"You mean how to dispose of them without a trace?"

"That's exactly what I mean. The first one was discovered when a raccoon intervened. The second one turned up because the killer didn't weigh it down well enough when it was thrown into the bay. Who knows how many other disposals have gone undetected? Maybe the body's all gone by now."

"Have you checked all the evidence they picked up at the trash can?" Melba asked. "Maybe you overlooked something."

"Maybe," said Samuel. "I'll go over it again."

"And maybe you're looking in the wrong places and at the wrong suspects," she said.

"What do you mean by that?" asked Bernardi.

"Maybe the dwarf and the witch shouldn't be the focus of your investigation."

"But so far that's where the evidence has led us," said Bernardi.

"Almost sounds like a waste of time," said Melba. "You haven't produced anything meaningful that implicates either of them."

Bernardi and Samuel both shook their heads adamantly. "We think they're both tied up in this," said Bernardi. "We just haven't figured out how."

After a minute or so of silence, something occurred to Samuel. "Maybe Melba's right. We could be missing something big, something that we've evaluated incorrectly or that hasn't yet shown its ugly head. Maybe the girl didn't disappear at all. Maybe she just went away for some reason. Wasn't she pregnant?"

"Mexican families are very close, just like Italians, and they love their children having children," said Bernardi. "She would only have only left voluntarily if there was a real family scandal, like incest or something like that."

"Well, what about incest?" laughed Melba. "Not unheard of in Mexican or American societies."

"I doubt that," said Samuel. "The father didn't fit the type and the mother is a pretty powerful figure. She'd never have put up with that kind of hanky-panky. Besides, I think the sister would have told us if that was going on. She's the talkative kind."

"You know the old saying," said Melba. "A hard dick has no conscience. Maybe that's why the girl left."

"In my experience, the father doesn't just go after one daughter," said Bernardi. "He goes after all of them, and from what I observed, it wasn't there."

Samuel didn't add anything, but he made a mental note of the conversation.

"Just asking," said Melba. "What about the other crime? Why would the dwarf kill the young man?"

"Jealousy," said Samuel. "He wanted the girl all to himself."

"You said the investigator McFadden was providing the preacher with a steady stream of young girls. You even witnessed some of that firsthand. So why would the dwarf bother? Plenty more where she came from, apparently."

"Maybe she didn't want him, and he was so obsessed with her that he decided to get rid of his rival and drug her into submission," said Samuel. "That might be the reason he had the doll and the herb in his dressing room."

"Now all you have to do is prove it," said Melba.

"That's what we've been trying to do, Melba," responded Bernardi.

"You say there's no way to match the semen found on the doll with the dwarf?"

"Nope," said Bernardi. "We don't have the science yet."

"Too bad, that could make the case. But aside from that, I agree with Samuel. Something big is missing. Your focus is too narrow. I think you should widen your investigation and look for someone else as the potential murderer."

* * *

At that moment, Blanche and Marisol walked into the bar together, both dressed to the nines. A white silk dress clung to Blanche's lithe figure and she'd pulled her blond hair back with a red headband. There was a touch of rouge on her cheeks. When he saw her, Samuel's heart missed a beat and he blushed with excitement.

Marisol was wearing a black, tight-fitting knock-off that she'd made herself, having copied it from a fashion magazine. It hinted at her curvaceous hips and voluptuous breasts in an elegant, understated way. Bernardi nodded his approval.

Melba laughed. "It's party time for the young ones. Have a drink. They're on the house, girls."

Bernardi introduced Marisol to Melba, and Marisol introduced Blanche to Bernardi. "I already know Marisol," said Melba. "Blanche worked with her on the Central American Project. Marisol tutored her in Spanish before Blanche went to Guatemala a few years ago to build latrines for the Indians in the mountain villages."

"You speak Spanish, Blanche?" asked Samuel admiringly.

"*Un poquito*," answered Blanche, smiling. "But it didn't do much good, because the Indians don't speak Spanish; they have their own languages. You'd think the powers that be would have known that."

"It's an ongoing educational process," said Marisol. "The governments down there don't want to admit that they don't have absolute control over the inhabitants within their borders, so they pretend the people all speak the same language— the language of the conquerors."

"What'll it be, kids?" commanded Melba.

"I'll have a vodka martini," said Marisol.

"And I'll have carrot juice," said Blanche.

"What's the plan?" asked Melba as the bartender mixed the drinks.

"I've been after Samuel to come to North Beach and try some Italian food," said Bernardi. "So tonight we have a reservation at Vanessi's, down on Broadway."

"Melba laughed. "Vanessi's? Heh! You know who owns Vanessi's, don't you? It's not an Italian, it's Bart Shea. He's as Irish as Patty's pig."

"Maybe," said Bernardi. "But his restaurant is devoted to Italian cuisine, I can guarantee you that."

"Say hello to him for me," said Melba. "He's an old friend."

"Will do," answered Bernardi.

The Ugly Dwarf

*   *   *

Bernardi parked his unmarked 1959 black Ford Fairlane police sedan in the bus zone next to the City Lights Book Store on Columbus Avenue, just below Broadway. In front of him, across from Alder Place, was a new green Studebaker Avanti. The two couples walked up to Broadway and headed east, passing some of the city's best-known restaurants and nightclubs along the way, including El Cid, Big Al's, Enrico's Café and Finnoccio's. Barkers did their best to entice them into a few of the clip joints that had moved up from the old Barbary Coast, down by Pacific Avenue and Jackson Street. Although civic reformers had tried to squeeze them out of their traditional turf so they would leave San Francisco, they had simply moved a few blocks up the hill to Broadway.

Samuel pointed out The Matador bar, which was just down the street from Vanessi's, at 492 Broadway. "That's a fun place to see movies of great bullfights, or listen to jazz," he said. "Let's stop in there after dinner."

"Okay, but no gore," said Blanche. "I'm an animal activist. I can't stand to see them hurt just so some macho guy can get an ear or a tail."

"I'm with you," said Marisol.

"I guess that takes care of that." Samuel shrugged.

By then they'd arrived at Vanessi's. The large neon and painted sign that covered the restaurant's pastel-colored, plaster façade made a defiant statement: There was still some class left in the neighborhood.

The owner recognized Bernardi as they entered, and motioned for the four of them to move to the rear of the restaurant. An elderly Italian man—dressed in dark pants, a wrinkled off-white shirt and a beret, with a multicolored scarf tied around his neck—was playing a haunting melody on a miniature xylophone. Samuel had never heard that particular sound before. As he put a dollar in the musician's tin can, he looked around the room, which was filled with cigarette smoke. On one side of the extended entrance aisle were booths jammed with patrons; on the other was a counter with seats that looked directly onto the kitchen.

The group approached the owner and Bernardi shook his hand. "Melba says hello, Bart. This is her daughter, Blanche, and this is my friend, Marisol. I'd also like you to meet another good friend of mine, Samuel Hamilton."

Bart Shea had on a gray double-breasted suit with an overdone flower-patterned tie. Though dressed in an Italian suit, his gray hair slicked back, he still looked like what he was: a handsome, blue-eyed Irishman. "You're all welcome," he said. "It's nice to meet you, Marisol and Samuel, and it's nice to see you again, Blanche." He ushered them around the corner to a comfortable booth in an area that wasn't so smoky.

When they were seated, Bernardi ordered a bottle of Camignano, a red wine from the Pistoia region of Tuscany, where his family was from.

"No offense, Bruno," said Bart. "But allow me to instead open a California George La Tour Cabernet Sauvignon from the Beaulieu winery. It's one of California's premium red wines, and it'll be on the house. I guarantee you'll enjoy it and it won't be the last time you order it." [1]

"How can we refuse?" replied Bernardi.

When Bart brought the Italian chef out from the kitchen, he immediately launched into an animated conversation in Italian with Bernardi. "The chef has promised us an inviting

---

1. Agustin Huneeus, the well-known California winemaker, has prepared a list of the best California red wines of the early 1960s, which can be found in the Appendix at the end of this novel.

entrée from the old country," said Bernardi. "He says we won't be disappointed."

Samuel raised his wine glass as the waiter delivered two small trays of antipasti and a glass of soda water for Blanche. "We've been talking about this for a long time. I'm glad we were finally able to do it."

The couples toasted the wine, and Samuel copied its name in his notebook as Bernardi signaled his appreciation to the owner. They chatted quietly, soaking in the ambience and the soft echo of the xylophone that carried to their corner of the restaurant. As they sipped their drinks, they nibbled on the mortadella, salami, and the hot Italian peppers.

Samuel was enjoying spending time with Blanche. She was particularly accessible this evening, he thought. Maybe he could make a move when he escorted her home after dinner...

As Samuel was fantasizing about how the evening might end, Marisol dropped a bombshell. "I don't think the dwarf killed anyone," she said. "I know him. I've talked with him about a lot of things, not just religion. He's not dangerous; he's just a pathetic, lonely man."

"Where did that come from?" asked a surprised Bernardi.

"I wouldn't be so sure about that," said Samuel. "There's a lot of circumstantial evidence that doesn't make sense unless he was doing something weird."

"That's what I mean," said Marisol. "He might have been doing weird things because he is weird, but not because he's a criminal." She looked at the detective, whose eyes were downcast. "Bruno tells me everything," she explained.

"But getting back to the dwarf—you have to add his personality flaws into the equation," she said. "Even his obsession with sex is more of a sickness than anything else."

"Having sex with minors is a crime," said Samuel.

"Even if you prove that, he's not necessarily guilty of

murder. But I bet you never prove anything. The girls would be too embarrassed to admit they were seduced by a dwarf, and the union people certainly aren't going to help you."

"You don't think he's capable of having cut Octavio up and then getting rid of him a piece at a time?" asked Samuel.

"He is absolutely incapable of that," Marisol assured them. "You should be looking for a twisted person with a history of that kind of behavior."

"We should look for an average citizen who's been accused of chopping people up in little pieces but who's out on bail?" taunted Samuel.

"You know what I mean," she countered, clearly annoyed.

"What about the witch?" asked Samuel, turning serious again.

"She might have helped him with black magic, but she's not stupid. She'd never intentionally be involved in killing anyone. She has too much to lose. Don't you think she knows how financially valuable her hocus pocus is in the Latin community?"

"What if she helped him kill the boy by accident?"

"That's improbable. Like I said, she's too smart for that. She knows exactly how much of each herb is necessary for what purpose. Even if someone wanted more, she wouldn't give it to them."

"She was lying about the henbane, then?" asked Samuel.

Marisol put her hand to her forehead and rubbed it gently with her fingers. She nodded. "I think so, and the aconite too. You probably have her on that. The only question is who was the henbane really for? I doubt that Octavio wanted it for Sara. That wasn't his style. Too macho, if you know what I mean. I bet the preacher used it to try and get in Sara's pants."

"That goes along with me seeing the doll in his dressing room," said Samuel.

"Great!" Bernardi laughed. "Aside from what you saw,

which we wrote up to get the search warrant, what can we prove?"

"You have to find Sara," answered Marisol.

"Do you think she's still alive?" asked Blanche.

"That's my hunch," said Marisol. "She's probably in Mexico."

"Where?" demanded Samuel.

"That's the $64,000 question. Use your combined talents to find her and the twisted one. Then the mystery will be solved."

The rest of the evening was devoted to the pleasures of enjoying an excellent meal in San Francisco, something that Samuel was just learning about from Bernardi. When they had finished the antipasto, the chef bought a platter of veal cannelloni covered with white sauce. It was smooth and appetizing, and went especially well with a second bottle of the George La Tour Cabernet. When it was time for dessert, the chef reappeared with a zabaglione made with Marsala wine and fresh raspberries.

After dinner they headed down the street to The Matador to listen to some jazz. Barnaby Conrad, the owner, was a socialite and a painter, and he ran an upscale joint. He had also once fought bulls in Spain under the name El Niño de California, which is why he screened bullfighting movies at the bar each Sunday night. He was well connected with the Hollywood crowd, so it was never surprising to see a star or two hanging around the bar.

When the two couples walked in they saw a gigantic bull's head protruding from the back of the bar. There was also glass-enclosed aviary that housed MacGregor, the owner's macaw. The well-known musician Miles Davis had brought his trumpet over on his night off at the Black Hawk to play bebop with the house piano player, John Cooper, an old friend. Miles also brought his seventeen-year-old drummer, Tony Williams, who had joined Miles' band just a few weeks before. The couples listened to the music until the bar closed at 2 a.m.

Samuel took Blanche home in a taxicab. As they approached her front door, she suddenly wrapped her arms around him and gave him a passionate French kiss. "You're a very sweet man, Samuel. Good luck with your search for Sara and the twisted one." Samuel wanted more but she disappeared before he had time to react.

Samuel returned to the cab dumbfounded. He touched his lips several times during the ride back to Chinatown, wondering if by some miracle his luck with Blanche was changing.

*   *   *

The next morning, Samuel was at the Medical Examiner's office as soon as it opened, ready to go over Octavio's evidence file. Turtle Face put him in a conference room and provided a clerk so that the chain of evidence wouldn't be broken. Samuel had forgotten that the entire contents of the trash bin and every single item surrounding it had been preserved. He spent an hour and a half going through each bit of material that had been collected. In the end, he decided his search had been a waste of time. It was incredible what people threw away.

Using a magnifying glass, he carefully examined the photographs of the saw marks on the piece of thigh, taking notes as he went along. When he got to the plaster of Paris molds of the various footprints, including the raccoon's and Excalibur's—which showed only that the ground was soft and impressionable—Samuel realized they meant nothing unless there was something specific to compare them with. Looking more closely at what appeared to be partial footprints, however, he noticed something new. Specks of something were mixed in with the plaster but he couldn't tell what they were.

Samuel asked the clerk to call the medical examiner. The man dialed a number, and within a few minutes Turtle Face appeared.

"After looking at every piece of evidence in this file, one thing that sticks out for me is the saw marks on the thigh bone," said Samuel. "Is there any way to figure out what kind of a saw was used?"

"Show me what you're looking at."

Samuel handed the examiner the magnifying glass and placed a photograph in front of him. Turtle Face studied the picture. "I see what you mean," he said, looking up. "The question is, could that have been done manually or was it done by some kind of a power-driven saw? We need an expert on this subject. I'll have to see who's available. I haven't used one since the McGilicutty case. The old man used a power saw to decapitate his wife." The examiner laughed. "Of course, she was already dead."

"I would hope so." Samuel shivered. "How long do you think it will take?"

"Don't know. That case was wrapped up ten years ago. If the expert is still around, it won't take long at all. If he's not, we'll have to search for a new one. Let's take it one step at a time. Call me on Monday," He stood up, pulling on the lapels of his white jacket. "Is there anything else?"

The reporter pointed to one of the photographs. "Can you also find out what these little specks are?"

*　　*　　*

Samuel had intended to go over his review of the evidence with Bernardi that afternoon, but time got away from him. It wasn't until the next day, Saturday, that he was able set up a meeting at Marisol's apartment with the detective.

He took the tram up Market Street to Church and walked towards Dolores Park. When he reached the café on the corner of Church and Eighteenth streets, kitty-corner to Marisol's apartment, he looked inside and caught sight of Dusty Schwartz sipping a cup of coffee and staring out the plate glass window toward her apartment. Samuel quickly averted his glace to avoid eye contact; he didn't want to deal with any of the dwarf's complaints of unfair treatment by the press or the police department.

Marisol opened the door and invited him into the kitchen where Bernardi, dressed in sports clothes instead of his usual brown suit, was lounging. Marisol offered Samuel a cup of coffee and he and Bernardi sat down at the table. The reporter brought him up to date on his visit to the medical examiner's office. When Marisol returned, Samuel told her what he'd just observed. "The dwarf's across the street in the coffee shop staring in this direction," he said.

"He spends a lot of time watching me from there."

"You mean this happens all the time?"

"Not all the time. He's been there every Saturday and Sunday since the cops shut down his church."

"Does he come up and knock on the door or look into your windows like a peeping Tom?"

"No, nothing like that. Sometimes he walks back and forth on the street in front here. I guess he's hoping that I'll come outside so he can approach me."

"Doesn't this bother you?"

"I know what you're thinking, Samuel," she said, almost defiantly, "I meant what I said the other night. This guy isn't a criminal, he's sick."

"What does Bernardi think about all this?" asked Samuel.

"He knows about it and he says the cops have an eye on

him, just in case he tries anything silly. But he won't, he's just a pathetic man."

"And maybe a dangerous one, too," said Samuel.

"If he's dangerous, he's a danger to himself, not to others."

"What do you think about this little twerp spying on your girlfriend," Samuel asked.

Bernardi gave him a dirty look and poured himself a cup of coffee. "I think the guy's lost it, myself. But Marisol's right; what he's doing isn't a crime. I have a couple of the boys watching the neighborhood. He only shows up on the weekends when he knows Marisol is more than likely to be home." Bernardi stood up and crossed his arms.

"This guy is a pervert," said Samuel. "We know that he has sex with underage girls. Isn't there something you can do about that?"

"Unfortunately, that's not my department. But I have vice looking into it. The problem is we need proof and so far we don't have it."

"What about that attorney. His investigator, McFadden, told me Harmony asked him to get young girls for the preacher in exchange for cases."

"That's what they're working on," said Bernardi.

"What if he starts showing up during the week?" asked Samuel.

"They'll notice it," said Bernardi. "He always uses the same perch. If he changes his pattern, we'll move in. He probably knows that."

He shrugged. "Anyway, you didn't come over here to talk about that jerk. Let's see if we can recharge our batteries and get moving again. I just can't believe that our trail has gone cold."

"That's only true if we listen to the opinions of the women," said Samuel.

"Yeah, our obsession with showing that the dwarf is guilty is just as unproductive as their ignorance of the facts that at least suggest it," said Bernardi. "But I've changed my mind a bit in the last few days. Right now, I'm more interested in seeing if the new leads you're following pan out."

"There really isn't much to go on. I have to wait until the examiner gets back to me on what kind of saw was used to cut up the body. The only other issue is identifying whatever got stuck in the plaster they made of the footprints. That one has me baffled."

13

Where's the Preacher?

WHEN DOMINIQUE CALLED SAMUEL, she sounded hysterical. "Dusty's been missing for several days now," she shouted, her voice almost an octave above her normal tone. "He's the most constant and consistent person in my life, never out of touch for more than a day. I haven't said anything until now, but I finally had to call someone."

"You do sound worried, Dominique," said Samuel. "But frankly, it's strange that you would pick me to tell your troubles to."

"It's strange for the Reverend not to check in with me," she repeated. "I know that you've been following him, so I'm sure you know something."

"It's flattering that people think I have eyes in the back of my head. When was the last time you heard from him?"

"He invited me to party at his apartment on Saturday night, but I didn't want to go. That's the last time I heard from him. I called the next day but there was no answer then or since then."

"It's only been a few days. I don't even think the cops would consider him a missing person yet."

"You don't understand," she said, her voice trembling and at a desperate pitch. "It's not like him. He needs people, but no one's heard from him. Even the lawyer he hired to defend him in his civil service case against the police department can't find him."

"You mean Hiram Goldberg?"

Her voice changed. "No, no. He has another attorney for that case. He's a specialist in civil service cases."

"Does the Reverend live in the same apartment that the police searched a few weeks ago?" asked Samuel.

"Yes. It's on Bartlett near Twenty-Fourth Street in the Mission." Dominique's voice turned pleading. "Please do something."

"Do you have a key to his place?"

"Of course not. Why would I have a key?"

"Just trying to make things easy."

Samuel thought for a moment. "Okay, I'll go over there right now, but you owe me one. And I collect all my debts."

"And I pay all of mine," answered the dominatrix.

*   *   *

Once Samuel got to Mission Street, Samuel took the electric trolley to Twenty-Fourth and Mission, which was the heart of the Mission District. He walked to Schwartz's apartment house, located on the 300 block of Bartlett, and went to the third floor. Samuel rang the doorbell, but there was no answer. After several rings, he went back downstairs and contacted the manager, a frumpy middle-aged woman with short-cropped gray hair who wore an apron over her washed-out housedress.

"We haven't heard from Dusty in three days," Samuel told her, as if he were a friend. Then he changed tacks, deciding on an outright lie. "He's one of our employees and we're worried."

"He had a party up there on Saturday night," the

landlady answered. "Everyone left by midnight. Since then, not a peep."

"Will you open the door?" asked Samuel.

"Even if I do, you won't be able to get in without breaking something if it's chained. Are you going to be responsible for any damage?"

"Of course," the reporter replied. "If the door's chained, he's probably in there and he's hurt or ill. Let's try."

They went back up to the third-floor apartment. The building was old, but in good shape. The light gray carpet on the stairs was expensive and well-taken care of, even though it had seen better days. When they got to the door of the apartment, the landlady inserted the master key. The door opened easily but stopped after about four inches, the length of the chain latch.

"I'm sorry, but I have to do this," said Samuel. He pushed hard against the door until the chain ripped from its socket, leaving a hole in the doorframe.

The hallway was dark, but there was a lighted lamp next to the sofa in the living room. Samuel had never been in the apartment; he only had Bernardi's description of it. He could see that the owner had good taste and plenty of resources. The furniture was of excellent quality, the watercolors on the walls were expensive, and the bookshelves, crammed with an eclectic selection of books, were made of solid mahogany. The preacher obviously liked to read—more books were stacked in piles all over the floor. In addition, an impressive collection of long-playing records was stacked next to a Thorens TD 124 turntable and a brand-new McIntosh MA 230 amplifier. An English-style leather chair, a small smoking jacket draped across its back, was situated near the window next to a reading light. On the other side of the room was a leather sofa in the same color and style as the chair, and a small coffee table.

Interestingly, there was no sign that there had been a

party. But Samuel noticed a strange smell coming from behind a closed door, which was now directly in front of him.

He approached it with a sense of foreboding. When he
pushed open the door, which opened onto a hallway leading
to the bedroom and bathroom, he gasped.

"Oh, my God!"

The dwarf's body was hanging from the doorframe of one
of the rooms at the end of the hallway, a cord wrapped around
his neck. Underneath him was a tipped-over barstool.

It took Samuel a moment to recover. He rushed to the
body. It was ice cold, and the odor of decay mixed with the
smell of fecal matter was almost unbearable. Operating on
autopilot, he ordered the landlady to go back to her apartment
and call the police. Then he picked up the phone and dialed
Bernardi. Since the apartment was a potential crime scene, he
knew not to touch anything with his bare hands, but he took
advantage of his solitude to use a handkerchief to open all the
drawers he could find in what turned out to be the dead man's
bedroom. In one of the drawers he found a letter addressed
to Schwartz from someone whose name he didn't recognize.
The return address listed a post office box in El Paso, Texas.
As Samuel copied the name and address in his notebook, he
noticed that one of the bedroom's walls was covered with ex-
pensively framed photographs, but he was too busy with his
search to stop and study them more carefully.

Within a short time, Bernardi arrived with a homicide
crew. By the time the photographer got all the shots of the
body and the tipped-over barstool, and the crime scene tech-
nician had collected the specimens from underneath the body,
Turtle Face had arrived. As usual, he was wearing a white coat
and an unreadable countenance.

"Well, Mr. Hamilton, we meet again," he said in a mono-
tone, studying the body dangling by the cord. "It's only been a
few days. Wasn't this little varmint one of your suspects?"

"Yeah, he still is," interrupted Bernardi, "but it's getting harder to pin anything on him."

"Maybe he took the easy way out, knowing you fellows were after his ass, so to speak."The examiner gave them a faint smile.

"I don't think he committed suicide," said Bernardi. "His death was probably an accident. The only thing he's wearing is an old T-shirt. You see the vial of amyl nitrate? He obviously inhaled some of that and then tried to choke himself slowly while masturbating. It backfired when he kicked the stool out from underneath him and hung himself. I've seen this kind of death before."

"Could be," said Turtle Face. "I understand from some of my assistants that there have been several close calls reported at General Hospital this year."

"I've got a different idea," said Samuel. "Maybe someone who knew we were closing in on him as a suspect killed him, thinking he would fold under the pressure and squeal on his partner in crime? Or maybe it was done to make him look guilty?"

"Maybe," said the examiner. "We'll check the semen pattern. You know he would have ejaculated when he died, no matter if he killed himself or was murdered. That's where all the shit came from too."

He told two officers to cut the man down. It took them several minutes, since one had to hold the body while the other cut the rope, and Samuel tried not to look at the dwarf's contorted face. Finally, they laid him gently on a gurney, covered him with a blanket and wheeled him away. Bernardi's team went into his bedroom, while Samuel went to the living room and called Dominique to tell her of her friend's death. Her sorrowful wail echoed in his ears long after he hung up the phone.

Bernardi called him into the bedroom to see the

photographs on the wall. The pictures were all of Marisol and Sara, and had been taken with a telephoto lens. "It looks like the pervert had a shrine," said the detective angrily.

"The poor bastard must have been crazy about both of them," said Samuel, thinking back to when he had seen Schwartz sitting in the café watching Marisol's apartment. "See the vacant spaces at the bottom left? It looks like there are some photographs missing."

Samuel remembered the voodoo doll doused with henbane that he'd seen in the preacher's dressing room. The little man must have been an abysmally lonely guy, he thought.

"Did you see any of these photographs when you executed the search warrant?" he asked Bernardi.

"Hell, no. If I had, I would've locked him up. It's disturbing to see my girlfriend's pictures plastered all over this bastard's wall."

"At least she's still with us. The fact that Sara's photos are here worries me more. I wonder what it means?"

"Do you think the missing photographs are of Sara or Marisol, or both?" asked Samuel.

"I have no idea," said Bernardi. "This case is getting more complicated by the minute." He called an officer over. "Take a photograph of those blank spaces and get the measurement, so we'll know what size frames fit there."

"Listen to me, Bruno," said Samuel. "Have your techs check for a rear exit, for prints and for any little thing that seems out of the ordinary. I have a bad feeling about this guy's death."

"You don't think it was an accident, then?"

"You see that scuff mark on the leg of the barstool? It could have come from someone kicking it out from under him," said Samuel. "And I bet you don't find any fingerprints on the vial of amyl nitrate."

"In order to do what he was doing in front of another

person, he'd have to trust them a lot, don't you think?" responded Bernardi. "Is there any way we can find out who was at his party Saturday night?"

"I may have the answer to that riddle—Dominique."

"Explain that to me," said Bernardi.

"She's the one who called me about the dwarf's absence."

"Do you think she could have killed him?"

"I don't know the answer to that yet," said Samuel. "But I need to talk with her and get some straight answers."

"You mean like the ones we got when I questioned her?"

"I mean straight answers," said Samuel. "We've heard enough bullshit."

They went into the kitchen. Several glasses and plates were on a rack by the side of the sink. There was also a load of silverware spread out on a dishtowel. The trash can under the sink was empty. Bernardi called the tech. "See what you can get off all this stuff. If Samuel's right, someone made sure there are no prints on anything in this place."

He turned back to Samuel. "When he's done, you can follow him down the back stairs. Just be careful not to contaminate any potential evidence."

After the tech finished his work in the kitchen, Samuel motioned for him to follow him to the back door and the back porch. Then he led him to the stairs, which were made of sturdy wood and painted green. Samuel watched the tech at work. "Interesting that the back door wasn't locked, and that there are no prints on the door or the light switch," he told him. "Will you make a note of that?"

The man complied. "What are you looking for, Mr. Hamilton?"

"Anything, just anything—a footprint, a fingerprint, who the hell knows?"

The tech took a photo of the light switch and put the burnt-out flashbulb in his apron pocket. "I suppose most people use these stairs in the evening."

"Probably. It looks like they're mostly used to take out the trash, since the cans are on Fern Street, on the other side of the fence at the back of the building."

Samuel stayed out of the way and as the tech slowly worked his way down the stairs. Suddenly, Samuel grabbed the tech's arm. "Hold it," he said, pointing to a single beige thread, which was caught on a nail "See that thing right there? Get a photo and then save it. Is there any way to tell what it's made of or where it comes from?"

"Sure, we have people who can do that," the tech answered. "It's just a matter of comparing it to known threads under a microscope."

"Bernardi will be proud of you," said Samuel.

At the bottom of the stairs was a gate, also painted the same green color. "I bet I don't find any prints on the gate either," said the tech.

"It doesn't matter, dust for them anyway and see what comes up," said Samuel. "If there aren't any, it just reinforces my point that someone cleaned up after him or herself."

When the tech was done, they walked out onto Orange Alley, where Samuel identified the trash cans that belonged to the apartment house. The tech dusted and found prints on all but one. Samuel lifted the tops with a stick and peered into one empty can after another.

"Looks like it was already trash day," said Samuel. "I wonder where they took all the stuff?"

"It will be almost impossible to trace, I'm sorry to say," said the tech. "We've tried before when we knew what we were looking for."

After they searched the area carefully, they went back upstairs and met Bernardi in the kitchen.

"Well?" Bernardi asked.

"Almost no prints, and a strand of some kind of material,"

said Samuel. "It looks like wool. But the trash was taken away, so if there were any clues, they're long gone." Samuel shook his head. "Not that it matters much. Whoever we're dealing with was too smart to leave anything behind."

"I'm not sure you're right about foul play, Samuel. I've investigated this kind of death before, and in all the other cases, it was a self-inflicted accident."

"You're not listening, Bruno," said Samuel. "There were no fingerprints on the vial or anywhere in the apartment where they should have been. And what about the scuff mark on the stool? Plus, the dwarf was too experienced to just kiss off his own life accidentally. Then there's the letter with the El Paso return address and all the photographs in his bedroom of both Sara and Marisol. None of that was there when you executed the search warrant. Remember?"

"That just means that someone at the SFPD tipped him off that we were coming."

"That's my point, Bruno. If he didn't think he had something to hide about Sara, he wouldn't have removed her photos. We can use the same argument for hiding the letter."

"What about his hiding Marisol's photographs?"

"For Christ's sake," said Samuel, rolling his eyes. "You know what you would have done if you'd found photographs of her on his wall. You'd have locked him up in a second.

"What about the letter you found in the drawer?" asked Bernardi.

"I don't know what to make of it yet," said Samuel.

"Let me think. Sooner or later we'll have to send someone to El Paso to check it out."

"I'll go," said Samuel.

"Really? You think the letter is the place to start?"

"I think Dominique is the place to start, and that's where I'm headed right now. I'll report back to you when I'm done."

* * *

Dominique sat on the edge of the sofa in her once well-appointed den. The spotlights that used to illuminate the statues of her many female goddesses now brightened vacant spots on the floor, accentuating the emptiness of the room. She hadn't bothered to tidy herself up, even though she had known that Samuel was coming to see her. She was haggard and looked like she hadn't slept for days. Her hair was disheveled, she had dark bags under her eyes and she wore no make-up, which made the burn scar on her face look raw. Samuel thought she looked like an actress getting ready for a part in a horror movie.

"I know you're in pain, Dominique," Samuel said, "but I kept my part of the bargain and now it's your turn. I'll tell you why I'm being so direct and so insistent. I think your friend Dusty was killed by someone who may also be responsible for Octavio's death and Sara's disappearance."

Taking a tissue, Dominique wiped her eyes and blew her nose. "All right," she said, speaking slowly. "I'll tell you everything I know."

Samuel took out his notebook and sat down.

"This is just between you and me, right?" she pleaded.

Melba looked up from the pile of bills in front of her on the oak Round Table and stubbed her Lucky Strike out in the ashtray. She wore thick glasses, like Mr. Song's, that Samuel had never seen before. He was about to comment when she spoke first.

"You look like shit, Samuel. It must have been a rough night."

"It's been pretty bad, Melba." The reporter slumped down in the chair nearest her. He told her about Dusty's death and how, as a result of it, he felt that his investigation was going nowhere. "And that's not even the worst of it," he said.

Melba turned to the bartender behind her. "Let's have a double Scotch on the rocks for my young friend here."

"That's not why I came to see you, Melba."

Melba turned around again, taking off the thick glasses. "This guy really needs to drown his sorrows. Make him two double Scotches on the rocks."

"The real reason I'm here is to see if you'll loan me two hundred dollars," said Samuel, his face red and his eyes downcast.

"It's that bad, huh?"

"I have to take a trip, and my boss is pissed off at me because he says I've spent too much time on this story without showing any results. So he cut me off money-wise."

"No more fancy expense account? What a blow to a big spender like yourself."

"Yeah, you know how I throw money around, and it couldn't have happened at a worse time. Dominique gave me some unbelievable information. But in order to confirm it, I have to take a trip to El Paso." He told her what the witch had confided in him. "I promise, Melba, I'll pay you back just as soon as I can."

"I'm not worried about you paying me back, Samuel," she said. "You always do. I'll help you. And while you're out there investigating this case, here are a couple of ideas that I think you should put into action." She lifted her beer bottle and clinked it against Samuel's glass.

14

Juarez

SAMUEL STOOD ON HIS TIPTOES on the Juarez side of the U.S.-Mexican border watching the crowd of mostly Mexican workers cross the iron bridge over the Rio Grande into El Paso, Texas. There were hundreds of them: female domestics, day laborers with straw hats, even children with books under their arms headed to an American school so they could get a better education, learn English, and land good-paying jobs.

He finally spotted Nereyda coming toward him, working her way against the crowd. She was taller, lighter-skinned and better dressed than most of the other people bustling back and forth. When she reached him, she smiled and gave him an affectionate hug.

"Long time no see, Gringo."

"Thanks for coming and thanks for doing this for me," he answered. He was dressed in his khaki sports coat, madras shirt and brown penny loafers, which were now covered with dust. "Any luck?"

"Yes, of course," she answered. "I found out where Daphne Alcatrás lives. Do you know much about her?"

"Not a whole lot."

"She has an interesting past."

"Dominique told me a little about that when I said I'd

found a letter from El Paso. Tell me what else you found out?"

"Gosh Samuel, I make this startling discovery and you're downright blasé about it."

"It's not that I'm blasé, it's just not what I'm after."

"I'm going to tell you anyway. It seems that Daphne was a famous hooker. In her youth, she was actually one of the brothel's main attractions. Your Dusty Schwartz was her son, though her pregnancy was unexpected. Fortunately for him, the father was a wealthy physician from the El Paso side of the border, and he paid for the boy's education. But he didn't have much else to do with him, according to my source."

"Did you find out where she lives?"

"That's the job you gave me, Samuel, and I never let a friend down. We have to take a taxi to her house but when we get there, remember that you can't bring up her past. She left the profession a long time ago and now lives a quiet life."

The body of the taxi was painted blue and the top green, but large areas were primed in gray, evidence of the extensive repairs done on the many dents the vehicle had sustained. Neyerda told Samuel that traffic in the thriving metropolis was so crazy that no one bothered to have their cars repainted, since they would likely be dented again almost immediately.

As they got into the cab, Neyerda gave the driver the address. *"Llevanos a 213 Avenida de Las Alamedas, por favor."*

"Sí, señorita," he replied, impressed with her looks and doing his best to get another look at her in the rearview mirror. He was very talkative as he whipped through the sandy back streets, keeping one eye on the road and the other on the rear view mirror.

Avenida de las Alamedas was lined with poplar trees—their

bright green leaves providing much-needed shade to what was otherwise a hot and dusty part of town. After the taxi rolled to a stop in front of the house, Samuel paid the driver and they got out.

"This must be an upscale neighborhood," he commented, indicating the sidewalk, rarely seen in neighborhoods outside the downtown area.

"Ladies of the night can sometimes make a decent living," said Nereyda, "especially if their name is Daphne."

"You said she doesn't work at that profession anymore," said Samuel. He lifted a questioning eyebrow.

"Shame on you, Samuel. I thought you came to Juarez on serious business, not monkey business."

He blushed and lowered his glance to avoid her mocking eyes. "I'm asking out of curiosity, not out of any pent-up desire."

"I'm kidding, Samuel. I really do think she's retired, but I don't know for sure. Do you want me to find out?"

"No. Let's talk to her."

The pathway to the house passed clusters of cacti and a few strategic plots of brightly colored spring flowers that were spread around the yard. They knocked at a heavy wooden door and an elderly Mexican woman wearing a white apron answered.

"*¿Está la señora Alcatrás?*" Nereyda asked.

"*¿De parte de quien?*"

"*El señor Hamilton y Neyerda Lopez.*"

"*Pasen, la señora les está esperando.*"

She escorted them into a living room with a pale blue couch covered with plastic. On the wall behind it was a large painting of the Virgin of Guadalupe. A small television set was in the corner, and next to it a radio console that was twice the size of the TV. The old woman motioned them to sit and left, closing the door behind her.

After a few minutes, it opened slowly and Samuel stood to greet the woman who entered. Looking down, he saw of a woman in her fifties. Daphne had a pug nose and was elegantly, if inappropriately, dressed in a green chiffon evening dress. She held a lighted cigarette in a twelve-inch holder, and a pair of glasses dangling from a silver chain around her neck rested on an exposed and generous cleavage. Her hair was tinted brassy red and she had eyes as blue as those of her deceased son. She was also a dwarf.

If she had been as much in demand as Neyerda said she was, Samuel thought that she must have been very experienced and seductive to compensate for such a misshapen body,.

"Hello, Mr. Hamilton," she said in accented English. "I understand you've been looking for me. Please have a seat and tell me what I can do for you."

"This is Miss Nereyda López," said Samuel. "She helped me find you. First, let me tell you how sorry I am about your son's death."

As Daphne nodded her head in acknowledgment, Samuel noticed that her expression remained inscrutable and her eyes dry. "Thank you for your kindness," she said. "He was too young to die, but he is in God's hands now." She bowed her large head, tapping the ashes at the end of her long holder into the ashtray.

"May I ask if you and *la señorita López* are romantically involved? I just want to be clear."

Nereyda and Samuel blushed for different reasons, and shook their heads emphatically.

"Would you like some tea?" Daphne inquired.

"Thank you," said Nereyda.

Daphne called to the maid in Spanish. After a few minutes, as they chatted about nothing of great importance, the old woman brought tea in a polished silver set and delicate porcelain teacups. The mistress poured each a cup and offered pastries from a separate tray.

"I know you are wondering why I came to see you, *señora*," said Samuel, blowing on the hot liquid.

"I have a pretty good idea, Mr. Hamilton."

"I need to talk with Sara Obregon. I know she is with you."

"That's not entirely true. She lives nearby, but she is not actually with me, as you say. What do you want from her?"

"She disappeared from San Francisco without a word to her family or anyone else, and they are anxious to find out about her. I haven't contacted the police or any other agency because Dominique told me that you would help me."

"I understand. But you will have to come back tomorrow. I do not speak for Sara, so I will ask her if she wants to see you. If her answer is yes, she will be here when you arrive. Shall we say four in the afternoon?"

"Thank you, *señora* Alcatrás. We'll see you then."

"I hope things work out for you," said Daphne, stubbing out her cigarette in the ashtray. She slid off the couch onto the floor and, with a sweeping motion of her arm, ushered them towards the front door. "Thank you for coming, Mr. Hamilton. You, too, *Señorita* Lopez."

When they returned the next day, the old woman once again showed them in. Daphne appeared a few minutes later, this time dressed in a powder blue full-length evening dress that would have been appropriate at a costume ball but that seemed out of place in a residential Juarez neighborhood.

When they were all comfortably settled around the coffee table in the small living room, Daphne nodded to the old woman, who left the room momentarily and returned with a baby in her arms. Behind her came a young woman dressed in a T-shirt and jeans. Samuel recognized her immediately. It was Sara Obregon, and she was even better looking than he expected.

"This is Sara and my only grandson," said Daphne, beaming with pride.

Samuel didn't know where to begin. His eyes were riveted on the child in the old woman's arms. Despite Daphne's words, he immediately thought back to the photograph of Octavio that he'd first seen in the Arizona border patrol office. The baby bore a strong resemblance to the dead young man.

"Your parents have been worried sick about you, Sara," he scolded when he was finally able to talk.

"I know," she responded. "And I'll explain everything to you a little later. Right now, I want you to meet Raymundo Schwartz, my son. Isn't he gorgeous?"

"He certainly is," said Nereyda, wistfully. "May I hold him?"

Sara took the baby from the old woman and gently handed him to Nereyda, who began cooing to him in Spanish.

Samuel turned to Daphne. "Can we spend some time alone with Sara?"

Daphne motioned to the old woman and they left the room, closing the door behind them.

Samuel waited a few seconds and then put his ear to the door to make sure no one was listening. "I need to ask you a lot of questions, Sara, and I need truthful answers."

"Don't worry. I'll tell you everything," she said with a sigh of relief. She could at last tell her side of the story. Her voice dropped to a whisper. "But I don't want what I tell you repeated by you or anybody else in front of Grandmother. Is that understood?"

"I understood that as soon as I saw the baby," said Samuel.

"She thinks it's her son's baby, and I was worried it would

be, which is why I let him send me here. I'm very happy that the baby is Octavio's and that he's normal."

"I guessed that you were involved with the Reverend," said Samuel.

"Unfortunately, I was. But it wasn't my choice; he forced himself on me."

"I figured that's what had happened," said Samuel.

"I was worried that I was pregnant with the preacher's child, but that's not the only reason I left San Francisco. I was also worried that even if it was Octavio's child, it would be deformed or retarded."

"What do you mean?" asked Nereyda.

"After Octavio and I got involved, if you know what I mean, my father warned me not to pursue the relationship with him. He told me Octavio was my brother."

"What?" cried Samuel. "How could that be?"

Sara sighed. "When my father was young he had a son with a woman in Mexico; this was before he courted my mother. The baby was Octavio. After he married my mother, they came to the United States. He never expected his son would show up in the same city or that his son would get involved with one of his daughters. He only spoke of it to me when he saw our relationship was serious and where it was headed. That didn't stop me, but when I got pregnant I feared for the child's health."

Although stunned by the coincidence, Samuel realized that something like this was possible in the small, tightly knit world of Mexican immigrants. He flashed back to the discussion he and Bernardi had had about incest, but they were talking about father-daughter; they never imagined it would be between brother and sister.

After a moment of silence, he said, "Tell me how you got mixed up with the Reverend. I heard that the labor leaders sent a lot of girls back to his dressing room. Were you one of them?"

"No way."

"I saw several go back there, and I couldn't believe they were actually attracted to him," said Samuel.

"That wasn't his appeal to me. I liked what he had to say about religion and that's why I started going to his church. When the issue of me having relations with my brother came up, I went to talk with him about it. While I was there, he gave me a cup of tea. The next thing I knew"—her voice grew angry—"he was on top of me, but I was too drugged to resist him. Then I missed my period. I became hysterical and threatened to call the police, but I don't think I would have actually done it. The shame of the rape was more than I or my family could bear. Not to mention that I had to make sure Octavio didn't find out about it, because he would have killed him.

"When I finally confirmed that I was pregnant, I was terrified I'd have a deformed child by either the dwarf or my own brother. You know, they warned us about these family things in school. And even though I tried to get rid of the baby, it didn't work.

"When did you finally decide to come here?" asked Samuel.

"The preacher tried to calm me down by offering to send me to his mother here in Juarez to have the baby, and he convinced me that no one would ever know. So this was my way out. But I couldn't tell anyone, so I just left San Francisco."

"You must have gone through hell, Sara," said Nereyda. "This Reverend guy was a real pervert and a shrewd manipulator."

"I'm sorry, Sara," Samuel agreed. "I can't believe this happened to you. But now that we know you're safe I need to ask you some questions about Dominique. You know who I'm talking about, don't you?"

"Yes, I know that bitch," she answered.

"Is it true she gave you something to end your pregnancy?"

"How did you find that out?"

"She said she gave something to you for nausea, but we didn't believe her."

"She didn't 'give' me anything. She 'sold' me a potion and said it would take care of my problem; meaning it would end my pregnancy. But when I took it, it only made me sicker. I chickened out and threw the contents away, but I saved the envelope, just in case she'd actually poisoned me."

"You didn't trust her?"

"Hell no. She was the Reverend's friend. I think she would have done anything to protect him."

"That may be important testimony, if you ever come back to San Francisco."

"What do you mean, if I ever come back to San Francisco?" she asked, looking confused. "That's exactly what I intend to do." Her voice once again dropped to a whisper, in case anyone was listening behind the door. "I haven't quite gotten up the courage to write Octavio, but I will soon because I want us to be together with our child, now that we know the baby's normal and it's obvious that Octavio is his father."

"Then you don't know?" asked Samuel, giving her a searching look.

"Know what?"

"That Octavio was murdered."

As soon as the words tumbled out of his mouth, Samuel realized he'd made a big mistake in describing Octavio's death so precipitously. He watched in dismay as her expression changed—almost in slow motion—from happy mother to horror-stricken lover. He would never forget what followed. The girl slumped to the floor and began to wail.

Daphne and the old woman rushed into the room, their eyes aflame, believing that something terrible had happened to the child.

Sara was crouched on the floor screaming, and Nereyda,

who had left the baby on the sofa, was on her knees trying to comfort her.

"*¿Que pasó, m'hija?*" cried Daphne, reaching out with her short arms. "*¿Le icieron algo al bebe?*"

"*No, abuela, nada así,*" Sara cried. "*Me dijeron que alguien mató a mi hermano.*"

Daphne gave Samuel a look of confusion. "I didn't know she had a brother."

"Yes. They were very close. I had to tell her that he was killed. I'm very sorry."

"It must have been drugs," said the worried grandmother as the old woman and Nereyda led the still-sobbing Sara from the room. "You know the problems young people are having with them in that crazy society across the border."

"As of right now, we don't know who did it or why," said Samuel, still anguished by what he'd done. "That's another reason why I wanted to talk with you."

Daphne looked puzzled and shook her head. "How do you think that I can help you with a horrible thing like that?"

"I don't want you to start naming possible suspects. I just want to know if anyone other than your son contacted you about Sara during the time she's been with you?"

"No one except him and that woman called Dominique. But you already know that because she told you where to find Sara."

"Did Sara tell you if she was running away from anybody else in San Francisco?"

Daphne squinted and put another cigarette in her long holder, calculating whether or not she should give away one of Sara's secrets. She lit the cigarette and took a long drag, blowing the smoke upward toward Samuel, who happily breathed it in. He needed a cigarette too, and it was all he could do not to ask for one.

"I don't remember her mentioning anyone else, besides

her family," she finally answered. "But she did talk about the shame at finding herself pregnant."

*   *   *

Nereyda and Samuel sat in a riverfront restaurant on the El Paso side of the border. From their window table they could see the bridge where they had met that morning. It was now empty of people, but the river glistened in the moonlight. On the far side of the Rio Grande was the sprawling city of Juarez. Although it was three or four times the size of El Paso, Samuel could see that no building stood more than two stories high.

"That poor girl almost went into shock," said Nereyda, pulling on her white napkin.

"Yeah, I handled that very badly," said Samuel, stirring the ice cubes in his Scotch with his finger. "I thought she knew that Octavio was dead. That is, until I heard her say that she was going back to San Francisco to be with him."

"It wasn't your fault. How could you know what her reaction was going to be?"

"She loved the guy and was looking forward to being with him, and then I opened my big mouth." Samuel looked sadly into Nereyda's earnest face.

"Don't you see," she said, "it doesn't matter. Even if you hadn't told her, she would have found out sooner or later. You just brought the reality home before someone else did." She patted his folded hands, which were cradling his drink.

"Let me just finish my thought," he said, sitting straight up in his chair. "Finding her and knowing she's okay is a big relief. It solves a part of the puzzle, but it shows we were only partly right about what was going on. Octavio's death is still a mystery and so is the dwarf's."

"Isn't there anything you found out here that will help you?"

"Confirming that she was alive was important. But other than that, I'm not sure. We were clearly headed in the wrong direction, so I have to fix that."

Nereyda nodded.

"Anyway, I'm sorry I got hung up on all that just now." He smiled at her. "Tell me what's going on with you."

"Not much to tell," she sighed. "I'm doing the same old stuff. I wish I could break the mold, but things just keep getting in the way."

"How about a change of scenery?" he asked, swaying toward her. "Like coming to California. There are lots of migrant farm workers who need the kind of help you provide. Besides, it's a place people escape to—a place to get a new start. That's what I did, and believe me I'm not alone in doing it. It's not called 'the new frontier' for nothing."

"I've thought of that," she said, "because I haven't had an easy life. But I don't believe in running away from my problems. They would only follow me wherever I went. I'd rather stay put and try to solve them right where I am."

"I'm surprised to hear you say that," said Samuel, lifting an eyebrow. "From what you told me the first time we met, I thought you had the perfect childhood."

"There's another side to my life that I haven't talked to you about. But we'll leave that for another time." Nereyda's voice was serene and Samuel knew that the door to that part of her was closed for the time being.

All he could do was nod and wonder whether he was capable of the same kind of resolve in facing his demons. At that moment, though, he was afraid to take anything further.

15

A Darker Side of North Beach

"THAT'S A TWIST I NEVER EXPECTED," said Bernardi when Samuel told him of the family relationship between Sara and Octavio. "Do you think that was enough of a threat for Schwartz to kill the young man?"

"I don't think so," said Samuel. "Look, the dwarf got it too, even if you don't accept that as a reality yet. So there must be something we've overlooked right from the beginning. I've been going over every detail repeatedly since I talked to Sara in Juarez."

"When is Sara coming back? I'd like to talk to her."

"She should be here within a week or so. In the meantime, I'm off to North Beach."

"Why there?" asked Bernardi.

"Dominique told me the Reverend spent a lot of time hanging around with beatniks, and that's their territory. If I can find out what joints he frequented, maybe I can also find someone who was at his party the night he died."

*　　*　　*

At Melba's suggestion, Samuel's first stop was Vesuvio's, right across from City Lights, San Francisco's best-known bookstore. The bar was noisy and quaint, its stained glass windows rendering it almost (but not quite) out of place in the neighborhood. Vesuvio's attracted an artistic crowd and smelled of North Beach's blend of cigarettes, marijuana, espresso and cheap red wine served and spilled by the glass. Always crowded, it had a happy atmosphere, one to which Samuel could have acclimated himself to had he not already been a habitué of Camelot. The patrons filling the small bar ran the gamut from hard-drinking beat types to snobbish readers who sipped their drinks with their noses stuck in the books they'd just bought across the alley. As he threaded his way through the tables on his way to the bar, Samuel passed a man with a beret and a scraggly beard reading Shakespeare; his female companion, her brown hair long and tangled, sat across from him perusing a comic book and smoking a joint.

Samuel bought the bartender drinks and made San Francisco small talk until both were intoxicated. Then he pulled out a photo of Dusty Schwartz that Bernardi had given him.

"Does this face mean anything to you?"

After glancing at the photo, the barman took a break from drying the glasses spread out before him on the bar. He studied Samuel for a long moment, thinking about what he wanted to say.

"Ordinarily, I'd stonewall you," he said. "But I know you're not a cop, and I know the little guy's dead. I liked him; he was generous with his tips, so I'm going to help you out. He used to hang around with Big Daddy Nord when he was running the Hungry I. You couldn't miss 'em because Big Daddy was six foot seven. They looked like Mutt and Jeff when they were together. But Big Daddy got run out of town after a scandal involving a teenage girl, and Enrico Banducci took over the Hungry I, so the dwarf began hanging out at the homo bars like The Black Cat down on Montgomery."

"Really. Are you saying that...?"

"I'm not saying anything," answered the bartender. He then launched into a half-hour lecture on how the payola system worked for San Francisco bars that catered to the queer community. Until the case of Stouman v. Reilly in 1951, the bartender told Samuel, it had been against the law to serve a homosexual a drink in California.

"But after that the State created the Department of Alcoholic Beverage Control and basically ignored the court's decision," he explained. "It was either pay off the cops or close your doors."

Samuel shook his head. "It sounds to me like these people have taken a lot of shit."

"They have, but they're a tough group. The queers always figure out a way to fight back against the restrictions the law places on them. You'd think the idiots that run the government would have given up by now. What are they thinking? That this is something new? Maybe, one of these days, we'll have some visionary politicians?"

Samuel rolled his eyes. The bartender laughed as he gave him the names of several other establishments in North Beach where Schwartz had hung out, including Finocchio's on Broadway and the Anxious Asp on Green Street.

His final words, however, confused the reporter.

"Remember," he said, "the little guy also liked hookers and he found plenty of 'em up at The Sinaloa."

"What's The Sinaloa?" asked Samuel.

"It's a Mexican nightclub right around the corner on Powell at Vallejo. They put on one hell of a show, even if you're not interested in the extras."

"Sounds like it's worth a look-see," said Samuel. "And where can I find Big Daddy?"

"Last I heard he was running a joint in Venice, down in Southern California. That's all I know about his whereabouts."

The Ugly Dwarf

Samuel had enough leads to keep him busy every night for the next two weeks so tracking down Big Daddy Nord would have to wait. The first question in his mind was where he going to get enough money to make it all happen. Breaking the story of Sara being alive and well had put him back in his boss' good graces, and he'd repaid Melba the two hundred dollars he'd borrowed, but that left him broke again. He decided that Bernardi would have to pony up some Homicide money.

*   *   *

Samuel set up a meeting with Bernardi at Camelot for the next evening. He arrived early, eager to spend some time with Blanche.

"She's at Lake Tahoe for the last ski run of the season," Melba told him. "She'll be back in a week." Samuel consoled himself by scratching Excalibur's head and doling out a few treats. He'd missed the worn-out mutt.

When Bernardi arrived, the three of them discussed the reporter's latest discoveries. "From what I'm beginning to see," Samuel said, "the little man had a much more complicated sex life than any of us ever imagined. Aside from his exploits with the dominatrix and the young girls, he liked homos, switch-hitters, cross-dressers, lesbians and whores."

"A man for all seasons," smiled Bernardi.

"Now you're on the right track," nodded Melba. "Somewhere in that group you're going to find an assassin who has enough of a twisted mind to kill the boy and the dwarf, and for little or no reason."

"What makes you think it was just one killer?" said Samuel. "It could be several."

"That's a definite possibility," said Bernardi. "Melba, what makes you think the murders are connected?"

"Oh, they're connected all right. I think we're dealing with just one perpetrator, not a team. I'll leave it to you two to find a connection between the young man's murder and the dwarf's. But I bet it's Sara, the girl."

"You mean some kind of a jealousy thing?" asked Samuel.

"Maybe," said Melba. "That's as good a place to start as any."

"Who do you think was jealous of whom?" asked Samuel.

"Shit! How do I know? I'm just thinking out loud, boys."

"I'd better put some undercover men into all those places that the bartender told you about, Samuel."

"That's the last thing you should do," said Melba. "If the police go snooping around asking questions, the word will get out and everyone will clam up and your suspects will go underground. Remember, the cops are trying to close down all those joints. I like the way Samuel got this far. Let him continue to be the gopher."

"Are you okay with that, Samuel?" asked Bernardi, acknowledging Melba's point.

"Yeah, I like the idea," he smiled. "Especially if the SFPD is picking up the tab."

* * *

Before Samuel started in on the dens of iniquity the bartender at Vesuvio's had described, he stopped off at the medical examiner's office. Turtle Face was sitting in his cluttered office, where the human skeleton lurking in the corner offered visitors a vivid reminder of whom they'd come to see. "Congratulations," he said to the reporter in his usual deadpan as he relaxed into his leather chair. "From everything I've heard, it's one down and two to go."

"I hope you're right, said Samuel. He assumed the examiner was referring to the newspaper articles he'd written about finding Sara alive and uninjured in Juarez. "I came to see what your people found out about the evidence that was picked up at the murder scene, and to see if you had answers to any of the other questions I left you with."

"I have some interesting revelations for you, Samuel. Where do you want me to start?"

"From the beginning, please."

"First, the two body parts were cut by the same power saw. We've determined it was probably a band saw like the one a cabinetmaker uses to make special cuts on pieces of wood."

Samuel was frantically taking notes. When the examiner stopped, he looked up in anticipation.

"That brings me to the second point you asked about," said Turtle Face. "We examined the plaster of Paris molds and identified those specks you noticed. They're tiny particles of pine sawdust. This is consistent with our conclusion that the piece of the thigh the dog found in the trash can was cut with a band saw."

"You mean whoever dumped the body part probably had sawdust on the soles of his shoes?"

"Yes, exactly."

"Did any of your molds produce a recognizable footprint?"

"No, no such luck. The area was too busy, as you could tell by the amount of trash in the can."

Turtle Face leaned forward and opened a folder on his desk. "The third item of interest, which I understand you found on the back stairs of the dwarf's apartment, was a beige alpaca thread."

"What is alpaca and where does it come from?" asked Samuel, furrowing his brow.

"It's pure wool from a South American animal similar to a llama. The wool is usually made into sweaters or shawls. And it's more expensive than your ordinary run-of-the-mill wool."

"So if it came from a shawl, we could be looking for a

woman?"

"Not necessarily. Men wear ponchos, too, but you're going too fast. Before you decide that the person involved in committing this crime was wearing a piece of clothing made from an alpaca, you have to establish he was there the night the victim met his end and that the killer left the material on the banister on the way down the back stairs."

"Right now, I'm not going to guess who did it," said Samuel. "I just want to get all the information I can. Sometime soon, I hope, it will all fall into place and give us the picture we need to catch the bastard who committed both of these crimes."

"You think the dwarf was murdered, don't you?" asked Turtle Face, rocking back in his leather swivel chair."

"Yeah, I sure do."

"And, do you think the same person was responsible for both deaths?"

"Our hunch is that it was the same person, and that it's a man, and he's a real sicko."

"You're probably right. These are two of the most bizarre deaths I've run across in my thirty years here."

There was nothing more for him to discuss with the examiner, so Samuel put his notepad away. "Thanks, Barney, you and your staff have been a big help." On his way to the door, he stopped and turned back to Turtle Face. "One last question: Do you have any record of any ritual killings coming out of the North Beach nightlife scene over the past few years?"

Turtle Face thought for a moment and shook his head slowly.

"Okay, I'll keep you posted on what I find out," said Samuel.

*　　*　　*

The Ugly Dwarf

Samuel hopped a quick Pacific Southwest Airlines flight to Los Angeles for his meeting with Big Daddy Nord. Once he'd rented a car, Samuel headed to Big Daddy's Shanty Town Bar in Venice Beach, which was tucked between Santa Monica and the airport. Made of bamboo and straw, the shack occupied prime real estate on Venice's Ocean Front Walk, overlooking the sandy beach and Pacific Ocean.

Despite its Polynesian decor, Big Daddy's bar was actually a hangout for Southern California beatniks. The clientele sported the ubiquitous beards and berets of the beats, but instead of black-on-black clothing they wore sandals and swimming trunks. They also mixed easily with the body builders from Muscle Beach, located on the sand right across the walkway.

After putting Big Daddy at ease by rattling off the names of his many San Francisco contacts, Samuel sat down on a barstool and the red-faced giant served him a piña colada. "It's on the house, he said," propping his elbows on the bar.

"So you want to know what Dusty the dwarf was up to in North Beach, do you?"

"It sure would be helpful to know who he was hanging around with in North Beach," said Samuel.

"Okay, I'm not a squealer and if the poor bastard wasn't dead I'd tell you to go fuck yourself," Big Daddy said, eyeing Samuel sternly. "But there is a person who can help you find out who he ran with up there, and so I'm going to give you that name and a few others, all off the record. Just remember it's a tip, and I don't want no one to know about it except you, my on-the-record-contact, and me. Understood?"

"You bet, Big Daddy!" exclaimed Samuel, who was flying high on the rum drink he'd already nearly finished.

Samuel and Big Daddy parted friends, and when he returned to San Francisco Samuel called Blondie, one of the contacts the giant had given him. Blondie invited him to meet him at Finnochio's the next evening, after the show.

Finnochio's was located on Broadway, on the second floor above Enrico's Café and the Swiss Chalet. The large neon sign on the roof was a San Francisco landmark, and people came from all over the world to see Finnochio's performers. Samuel had never been to the show before, which featured a parade of beautiful and elaborately costumed "women" dancing and singing at the front of the small auditorium, which seated around a hundred and fifty people. When the show ended, the performers stripped to their waists to show their clean-shaven chests, thus proving to the audience that they were in fact men. The crowd responded with lengthy and effusive applause, throwing flowers and wads of bills and coins onto the stage, as well as love notes and business cards with phone numbers underlined.

When things had quieted down, Samuel went back-stage to the dressing room, introduced himself, and thanked Blondie for agreeing to meet with him.

"Having Big Daddy give the okay was the key," answered Blondie, a huge man wearing a blond beehive wig that made him a full six inches taller. He sat in front of three mirrors, which had makeup lights running across the top and down the sides. After taking off his false eyelashes, he rubbed cold cream onto his face to remove his pancake makeup.

"Big Daddy said you'd talk to me," said Samuel, "and that you knew Dusty Schwartz pretty well."

"I liked Dusty," said Blondie, whose voice was slightly af-fected. "It was a big shock to me to hear of his passing." He removed the wig to reveal a buzz cut that made him look more like a Marine drill sergeant than the diva soprano Samuel had seen on the stage. "He used to come to the show quite often in the days before he started his church. He'd come backstage and sit in my lap after the show. He wanted to have sex with me, but that's not my thing. I like to dress up like a woman and sing soprano, but I'm not a homo or bi like the dwarf."

Samuel noted that even though the man was over six-feet-two-inches tall, he had a feminine air and a girlish sweetness to him.

"I thought it was cute that he wanted to sit in my lap; it made me feel like I was mothering him," said Blondie. "But when he started his church, Dominique took over and I didn't see him anymore." His voice turned sad. "He was a guy who needed a lot of love. You know, he really was a very sad and lonely person."

"Tell me about Dominique," said Samuel. "Did it make you jealous that she took him away from you?"

The man reddened and turned abruptly from the mirrors. "A little, now that you mention it. But she was a dominatrix and could give him the kind of pleasure he was after. And she did a lot for the little guy. Look at the success of his church. He couldn't have done that by himself. I was happy about his achievements. I admit I don't know much about that woman. Some people say she's a witch."

"Tell me what you heard about that."

"Only that if someone wanted a spell cast or some kind of black magic she would do it."

"Did you ever take her up on that?"

"Not me! I only know the lady by her reputation. I never wanted to get the shit beat out of me or put a curse on another human being."

"Do you know anything about a party Dusty had the night he died?"

"Is that how he died—at a party?" asked Blondie, raising his eyebrows. "Good way to go out, don't you think?" He broke into a belly laugh that thundered throughout the room.

Samuel changed the subject, taking care not to say he suspected foul play the night of the party. He knew that if he said those words, the flow of information would dry up. "Can you give me the names of some of his friends I can talk to, to find out more about him and the last party that he threw?"

"Sure," said Blondie, writing a few names and numbers on a piece of paper. "You can tell them I told you to call. Maybe one of them can help you find what you're looking for." Still bare-chested, he stood up. Traces of cold cream under his eyes were smeared with cyc makeup, and he looked as though he were wearing a half-mask. As Samuel left, Blondie blew him a kiss.

*   *   *

The list of witnesses Samuel needed to interview came not only from Dominique, Melba, Big Daddy and Blondie, but also from Bernardi. One of them was the attorney, Michael Harmony, whom he had seen at the Reverend's church. The police suspected Harmony had provided Dusty with young girls in return for injury cases. Based on what Dominique had told him, however, Samuel knew the man had other issues as well. He wasn't sure whether to question the attorney directly at his office or to arrange an encounter that would appear to be accidental, in which case he might catch Harmony off guard. Samuel had tried to contact him when he was writing the story of Schwartz and his church, but all contact with the attorney had gone through Harmony's secretary, Mary Rita La Plaza. She, however, no longer worked for the attorney. Samuel asked around and eventually found out that Harmony usually spent cocktail hour at Paoli's, on California Street at Montgomery, so he made sure he showed up at the right time.

Paoli's was a downtown watering hole popular with office workers. A table in the center of the bar was loaded with antipasto, where many of the workers collected their evening meal.

When Samuel entered around six-thirty that evening, he saw Michael Harmony, dressed in his electric blue suit, sitting alone at the bar and drinking a martini, straight up. He made his way through the crowd and slid onto the stool next to him.

"Hello, I'm Samuel Hamilton," he said. "Remember me? I met you at Dusty Schwartz's church a while back."

Harmony's shoulders tensed as he turned to face Samuel. In the overhead lights, his blondish hair, which was carefully coifed, looked like a wig. "I meet a lot of people," he said coldly. "What's your line of work?"

"I'm in the newspaper business," said Samuel, broadening his job title a bit.

Harmony studied him in silence "I remember," he finally said, disdain dripping from his voice, which was strangely affected. "I've read your articles about the closing of the church and about the lost girl you found in Texas. I know you by reputation, Mr. Hamilton." He got up and placed five dollars on the bar. "Why in the world would I want to talk to you about anything?" He turned and walked away.

As Harmony moved prissily towards the exit, Samuel gave him the finger. He didn't like being brushed off. But he knew he wasn't ever going to get anything relevant from the attorney. The man was much too smart to incriminate himself.

Rather than moping in Paoli's, Samuel decided he'd rather be in the familiar environment of Camelot. He walked quickly went up the hill to his favorite bar, ordered a Scotch on the rocks and phoned Mary Rita La Plaza.

"I just got the kiss-off from your ex-boss," he told her. "Can I talk you into coming to Camelot and having a drink with me? I know you live just around the corner."

Twenty minutes later, she was sitting across from him, dressed in the working outfit of most of the secretaries employed in the financial district: a stylish skirt, a white blouse, and a cardigan sweater to protect against the chill in the San Francisco air. Her medium-brown hair, which she wore in a pageboy, and her dark eyes contrasted with her fair complexion. A fan of laughter wrinkles around her eyes, gave her a soft, even reassuring, expression.

When Mary Rita looked at Samuel, he could tell from the intensity of her gaze that she was a serious person, and when she spoke, it was with a calculated coolness that couldn't completely hide her bitterness.

"Mr. Harmony treated me unfairly," she said. "I worked for him for over twelve years. When I started as his secretary, he was nothing. I helped him build his business and he continually promised me that I would never regret it—he would make sure that I would be taken care of. Once he became a successful personal injury attorney, however, he didn't need me any longer. A few weeks ago he came in and said I was being replaced. He brought in a young, good-looking chick to sit at my desk."

"What was his beef?" Samuel asked.

"I knew too much."

"Really? Then I've contacted the right person."

"Maybe, Mr. Hamilton, and maybe not. We'll see."

Samuel got out his note pad. "What's the connection between Harmony and Dusty Schwartz?"

"Mr. Harmony is a closet homosexual."

"I've heard that from other sources," said Samuel. Her words affirmed some of what he'd already learned from Dominique.

"He and Mr. Schwartz had a fling after they met in one of those bars or sex clubs that queers frequent. But they had business dealings that went beyond that. That was their real connection."

"Sex clubs?"

"Yes, they'd meet and participate in orgies there. Well, that's what I've heard anyway."

Samuel looked surprised. "Where are they located?"

"Take your choice," she said with a nonchalant air. "They're all over the place."

"Are you kidding?"

She laughed. "I thought you knew San Francisco, Mr. Hamilton."

"Not well enough." He smiled. "Which ones did Michael Harmony hang out at?"

"He mostly went to the ones South of Market."

Samuel looked puzzled. "What about North Beach?"

"I'll have to check, I'm not sure."

"What kind of business dealings did they have?"

"Mr. Schwartz sent injury clients to Mr. Harmony in exchange for dates with young girls at the church. The attorney arranged those through several labor leaders."

"Didn't that cause a conflict between them as lovers?"

"The were not real lovers, they just had casual sex. Both men were complete hedonists. All they could think about was their own pleasure, so I'm sure neither of them was bothered by it."

"Do you think that Harmony got jealous and hurt Dusty?"

"I told you, no!" She pressed all ten fingers against the table to emphasize her point. "Harmony didn't care who the dwarf had sex with. He was looking for multiple male sexual partners, not long-term relationships. He's promiscuous, and you know that Schwartz was, too. It seems that's frequent among male homosexuals."

"That's a generalization, isn't it?"

"Well, Mr. Hamilton, that was exactly the case with Michael Harmony. I saw it with my own eyes. He can't admit what he is publicly, of course, but he couldn't hide it from me. I assure you that he didn't want a monogamous relationship with another man, let alone a woman. But if anyone outside his circle ever discovered his proclivities, his business with the labor people would be ruined."

"He told you that?" asked Samuel suspiciously.

"He told me that," she said emphatically, her fists clenched so tightly that her knuckles turned white.

Samuel thought for a moment. "At some point, did his relationship with Schwartz run into some kind of trouble?"

"I don't know if 'trouble' is the right word?" she said. "When Schwartz's church closed, Harmony couldn't use him anymore because the Reverend was no longer able to provide injury cases. And he was already tired of the dwarf sexually, so it was bye-bye baby."

"You certainly are well informed," said Samuel.

"He told me everything, Mr. Hamilton. I was Michael Harmony's confidante."

"Kind of stupid of him to get rid of you, don't you think?"

"He'll live to regret it," she said in a steely voice. Her dark eyes glistened and the reporter realized he had made a valuable ally.

"On the night Schwartz died, he had a party," Samuel said, giving her the date. "Do you know if Harmony attended it?"

She thought for a moment. "I don't know. They were on the outs by then. I was still working for Mr. Harmony when the dwarf died, and he never mentioned anything about a party. In fact, he made a point of telling me he was in Las Vegas that weekend."

"Was he?" asked Samuel.

"I don't think so. I'm pretty sure he was trying to cover something up, but I don't know what."

"Like going to the dwarf's party?"

"Like going to the dwarf's party," she answered.

"That's important," said Samuel. "I'll pass that on to Lieutenant Bernardi."

He guessed there was a lot more Mary Rita could tell him

about Harmony. Under ordinary circumstances, he would have milked her for that information, but for the time being he was after a killer, and everything else had to be put on the back burner. He thanked her, and they agreed they'd stay in touch.

As he watched Mary Rita walk out of the bar, he wondered if he would be able to establish a motive for Harmony having the Reverend killed out of jealousy or to silence him in case the little man was preparing to disclose Harmony's proclivities. According to Melba, blackmail was always a good motive, but Samuel couldn't perceive of even the remotest possibility that Harmony knew Octavio or would want to harm him. He grimaced. Was there something in the underworld that he'd ventured into that connected the two of them? In any case, he had enough for Bernardi to start pressuring Harmony, who apparently didn't want to account for his whereabouts the weekend of the dwarf's party.

*　　*　　*

Based on the information Samuel gave him, Bernardi called Harmony down to headquarters for a chat. The attorney arrived in his usual electric blue suit, his blond hair sprayed into an immovable object. He also brought along his expensive lawyer.

Samuel stood behind the same opaque two-way mirror in the soundproof observation space where he'd listened to the police grill Dominique. Once again, a lone speaker carried sound from the unventilated interrogation room. Bernardi sat on one side of the table—which held a tape recorder and two empty ashtrays—with Charles Perkins, from the United States Attorney's Office; a captain from the SFPD vice squad; and two assistants. Harmony and his lawyer sat on the other side of the table, their backs to Samuel.

"Good afternoon, Lieutenant Bernardi," said Harmony's

lawyer. "My distinguished client, Michael Harmony, doesn't want to waste your or anybody else's time in this interview, so I'm advising you on his behalf that he's taking the Fifth."

"We haven't even asked him any questions, yet," said Bernardi with a smile. "Like, does he want a cup of coffee?"

"Very funny, Lieutenant," retorted the lawyer.

"Let me introduce Charles Perkins from the United States Attorney's Office and Captain Markle from our vice squad. They, as well as myself, are very interested in getting some information from your client. Now, we can do it the easy way and find out what we want to know in this informal atmosphere, or we can do it the hard way and go to a grand jury. Which is it going to be?"

"My client has nothing to say to you gentlemen," said the lawyer.

"Very well," said Perkins impatiently. "The United States Government wants your client to know that he is a target of an investigation into violations of the Mann Act. And in case you don't know what that is, it's the law that prevents people like him from taking women, or in this case, young girls, across state lines for immoral purposes."

Or little boys, Samuel thought to himself.

Captain Markle spoke up for the first time. "The San Francisco Police Department is investigating your client for his alleged involvement in providing Mr. Schwartz, now deceased, with teenage girls for immoral purposes, and has arrested your private investigator, Mr. Art McFadden, on the same grounds. We have evidence that Mr. McFadden, in fact, procured the girls for Mr. Schwartz, and that he did so in the course and scope of his employment with you."

"And that's not all," chimed in Bernardi. "Homicide is investigating your client as a suspect in the murder of Mr. Schwartz, since he can't, or won't, account for his whereabouts on the night of Mr. Schwartz's death."

The Ugly Dwarf

"If you gentlemen had the goods on Mr. Harmony, you'd arrest him," said the lawyer. "So if that's all, we'll say good morning, and maybe we'll see you all in court." The lawyer and Harmony got up and left the room, slamming the door behind them.

"What an arrogant prick," muttered Perkins.

Samuel laughed to himself. He should talk, he thought.

"I thought he'd give us something," said Captain Markle. "Like maybe serving up his investigator as a loose cannon. But this guy is tough."

"He has a lot to lose," said Bernardi. "If it gets out that he's a homosexual, he'll lose a lot of his clients. If we can prove that he was providing Schwartz with young girls, he goes to prison. And this is all before we even deal with a potential murder charge. Speaking of which, I have two men investigating his lack of an alibi for the night Schwartz was killed."

Samuel entered the interrogation room. "I didn't think you'd get much from him. Bernardi's right, he does have a lot to lose. But I guarantee you this, Art McFadden's not going to do time for this guy. It will be interesting to see him turn on his boss to save his own ass."

*   *   *

On Melba's advice, Samuel made a reservation at The Sinaloa for the midnight show. He arrived early, at ten-thirty, which would give him enough time for a couple of drinks and to meet with one of the girls he was interested in questioning. He recognized her immediately from the description he'd been given. She was in her twenties and had streaks of bleached-blond hair scattered throughout her dark beehive hairdo, high cheekbones and a more than adequate cleavage. She was seated at the end of the long bar in the cocktail lounge with five other young women. There was an empty seat next to her, so Samuel sat down, though he wasn't sure exactly how to proceed.

"What's yous name, stranger?"

"Samuel. What's yours?"

"Veronica. Why don't yous buy me a drink?"

"Sure, what's your pleasure?"

"Da usual, Charlie."

The bartender, a man in his fifties with gray hair and a pudgy face, deposited what looked like a glass of colored water in front of her. It had a green plastic swirl stick in the form of a cactus, and two maraschino cherries floated on top. "Three bucks, please."

Samuel reacted with a start, knowing he was being ripped off, but thought better of saying anything given his reason for being there in the first place. He pulled out a ten and slapped it on the bar.

"What's yours, Mister?" the barman asked.

"Scotch on the rocks."

That took longer to deliver, since it was a real drink. In the meantime, Samuel tried to focus on the task at hand.

"Yous ain't a cop, is yous?" she asked.

By the way she talked Samuel decided that she was part farm girl and part lower-class slum dweller who had probably dropped out of school no later than eighth grade. He laughed and almost said he was too broke to be a cop, but he caught himself. "Naw," he said, smiling. "I just heard this was a good place to meet women and see a great show. I'm a salesman."

"I likes company, Samuel. How 'bout buying me another drink?" she said, quickly draining the glass in front of her and raising her arm.

Charlie was there within seconds with another concoction. "Three bucks," he commanded.

"Business must be tough," said Samuel, arching an eyebrow as he placed another three dollars on the bar.

Veronica smiled. "It's the price yous pays for the pleasure yous get."

"What does that include?" asked Samuel.

"Depends on what yar after."

Samuel thought for a moment. He wasn't ready to get down to basics, but he had to keep her interested. "I'd actually like to talk to you," he said, realizing that it sounded phony. In the back of his mind, he admitted that her attributes were starting to interest him.

"I kin do dat, too," she said, "if that's the way yous want to spend your dough."

"How much will it cost me?"

"Twenty dollars an hour and you pay for the room."

"Can we go now?" he asked.

"My boss wants dat you buys me dinner and see da show. Any problem with dat?"

"No, no," said Samuel, mentally counting the money he had in his wallet, worried he wouldn't have enough to get the information he needed, and hoping he could stay focused on the business he was there for.

"Don't worry, yous only have to buy me two bar drinks and a bottle of wine with dinner. Yous can afford dat, can't yous, handsome?"

"Sure. You're worth every penny," he said earnestly, since he knew that he had the right girl.

Just before midnight, they were ushered into a large room filled with a hundred or so small tables crammed together. They were given a pretty good table near the stage. The meal was Mexican—modified to satisfy tourists' tastes—featuring chicken enchiladas and plenty of guacamole. The bottle of wine that came with the meal was cheap, but it went down easily. Samuel was anxious to get down to business, but the clatter from the dancers and singers in the floorshow made talking impossible. Watching the almost-naked women rotate through the numbers and stealing an increasing number of glances at Veronica's cleavage didn't make his job any easier. The show was over by one-thirty. The room was now filled with smoke and there wasn't an unhappy soul in the place. Veronica grabbed Samuel's arm and they went out into the fresh morning air. She guided him down Powell Street towards Columbus until they came to a sleazy hotel. They went up the rickety stairs, which were covered with a worn and faded red carpet, and walked to a room at the end of the second-floor hallway. Veronica took a key out of her purse and opened the door. Once inside, Samuel saw that the dingy room contained a double bed with a faded blue cover that reminded Samuel of his grandmother's bedspread, a small table, two chairs and a dresser. The room's only window looked out onto Powell Street, where The Sinaloa's red, white and green neon sign blinked from a few buildings away.

Veronica sat down on one of the chairs by the table and took off her high heels. She smiled at him. "First yous pays, and den we plays, and don't forget the fifteen bucks for the room."

Samuel peeled thirty-five dollars from what little remained in his wallet. He laid the money on the table between them. "I didn't come here to play, Veronica," he said with the straightest face he could muster, pushing aside his ambivalence. "I came here for information."

She laughed. "Dat's what they all says. But you'd better hurry up and make up your mind what ya want. Yous only has an hour."

He cleared his head. "I want to know everything you know about Dusty Schwartz."

She paused and then squinted. "Yous means da preacher man?" she asked, raising a palm to her waist to indicate his height.

"That's who I'm talking about."

"How did yous know dat I knew him?"

"Word gets around. This is a small town."

She was silent for several seconds, as though she were sizing him up. Samuel began to worry that she would clam up. "There's ain't much to tell," she finally said. "I was wit him and his friend a couple of times but dey got so kinky that I kissed 'em off."

She started to speak again but he interrupted her. "Wait, wait. Tell me about the friend."

She scrunched one eye closed in thought and was silent for a moment. "He was tall wit a good build, and pretty well hung, but he was a pervert."

"Describe him to me."

"Jesus Christ!" Her face reddened. "I just did."

"No, I mean, be more specific. Give me details so I can pick him out of a crowd without having him get undressed."

"I gotcha," she said, laughing. "Da guy had gray curly hair. He was a little on da heavy side but, like I said, he had a good build. I thinks his eyes was brown, but I ain't for sure, since I only seed him at night. He also had a foreign accent."

"Could you tell where he was from?" asked Samuel, knowing he probably wouldn't get much from her. Still, he had to try.

"No. It was an overseas accent when he talked English to me. He and the dwarf talked to each other, but I couldn't understand what they was saying."

"Were they talking Spanish?"

"Maybe. But like I told you, I couldn't understand."

"Did the friend have a name?"

"I never asks those questions—it's bad manners."

Samuel laughed to himself, thinking about manners and where he was and what he was doing. "What do you mean he was a pervert?"

Veronica was now perched on the edge of her chair, an

elbow on one knee and her chin cupped in her hand. "He set it up so the dwarf stood on a chair and had me from the front, and he had me from behind. That part didn't bother me. But when he wanted to tie me up and hang me from the ceiling and stick things like soda bottles in there while the dwarf took photographs, I told 'em both to get lost."

"I can understand your reluctance," said Samuel, dead serious.

"They wanted to leave me hanging up der and come back once every hour to try something new. Sorry! There's ain't enough dough in the world for that kind of craziness. Besides, der was something mean about the friend. It was a feeling I had that I can't describe. It just told me not to go any further with him."

"Can you say more about that meanness?"

"I can't. It was just a feeling. He was a mean son of a bitch. It was his attitude; dat's all I can say. If yous ever meets him, yous will know what I means."

"Did you ever see either of them again after the night they tried to hang you from the ceiling?"

"Only the little guy. He came around once in awhile for a poke."

"When was the last time you saw him?"

"About six weeks ago."

"Do you know anything about a party at Schwartz's apartment?"

"Only what I heard on da radio. He died at his pad after a party. I was not invited and woulda not gone if I had been."

"Can you tell me anything else about this friend that would help me identify him?"

"I sure can't." She stuck her chest out in Samuel's direction. "Yous knows, your hour is almost up. Don't you want a quickie, or a blowjob at least?"

Samuel didn't give himself time to think. It would be easy

to just go for it but he might need more information from her down the road, so he convinced himself to keep things the way they were. He walked down the worn out stairs and left the shoddy hotel. It was almost three in the morning, and even The Sinaloa's neon sign was turned off for the night.

He walked the few trash-filled blocks back to his tiny flat, his head bowed against the wind. His mind was working overtime trying to figure out who the foreigner with kinky tastes might be.

16

The Painting

"WHERE THE HELL YOU BEEN?" yelled the voice on the other end of the line as the groggy reporter fumbled with the phone, trying to sort out where he was and who was calling.

"What time is it?" he asked in a muffled tone, trying to clear his throat and open his eyes.

"What?" The voice bellowed in his ear.

"What time is it?"

"Have you started drinking again? This is Perkins, your old college buddy. It's ten-thirty in the morning on a workday, and you're lying in bed hung over."

"Oh, Charles," Samuel said blearily, trying to focus on the dirty window of his flat. "Hi there. I just had a late night running down some leads and I didn't get home until way after midnight."

"Yeah, sure. Tell me all about it. I need you down here right away. I have some interesting information about that painting you sent me."

"What kind of information?" asked Samuel, vaguely remembering that he and Bernardi had turned over the large painting that Schwartz used in the church to the assistant U.S. attorney to see if his people could trace its origin.

"Get your ass down here with that lieutenant friend of yours."

"Can you give me some kind of a hint?" asked Samuel, still trying to clear his head.

"Yeah, I'll give you a hint. I'm interested in the case of the painting. Now get your ass down here, *toute suite.*" Perkins hung up.

*   *   *

It was past one in the afternoon when Samuel dragged Bernardi into the assistant U.S. attorney's federal building office.

On the way over, Samuel had filled Bernardi in on his evening at The Sinaloa and his conversation with Veronica.

"Any ideas on who she was describing?" asked Bernardi.

"I don't have a clue. No one has ever mentioned this person before and there's no evidence that gives any information about who he is. But if you think about him and the victim cavorting together, and then you think about what your people didn't find at the apartment, he could have been the one who cleaned up after himself on the night of the murder."

"You're making some big assumptions there, Samuel."

"Right now, it's all beside the point. We have to deal with asshole Perkins and see what he has to offer and what he wants for the information he's about to give us. One thing I can guarantee, it won't be for free. There has to be something in it for him."

Perkins kept them waiting until two. When he finally ushered them in, Samuel noticed he was wearing what appeared to be a new three-piece Cable Car variety suit. It still didn't fit him correctly—one sleeve was almost an inch shorter than the other—but he looked neater than usual, with a freshly starched white shirt and his limp blond hair plastered to his scalp with pomade.

Perkins walked over to his cluttered desk and stood next

to a full-sized photograph of the oil painting taken from Schwartz's church. White lines were drawn across the picture, each one connected to notes tacked to the edges.

"We've identified your painting. The Germans stole it from an Italian church in Rome in 1944. You see all those white lines? They all lead to points of authentication. The only thing we don't know is how the painting got here. Tell me again how the woman said she ended up with it."

"She told us she got it from a client," said Bernardi. "For services rendered."

"Does that mean what I think it means?" asked Perkins, wide-eyed and smiling.

"She's a dominatrix," laughed Samuel. "You wanna date?"

Perkins adjusted his tie as if to say, *how dare you.* "Did you get the identity of her client?"

"She said she wouldn't give it to us as it was confidential. At the time, we didn't see any reason to push the matter."

Perkins sat up and smirked. "Vlatko Nikolić was a Croatian SS general. He's wanted for war crimes, and his fingerprints are all over the painting. It's a federal crime to knowingly possess war loot, and it's an even more serious crime to hide a war criminal. If Nikolić really is her client, she has a lot of explaining to do."

"That's not her only problem," said Bernardi. "The D.A. is preparing to haul her before a grand jury for practicing black magic and for committing perjury."

"Maybe we should get to her first. If she's indicted, she'll clam up and then we may never know how she got the painting."

"Is this a major work of art or just a rip-off?" asked Samuel.

"Major, major!" Perkins smiled, enjoying the fact that he'd scored a coup when his people discovered the origin of the artwork.

"Can you tell us its value?" asked Bernardi.

"Priceless," said Perkins, gloating. "I mean, it's priceless,"

"Who painted the picture?" asked Samuel. "Have I ever heard of the artist?"

"I've got the name somewhere. I'll tell you later."

"Does it have a title?" asked Bernardi.

"Yeah. I'll get that for you, too."

Samuel knew Perkins wouldn't give them any more information about the painting. That way they couldn't act without consulting him. Nonetheless, Samuel was willing to play Perkins' game.

"Who would have thought," he said, "that this masterpiece would be found in a broken-down church in San Francisco's Mission District, where it was being used as a stage prop by a quack preacher."

"When you write the story, you'll give us full credit for identifying it," said Perkins.

"Can I run with this story now?" asked Samuel. "If so, I need to know the name of the painting and of the artist who painted it."

"We're not ready release this information to the public yet," interjected Bernardi. "If there's an outside chance that the painting is connected to the unsolved murder of Octavio or, as you contend, Schwartz, we may be letting something out of the bag that will ruin our chances of catching the killer or killers."

"I'm in charge of this case," said Perkins, perturbed that publicity for the identification his team had made would have to wait, but still determined to withhold the title of the painting and the name of the artist.

"I know you know the rules, Mr. Perkins," said Bernardi, his voice stern. "Just as I wouldn't do anything to jeopardize an investigation of yours, I'm sure you'll respect my judgment on this."

Perkins pouted like a castigated child. He was about to start an argument when Samuel intervened. "Look, when I break the story of the painting I'll give you plenty of coverage and credit."

"How long do I have to wait?" demanded Perkins.

"Until we're sure we have our man and we have enough evidence to convict him and get him off the streets," said Bernardi.

"I'll give you two weeks," said Perkins, clearly annoyed. "If you're not ready to go public, I'll go through other sources. And in the meantime, we'll have a talk with this person who says she got it from a client."

"You'll include us in that, won't you?" said Bernardi.

"Of course," said Perkins. "You're part of the team."

Samuel smiled. He knew what that meant, which wasn't much. Now that Perkins thought he had the upper hand, he would make sure he was the star and that everyone else was relegated to minor roles. It only mattered if the painting shed light on the deaths of Octavio and the dwarf. If it didn't, it was a one-day story and Perkins could easily disclose information about the painting through a myriad of sources. But if Perkins disclosed that information prematurely, thus preventing the police from catching a killer, the reporter would never forgive himself for putting the painting in the hands of such an egotistical and overbearing man.

"Let me ask you another question," said Samuel. "Are you having any luck with your investigation of Michael Harmony on the Mann Act charges?"

"Naw," said Perkins. "I never thought much of that case. I just went down there to scare the shit out of him and to help Bernardi. They have him on providing this Schwartz guy with young girls. McFadden is singing like a bird, and I'd guess Harmony will get ten years."

"What about the murder charge?" asked Samuel.

"That's not my concern. You and Bernardi are supposed to be on top of that one."

Samuel was simply fishing to see what Perkins knew. In any case, he wasn't about to let on what he'd learned. That was between him and Bernardi. The two of them thanked Perkins and left.

17

Catching the Twisted One

LATER THAT DAY, AROUND FOUR, Samuel brought Bernardi to Camelot. Melba, seated at the Round Table with Excalibur at her side, lifted her half-empty glass of beer in salutation. The dog pulled at his leash on seeing Samuel, but Melba waved the reporter away. "He's on a diet," she laughed. "Doctor's orders."

Bernardi went over and grasped her hands with affection. He then made himself comfortable and chatted with Melba while Samuel sat down hard on the oak chair next to her. "I'm worn out," he declared.

"Parties, women and booze?" she asked.

"I wish," he said. "All those late hours, night after night, and a shitty meeting with an asshole." He then proceeded to tell Melba what he'd learned from his investigation in North Beach and about the afternoon he and Bernardi had spent with Charles Perkins.

"Were you actually surprised all that was going on in San Francisco?" she asked.

"I was," said the reporter. "At first I thought it was just North Beach and the beatniks, but there are other worlds out there that are never talked about in polite society."

"Like everywhere else," said Melba. "It's just under the surface, boy. And sometimes what's fringe behavior becomes mainstream."

The Ugly Dwarf

"It sure isn't what I learned in school," laughed Samuel.

"My life as a homicide detective has given me a broader perspective," said Bernardi, taking on the pose of a wise elder.

"Let's get back to what you fellas are after," said Melba. "What have you learned that I should know about?"

Samuel started to talk, but Bernardi interrupted him. "The first thing I have to admit is that Samuel is probably right about Schwartz being murdered, and I think he's also right that it was the same person who killed the Mexican boy."

"What made you change your mind?" Melba asked Bernardi.

"The story the young woman at The Sinaloa told Samuel about the little guy and a man with a foreign accent spending time with her. She said that Schwartz's companion was a perverted and mean son of a bitch. From that interview I put several things together."

"Like what?" asked Melba, handing her empty glass to the barman and accepting a new one, filled to the top with beer.

Bernardi began to explain, but she held up her hand. "I'm sorry, boys, that was rude of me. What are you drinking?"

"I'll have a glass of red wine," said Bernardi.

"I'll have the usual," said Samuel.

"Double Scotch on the rocks and a Dago red," Melba yelled over her shoulder. "Now, go ahead," she instructed Bernardi.

"Putting the girl's story together with what happened at the dwarf's apartment and the way the boy died, it just changed my mind," said Bernardi. "Let's remember we only have pieces of a body. It takes a pretty strange killer to keep body parts in a freezer and dispose of them one by one. Then there's Schwartz's death. He's found hanging from a door-frame and, at first glance, it looked like he did himself in. I've seen that kind of death before and it's always been a solo job." Bernardi took a drink of his wine, which had just arrived.

"But here I have to give credit to Samuel. Someone was probably helping him, like the pervert the woman described, so it seems very plausible that once he was up on the stool and in the process of choking himself while he masturbated, his killer kicked the stool out from under him and left him there to die. Then he cleaned up the apartment to remove any evidence of his ever having been there. But he left a couple of clues—the mark on the stool and the wool fiber on the rail of the rear stairwell."

"Why do you think the fiber came from the killer?" asked Melba.

"Right now it's just a guess, but remember he probably doesn't know we have it. If we find something in his possession that matches the fiber, then it becomes powerful circumstantial evidence."

"Why so?" asked Melba.

"Because he's had plenty of time to come forward and say he knew the victim and that he hung around with him," explained Bernardi. "His silence about their relationship and his presence at his apartment is damning. That's what circumstantial evidence is all about."

"Have you found anybody who admits he was at the party?" asked Melba. "I mean, beyond the fact that you both suspect Harmony was there."

"We haven't been able to prove that yet," said Samuel, taking a pull on his drink. "But we're still looking. I just found out about the pervert. I'm hopeful I'll get more information about him in the next few days, now that I know who we're looking for."

"Is there still a case that Schwartz killed the boy?" asked Melba.

"That's a good question," answered Bernardi. "I'm not sure yet. There's a solid argument that he killed the boy and just couldn't take the pressure of being pursued by the police and having his church shut down, so he just ended it."

"I'm sure it didn't happen that way," said Samuel. "That's exactly the picture the pervert was trying to paint. But he made a big mistake. He cleaned the apartment after he kicked the stool out from under the dwarf. It brings all the attention back to him."

"And of course you still haven't totally eliminated Harmony, have you?" asked Melba.

"He was on my list of suspects until yesterday," said Samuel.

"What happened that changed your mind?"

"I learned about the pervert with the foreign accent."

Melba smiled. "Tall, dark and handsome, with a foreign accent. It has the making of a great movie, starring... let me think for a moment." She tilted her chin upward and blew the smoke from her cigarette towards the high ceiling.

"It sounds like a cliché, but it's happening right here under our noses," said Bernardi.

Melba stubbed her cigarette out in the already full ashtray. "You're getting close, Samuel. All you have to do is find the connection between the dwarf, the accent and Octavio, and then you'll be the hero. I've already told you where I think the connection is."

"It's not about being the hero, Melba, it's about getting at the truth," sighed Samuel, feeling more fatigued by the minute.

"Bullshit!" she laughed, lifting her glass to her lips. "Everyone wants to be a hero."

She lit another cigarette and looked at Samuel appraisingly. "I'm seriously wondering about your health Samuel. You haven't once asked about Blanche," she teased. "She'll be in later if you're still interested."

Samuel turned red. "I'm interested, but I don't have the energy to do anything about it right now." He got up and scratched the dog's head, leaving Bernardi and Melba talking at the table. He walked out into the brisk late afternoon San Francisco air and went back to his flat, where he promptly fell asleep and didn't wake up until the next morning.

*   *   *

Samuel was at the The Black Cat on Montgomery Street when it opened at five o'clock. He'd already learned that that was when the night bartender came to work. Although the exterior of the nightclub was dark, drab and unexceptional, Samuel found the interior surprisingly elegant. Opulent chandeliers hanging from the ceiling illuminated a long bar and several small tables, which were draped with white tablecloths and set for dinner. A silent piano waited in a corner by the door.

Samuel sat down on a bar stool and ordered a drink. The young man who served him wore a tight-fitting T-shirt that emphasized his wiry physic. He had short hair and his ready smile showed almost perfect teeth. He was easy to talk to and Samuel quickly engaged him in conversation. The only problem was that the young man wouldn't have a drink himself, and Samuel calculated that if he didn't get down to business soon, he would be drunk before he had a chance to pump the bartender for information.

"Do you know Michael Harmony?" he finally asked.

"Is he a friend of yours?"

"I know him through some mutual acquaintances."

"What do you want with him?"

"Nothing. I was just wondering if he'd been in here?"

"Yeah, he's been here a few times, but he's not a regular," said the bartender. "What do you really want, Mister? You didn't come here to talk about Michael Harmony."

"You're right. I came here to ask if you know anything

about this man." Samuel pulled out a photograph.

The bartender laughed, his teeth sparkling in the light from the chandeliers. "The preacher man, Dusty Schwartz. He was a regular here before he opened his church. I didn't see him around much after that."

"Did you ever see him hanging around with a bigger man with curly gray hair and a foreign accent?"

"Yeah, they trolled together."

"What does that mean?" asked Samuel.

"They would come in around ten o'clock, looking for targets. They liked to pick up one guy for the both of them."

"Do any of the men that they picked up together still frequent your bar?"

"Probably not. It doesn't work the way you think it does. Targets roam from bar to bar. Most of the time, you never see them again. I just remember those two because they kept coming back here to pick up dates, and one of them was a dwarf," He laughed. "How could I miss that?"

"Can you tell me anything else about the big guy with gray hair?"

"Only what you've already said, that he spoke English with a foreign accent."

"What was his accent?"

"I'd have to guess. I'd say European. But which country I couldn't tell you."

"You know that Schwartz is dead, don't you?"

"I read it in the newspaper."

"He died at a party in his apartment. Did you know about the party or anyone who attended it?"

The bartender eyed Samuel suspiciously and speeded up drying glasses with his dishtowel. He hesitated before he said anything further, clearly uncomfortable.

"No. Like I said, he and his friend stopped coming in here when Mr. Schwartz opened his church. That was a couple of years ago. Who are you anyway? A cop? Or are you from the ABC?" He raised his arm and gestured towards the front door, as if he were signaling someone.

"No, no, don't worry. I'm just a friend, trying to find out what happened to the little guy. Given that the world he lived in is pretty much underground, people like yourself are reluctant to give information."

"Can you blame us?" the bartender asked impatiently.

The bar was almost full now, and single men sat at the tables and the bar, eyeing one other in a way that was unfamiliar to Samuel.

"I'm really trying to help, and one way to do that is to find out who was at Dusty Schwartz's party."

The young man shook his head. "I've told you all I know and I've probably said more than I should have. Now let's see if it comes back and kicks me in the ass."

"I understand your concern. Believe me, I'm not trying to hurt anybody."

The bartender gave him a cynical smile. "Sure, Mister, I understand."

Samuel thanked him, left a tip and got up to leave. A piano player was now belting out familiar tunes. A couple of men in the crowd motioned for him to join them, but he escaped with as much dignity as he could gather and exited the door onto Montgomery Street. The buff bouncer in a black T-shirt who was manning the door had obviously received the signal from the bartender; he eyed Samuel with suspicion and flexed his bugling biceps, indicating clearly that Samuel had worn out his welcome.

Thinking over his conversation with the bartender, Samuel wondered if Octavio was a homosexual and had been picked up on a troll by the mysterious stranger and Schwartz. That was an aspect of the case he'd considered only briefly when he'd learned of Harmony's activities, and he'd stored it away until this very moment. In order to make the theory work, however, he needed evidence of all three of them being at the same place for the same reason. He went over what he already knew and came up blank. That wasn't the way it happened, he decided.

Since he was just around the corner, he walked up to Broadway and had dinner at the counter of Vanessi's, where he, Blanche, Bernardi and Marisol had eaten the night of their double date. It gave him a chance to listen to the old Italian man play his melodic tunes on his miniature xylophone.

After dinner, he walked up Grant Avenue, passing La Pantera Café, a well known family restaurant located next to The Saloon, and continued on past several of the city's most famous beatnik bars, which still packed in tourists looking for Jack Kerouac and Neal Cassidy. He went right past Gino and Carlo's, the old North Beach hangout for locals on Green Street, and went into the Anxious Asp, the lesbian bar that the bartender at Vesuvio's had told him about. He laughed when he saw a 1958 Edsel Pacer four-door sedan parked out front. What a disaster that car was, he thought.

It was after nine on a Friday night and the place was packed with women, some of them dressed as men. Looking more closely, Samuel realized he was the only male in the place. He sat down on a stool, the only vacant place in the bar, and ordered a drink from a woman in a white T-shirt. She wore no bra and—in sharp contrast to her masculine crew cut—her nipples showed through the material like pebbles. When his drink arrived and he paid, Samuel took out a photo.

"Have you ever seen this man in here?"

She squinted and smirked. "Are you kidding, Mister? This is a dyke bar."

"Yeah, I know. But, maybe, just for a visit with a friend."

"Look around, buddy. Do you see any men here, except for yourself? Fuck off!" She turned her back on him and walked to other end of the bar. He finished his drink, walked home and went to bed thinking he'd wasted his time, and that if he'd had one more drink his liver would've exploded.

During the night he found himself in bed with Blanche, slowly touching her breasts and kissing her passionately as he slipped her panties off. Just as he was about to consummate the relationship with the love of his life, Samuel woke up panting and in a cold sweat.

*　　*　　*

Exhausted after his long week of late-night wanderings in North Beach, Samuel's dream made him even more desirous of Blanche than usual. Earlier in the week he'd made a date with her for that very evening, and when he woke up, he decided that he wanted to cook something himself at his small flat. If everything went according to plan, he would repeat the moves he'd made on her during his nocturnal fantasy.

Samuel remembered the delicious enchiladas he'd enjoyed at Rosa María Rodríguez's house, so he called Mi Rancho Market and asked her if he could drop by and buy the ingredients so he could make them for Blanche. Rosa María laughed when she heard what he was up to and agreed to help him, but she told him that that recipe was too complicated for him. Instead, she told him, she would give him a simple Mexican recipe that would impress Blanche.

When he arrived at the market around noon, Samuel walked in past the packed aisles of canned and dry goods and headed toward the checkout counter, behind which Rosa María was standing. She was clad in a flowered dress that was partially covered by a white apron. She greeted him with her usual contagious smile.

"Hello, Mr. Hamilton. We haven't seen you around here for some time. How is your case coming along?"

"We solved part of it, thanks to your kids."

"You mean the part about Sara's whereabouts?"

"Yes."

"We read that in the newspaper," she said, placing her hands on the counter. "Marco was disappointed that you didn't mention his name next to the funnies. But he got over it."

"Tell him not to worry," exclaimed Samuel. "If I ever solve Octavio's murder, I'll give both kids full credit." Just then, Ina and Marco came through the curtain from the office and stood next to their mother.

"Hello, Mr. Hamilton," said Marco. "It's nice to see you again."

As usual, Ina was trying to hide behind Rosa María. She wore a blue spring dress over a starched white cotton blouse, and her long black hair was woven into a single braid that hung down her back. "We liked the story about Sara that you wrote," she said, peeking out at him. "Our mother read it to us."

"Sara visited us when she came back to San Francisco," Marco interjected. "She even let us play with her baby when the butcher called her over to talk."

"Your butcher?" asked Samuel, glancing at the man behind meat counter.

"Yes, he's been fussing over her ever since she started coming here," said Marco. "That was before she knew Octavio."

"That's very rude of you, Marco, butting into other people's business." Rosa María interrupted him before he could say any more.

"Please, Rosa María, let him continue," pleaded Samuel. "Kids notice more than you think they do."

"He used to give her free samples," said Ina, not wanting to be left out of the competition.

As Samuel looked over at the butcher again, the color drained from his face.

"I've copied a recipe for you Mr. Hamilton, said Rosa María, who had not noticed the reporter's reaction to the butcher. "It's easy to make and I think it will put Blanche in a romantic mood."

"Tha…thank you," Samuel stammered. "I'll have to take a rain check. I'm sorry." He rushed out of the market, ran up to Mission Street and caught a trolley downtown.

* * *

By ten o'clock the following morning, Mi Rancho Market had been cordoned off by swarms of police officers from Homicide, and crime technicians and staff from the medical examiner's office were clustered inside. The smell of *Mexican pan dulces* wafting over from the in-house bakery mixed with the aroma of the market's freshly made coffee.

Captain Doyle O'Shaughnessy, puffing on his usual Chesterfield, stood with an entourage of Mission Station patrolmen on the sidewalk outside the market. He was red-faced and angry. "Why wasn't I informed of this bust?" he bellowed.

Bernardi, who was directing the last of several crews to arrive, heard the commotion and walked outside to confront the furious officer. "Relax, Captain," he said, pushing his hands down as if trying to smother the flames of a fire. "This is a homicide investigation. Nothing has happened yet. We're executing search warrants and looking for evidence. If we find anything, you'll be the first to know."

"Oh, yeah! Then what's that reporter bastard doing behind police lines?" The spittle flew from his captain's mouth and his fists were clenched.

"He's just observing, with the understanding that he can't print anything without my permission. You can come in, too, if you like."

"No, no," said the captain, taking a deep breath and

calming himself down. He realized he was making a fool of himself. "I'm still in charge in the Mission, and I don't appreciate being left out of what happens on my own turf. You keep me informed."

"You bet, Captain," said Bernardi with a conciliatory smile. "You're the boss; we know that."

Any irony was lost on the captain. He motioned to his entourage and they scrambled into their vehicles and quickly departed. Bernardi watched the three squad cars drive away; then, turning to the onlookers on the sidewalk, he encouraged them to leave as well. He walked back to the meat counter inside the market. There he found the butcher, Pavao Tadić, seated between two police officers. His pudgy face was blotchy and his gray curly hair disheveled. Tadić folded his arms across his chest and glared at Bernardi, his blue eyes blazing with anger.

"I am entitled to speak with a lawyer," he growled in heavily accented English.

"You haven't been charged with anything and we haven't even asked you a question yet, sir," answered Bernardi. "When and if we start asking, we'll give you an opportunity to call your lawyer. Right now, we just want to look around. But at the same time, we'd like to make sure we know where you are while we're doing it."

Bernardi moved over to a group of technicians standing with Samuel near the meat counter, making sure he was out of ear shot of Tadić before speaking. "I want all the sawdust on the floor of this shop swept up and put in boxes so it can be tested for human blood and compared to the samples we have from around the trash can." He looked at Samuel. "I know that's a long shot, but if either turns out to be a match we're one step closer." He turned to the technicians again. "When you're finished with that, dismantle both of those meat-cutting saws. The examiner needs to do some microscopic studies on the blades to see if they could have created the patterns that were found on the bones."

Bernardi gave a few more orders and walked back to the butcher. "Do you have a deep freeze in the shop or inside the meat locker?"

Pavao squinted at him. "I don't have to answer your stupid questions," he said. "I know my rights and I want a lawyer."

"Okay, have it your way."

But Samuel was already one step ahead. He beckoned to Bernardi to follow him to the rear of the building, calling out to the medical examiner to join them. Once there, he showed them a deep freeze hidden behind an old screen covered with a painting of a muscular Aztec warrior with a feathered headdress standing beside a flaming volcano. The medical examiner used his gloved hand to open the deep freeze. It was empty, but the ice that had caked on the sides and bottom was stained with what appeared to be blood.

"Let's not unplug the freezer," said the examiner. "We'll just take samples and have them tested. In the meantime, I'll seal and lock it so that no one can get into it or take anything out."

By then it was past ten o'clock. They'd been in the market for more than two hours. Samuel walked out to the grocery counter and saw a distraught Rosa María standing on the sidewalk, talking earnestly to one of the officers who wouldn't let her past the police line. She spotted Samuel inside the store and gave him a searching, angry look. He retreated and found Bernardi.

"Rosa María Rodríguez is outside and she's furious that we've taken over her store. You have to explain it to her. Please don't be harsh; she's given me a lot of help on this case."

"Don't worry," said the detective. "I'll calm her down, if I can." They headed outside to join her.

"How long will you have my market closed?" she said to

Bernardi, ignoring Samuel.

"Please come inside, Mrs. Rodríguez. We're sorry to cause you all this trouble."

She turned to Samuel. "What's going on here? I thought you were my friend!"

Samuel was about to answer when Bernardi interrupted. "We'll be out of here as soon as we can, Ma'am."

"Why are you *here* in the first place?" she shouted.

"All I can say is that we're investigating a murder, Ma'am. But as soon as my men are out of here, I'll have Samuel explain everything."

Rosa María saw the butcher sitting between the two officers. "Is my butcher under arrest?" she asked, confused. "What did he do? And what about my market? You understand I'm running a business, don't you? The doors have to be open so people can do their shopping, and I need a butcher to cut the meat."

"I understand that very well, Mrs. Rodríguez. You may have to get along without your butcher for today at least, maybe longer. I have to take him to his apartment and search it. After that, I need to ask him some questions."

"Are you accusing this man of a crime?" she asked.

"I'm not accusing him of anything," said the detective. "I'm conducting an investigation and that's all I can say."

Rosa María was still angry but she seemed resigned to the reality she was facing. "That means I'll have to call the union and get another butcher. When can I open my doors?"

Bernardi thought for a moment. "We should be out of here within the hour."

"I'll hold you to that," she said dryly, looking directly at Samuel. "You, young man, have some explaining to do." She turned abruptly and walked out to her car, which was parked on the opposite side of the street.

Bernardi's voice followed her out the door. He spoke as

loudly as he could without yelling. "I'll see you shortly, Mrs. Rodríguez. I have a couple of questions to ask you." She pretended not to hear and drove away.

Samuel turned when he heard Bernardi say he wanted to talk to Rosa María. "You don't think she had anything to do with this mess, do you?"

"Probably not, but I need to know how long the butcher has been here and whether she noticed anything out of the ordinary about him. I also want to hear about the circumstances under which she saw the man with Sara and Octavio."

By the time Rosa María returned, now completely in control of herself, the police lines had been dismantled, the technicians were gone and only Samuel and Bernardi remained in the store. "I saw Pavao in the back seat of your police car with his hands behind his back," she said to Bernardi. "I thought you weren't charging him with anything."

"Right now, he's only in custody as a material witness. He has to be handcuffed because we can't have a citizen in a patrol car with freedom of movement. That's to protect our officers."

She nodded but didn't believe him. "Samuel, we have to talk," she said briskly.

"I'll tell you what I can," he said. He took her over to a corner by the canned goods and explained the chain of events that led him to suspect the butcher and how, when he finally figured out the man's probable involvement, he called Bernardi, who took immediate action.

Rosa Maria looked both distraught and confused. "I can honestly say I never noticed anything unusual in the way he treated any of my customers, including Sara and Octavio. I didn't know that he flirted with Sara until the kids said something, but that's a Latin thing, and Pavao spent enough time in Argentina to learn all about that."

"Do you know how long he was in Argentina before he came to the U.S.?" asked Bernardi.

"I only know that he was a refugee from Yugoslavia and that he escaped Tito's takeover by going to Argentina. Then he emigrated here, but I don't know when."

"Did you ever see him with Octavio?"

"Only when he and Sara were back there together buying meat."

"Did you ever see any friction between the two?"

"Never," answered Rosa Maria. "Why don't you ask Sara? She would know better than anyone, I think."

Bernardi handed her his card. "Okay. If you think of anything else, I'd appreciate a call. Sorry for tying up your business this morning."

"I hope you're on the right track, Lieutenant," she snapped. Her hands on her hips, she watched as the men exited the market.

*　　*　　*

Pavao Tadić lived on Twenty-Fourth Street, just around the corner from Dusty Schwartz, a fact that wasn't lost on either Bernardi or Samuel as they put the affidavit together for the search warrant.

After reading the butcher the warrant, they used his key to open the door. Tadić had agreed to give it to them so they wouldn't have to break in.

The building he lived in was a small four-story structure. Tadić's apartment, which Samuel noticed was immaculate, was on the first floor. The hardwood floors were covered with woven rugs from South America, and the walls were covered with prints of European paintings by some of the masters. The furniture wasn't new, but it was in good shape.

Bernardi handed the officers the list of things that the search warrant entitled them to confiscate, and the team spread out. After a few minutes, one of the officers brought a beige Alpaca wool sweater to Bernardi. "I found this in the dresser in the bedroom," he said.

"Does this sweater belong to you?" Bernardi asked the butcher.

"I won't talk to anybody without my lawyer," he answered.

"Yeah, it looks like you'll need one."

Bernardi took Samuel and a tech with him to the rear of the flat, where they looked for a freezer, but found nothing. They also checked for saws and unusual knives, and while they didn't find anything out of the ordinary, they did confiscate a meat grinder. Then, returning to the living room, they looked through the books on the shelves in the living room, which featured a collection of literature in several languages that Samuel found to be surprisingly diverse.

"Let's look in his bedroom," said Samuel. Bernardi accompanied him and they checked everything in sight. On the table beside the bed, they saw a photograph of Sara.

"I'll be damned!" exclaimed Bernardi. "This is important. Measure it and put it in a plastic bag so we can compare its size with the empty spaces on Schwartz's bedroom wall."

They went back out into the living room, where the hand-cuffed butcher was still standing. "You're going downtown, Mr. Tadić," said Bernardi, "and then you can call your lawyer."

* * *

The next stop for Bernardi and Samuel was the Obregon family home in the Mission. They climbed the steps of the rickety porch and knocked on the door. Sara Obregon greeted them warmly as her mother, whose gray hair was neatly combed this time, stood next to her with the baby in her arms, smiling at Samuel.

Sara ushered them into the small living room. As the two men settled into their seats, Sara's mother chatted away at them in Spanish, which neither man understood.

"She's so happy that you found me and the baby and that we've come home," explained Sara. "She thinks it was all Mr. Hamilton's doing, so she calls him uncle and told me to tell him that he's welcome here anytime."

Samuel blushed.

Bernardi took over. "We need to ask you some more questions, Sara. Some of them may not be pleasant and others may test your memory."

"You want to ask about the preacher or about Octavio?"

"I want to know anything you can tell me about the butcher from Mi Rancho Market."

"The butcher?" she repeated, with a startled look. "I don't know much about him. He would flirt with me when I went to buy meat, and sometimes he gave me a little extra. He always told me I was beautiful, but I am sure he said that to many women. Other than that, I don't know anything."

"What about Octavio? Did he ever go to the meat counter with you?" asked Samuel.

"Yes, of course. He did say that the butcher was a dirty old man and asked me not to buy meat from him. He always said the man had evil intentions towards me."

"Did Octavio ever threaten him?"

"I wouldn't call it a threat. They did have words, so I stopped shopping for meat when I was there with Octavio."

"What did they say?"

"Octavio called him *un viejo verde*. It means dirty old man."

"What did the butcher say to that?"

"He was sharpening a knife at the time, and he just started

doing it faster and faster. I didn't want any trouble between them so I dragged Octavio out of the market.

"You don't think...?" She gasped, clapping her hand over her mouth.

"I don't know yet," said Bernardi. "Right now, we're just trying to get as much background as we can."

"I hope you find whoever killed Octavio," she said, tears rolling down her cheeks. Her mother handed the baby to Sara's sister and went to her side as the two men took their leave.

"Melba was right," Samuel said once they were in the street.

"What do you mean?" asked Bernardi.

"She said Sara held the key to this whole mess."

"How could she know?"

"The old broad has instincts," said Samuel. "Sometimes she scares me with her powers of divination. I wouldn't want to have her as an enemy."

*　　*　　*

"I have instructions from Mr. Perkins that he's not to be disturbed this morning," the secretary told Samuel when he showed up a few days later and tried to get an unscheduled appointment with the assistant U.S. attorney.

"Tell him, it's Mr. Hamilton, and that he's ready to go to press. He just needs to check out a few facts about the painting."

"You know how grouchy he is," she said nervously. "Are you sure you're giving me enough information so that he won't blow up at me?"

"Trust me. Once you say the words 'ready to go to press,' he'll rush out to greet me. Samuel knew the man was eager to get credit for the stolen painting story."

She nodded hesitantly and buzzed the attorney.

The Ugly Dwarf

Just as Samuel had predicted, Perkins bolted out of his office. "Hello, Samuel. Getting ready for the big story? How can I help? Come in, old friend, come in!"

The secretary looked baffled as her moody boss ushered the reporter into his office.

Samuel didn't even bother trying to find a place to sit in the messy room. He took out his notepad and a pen and put one foot up on one of the many boxes that littered the floor.

"Here's what I have so far," he explained. "Pavao Tadić, the Croatian butcher who worked at Mi Rancho Market, has been arrested for the alleged murder and dismemberment of the young man, Octavio Huerta. The band saw in the meat department was used to cut up the boy's body, and the blood found in his freezer and on the meat grinder was type AB positive, the same as the victim's. The D.A. says the probable motive for the slaying was jealousy, as the butcher wanted Octavio's girlfriend for himself. He isn't sure yet if he has enough evidence to charge him with the alleged murder of Dusty Schwartz, but the fiber found on the rail of the back stairwell came from a beige alpaca sweater found in Tadić's apartment. In addition, a photograph of Sara Obregon was also found there, and we have proof that it came from Schwartz's apartment. The D.A. says that if the grand jury indicts Pavao Tadić, he thinks he can prove the same motive: jealousy. Schwartz had sex with Sara and the butcher thought the dwarf knocked her up. That infuriated him, since he probably had plans of his own for her."

"You came over here just to tell me this?" said Perkins. He looked irritated. None of what Samuel had discussed thus far related in any way to the help he had provided.

"Just a minute," said Samuel. "I haven't finished. Bernardi sent Tadic's prints over to your people as requested, and a rumor came back that he was more than just a butcher."

"I get it," said Perkins, puffing himself up self-importantly.

"You heard that the man was a war criminal and you want some quotes from The U.S. Attorney's Office for your story."

"Now you're talking, Charles. What can you give me?"

"Interesting how you always ferret out the connection between things," said Perkins, throwing the reporter an offhand compliment.

"But wait," he continued. "There's more. "Bernardi sent over Tadić's prints and they match the prints on the painting, which I previously told you belonged to a well-known Nazi SS general, Vlatko Nikolić."

"This is big news, and it makes the story even bigger," said Samuel. "Tell me more. I'll identify Pavao Tadić for who he really is."

"You will, of course, give credit where credit is due," said Perkins.

"I've already told you I would," said Samuel. "That's why I'm here. But I can't go to press without the full story."

"So the storyline will read that the reporter learned from Assistant U.S. Attorney Charles Perkins that the accused murderer, Pavao Tadić, is one and the same person as Vlatko Nikolić, the Croatian Nazi SS general wanted for war crimes and for plundering art from Italian churches during the Second World War."

"What war crimes is this man wanted for?"

"Genocide. In other words, the murder, pillage and rape of innocent human beings for no reason whatsoever. He was a cohort of Andrija Artuković, The Butcher of the Balkans, and a big shot in the puppet state of Croatia, which was created by the Nazis in 1943."

"Can you tell me more about the painting?" inquired Samuel.

Perkins gave him the title of the painting, the name of the artist and the church from which it was taken from in Rome.

"Can I put all this in print?" asked Samuel.

The Ugly Dwarf

"I want you to. The case of Andrija Artuković is a good example of the political battle currently being waged in the U.S. There is a powerful group here that wants to prevent the extradition of Nazi war criminals to Communist countries such as Yugoslavia. It's good that there are other charges against Tadić."

"What do you mean by that?" asked Samuel.

"Artuković has been here in California since 1948. He was arrested and ordered deported in 1952, but in 1957 the U.S. Supreme Court sent the case back to the immigration court, and they threw it out, claiming that the affidavits setting out the war crimes were not believable. But by bringing this case to the public's attention, maybe we can get Artuković's case back on track."

"What about the dominatrix?" asked Samuel.

"I'll give her immunity if she'll testify that Tadić/Nikolić loaned her the painting and that he claimed to be the owner."

"She's not going to get off so easy on the State's charges," said Samuel. "She's going to do time for practicing black magic and for perjury."

"I couldn't give less of a shit," said Perkins, rolling his eyes impatiently as he prepared to show Samuel out of the office. "Just spell my name correctly when you write the article and give me all the credit you've promised here today."

* * *

Two days later, Samuel was sitting at the Round Table at Camelot showing Melba his article, which had just appeared in the morning paper under the headline ANOTHER BUTCHER OF THE BALKANS CHARGED WITH MURDER. It explained the complicated nature of Tadić's crime and how the assistant U.S. attorney had discovered the true identity of the accused. It also outlined how Marco and

Ina Rodríguez had provided important clues in solving the crime. The article ended next to the funny pages.

"This is a big boost to your career, Samuel. Three big cases in a row. They couldn't have done it without you. Drinks are on the house."

The reporter blushed. "Thanks, Melba, but it's only eleven o'clock."

"So what? Who's watching? Give this man a double Scotch on the rocks, and I'll have the usual," she yelled over her shoulder.

"I've got to hand it to you, Melba, for saying that Sara was the key. I always kept that in the back of my mind. One Saturday I went to Mi Rancho Market to ask Rosa María for help in preparing the dinner I was going to cook for Blanche, and the kids told me the butcher was always making a play for Sara. In that instant, it all came together for me. That's literally what led to breaking the case."

"That isn't entirely true. Your legwork was the actual reason the case came together, but complimenting me is always good public relations." Melba smiled.

"What's going to happen to Michael Harmony?" she asked. "Ever since you cracked this case, no one talks about him"

"That's my next story. He and McFadden and a couple of labor leaders are going to do time for procuring the teenage girls for Schwartz."

"Did you ever have dinner with Blanche? You know, the one you were going to prepare in the romantic setting of the dump where you live?"

"As a matter of fact, I'm on my way over to Mi Rancho right now to thank the kids and to pick up a recipe Rosa María is giving me. I'm cooking dinner for Blanche tonight. I was going to make the shrimp enchilada dish we had at Rosa María's house that night, but she said it was too complicated."

The Ugly Dwarf

"What do you have in mind?"

"A romantic evening."

"Oh really? If I were you, I'd have a plan B," said Melba, chuckling.

*   *   *

Ordinarily, Rosa María would not have been happy to see Samuel. But when he walked towards the checkout counter, she had a smile on her face. "You kept your word, Mr. Hamilton. The kids were thrilled to see their names in the paper right next to the funnies."

"They played a big part in solving these crimes, so I'm grateful to them. But I am sorry I disrupted your business."

"No I'm the one who is sorry. Now that I know what that man is accused of, I'm mortified that I didn't catch on to what he was up to. To think he was using my place to carry out his crimes. I told the police that I didn't want anything returned—not the saws, not the grinder, not the freezer." She shook her head in disgust.

"You will thank the children for me, won't you?"

"Of course. Now, here's a list of the ingredients you need to prepare your dinner for Blanche. I know it will put her in the right mood."

Samuel went over the list. "What is all this stuff?" he asked, a bewildered look on his face. "And where do I get it?"

Rosa María got a basket and beckoned for the reporter to follow her. As they rolled up and down the different aisles of the market, Samuel watched carefully as she selected several cans. Then she took him to the produce section, where she chose mushrooms with a pungent odor. As she picked out each item, she explained how he was supposed to incorporate it into the recipe.

"Make sure not to put in too much pomegranate juice,"

she warned. "And, most important, measure out exactly one cup of the mushrooms. If you put too many in the mix you will overexcite her, and you'll have more on your hands than you bargained for."

After Samuel paid for the items, Rosa María loaned him a canvas shopping bag emblazed with the logo of Mi Rancho Market. He grabbed it by the handles, thanked her and walked out of the market whistling. His only thoughts now were about how he was going to get Blanche to make love to him after their romantic dinner. Despite Melba's suggestion, he didn't have a plan B. He wouldn't allow himself to think he needed one.

Appendix: The Best California Red Wines of the Early 1960s

1. Beaulieu Vineyard's Georges de Latour Private Reserve. Known for its lush richness, this wine was by far the most recognized and sophisticated of the California reds of the 1960s.
2. Inglenook "Cask" Cabernet Sauvignon. Another connoisseur's wine, this one was a rival to B.V.'s Georges de Latour bottling. It was known for its detailed austerity and propensity to age well over decades.
3. Charles Krug Cesare Mondavi Vintage Selection was the winery's top-of-the-line vintage. The grapes came from the famed To-Kalon vineyard in Napa Valley's Oakville, which later became the prized property of Cesare's son, Robert Mondavi, who launched his eponymous winery there.
4. Simi's Cabernet Sauvignon gave Sonoma County a seat at the table of fine Cabernets in the 1960s.
5. Paul Masson Cabernet Sauvignon was originally produced in the Santa Cruz Mountains, where its namesake owner first established a winery near Saratoga. While not in the same league as the others, it still bears mentioning.
6. Hanzell Pinot Noir was a rare find, as so little wine was produced from this artisanal winery. It was—as one critic put

it—as rare as a unicorn. Hanzell was the well-funded effort of James D. Zellerbach, who made his fortune in paper manufacturing. Zellerbach sought to create the California equivalents of his beloved red (Pinot Noir) and white (Chardonnay) Burgundies. The winery's name is a contraction of his wife's first name, Hana, and the beginning of his last name.

—Agustin Huneeus

Acknowledgements

When I was in Mexico City in 2006 for the presentation of my first published book, *The Chinese Jars*, my very good friend, the late Maria Victoria Llamas Seid, arranged for the well-known Mexican writer Victor Hugo Rascón Banda to introduce me and my book to the Mexican public. During the presentation I was asked the usual question: if this was my first book. I gave my usual answer, that no, my first book was about an oversexed dwarf. Victor Hugo then mentioned that there had been a well-known house of ill repute in Juarez, Mexico, in the early 1900s that was staffed only with dwarf prostitutes. After the presentation I went to dinner with Maria Victoria and several of her friends. One of them, the photographer Lourdes Almeida, said that she remembered reading a book by Ignacio Solares entitled *Columbus*, which dealt with the issue, and she asked if I would like a copy of his book. I said that I would, and she sent it to me. So thanks to Maria Victoria, Victor Hugo, Lourdes Almeida and Ignacio Solares, Dusty Schwartz has an origin instead of being just another oversexed dwarf.